+Plus One

Also by Kelsey Rodkey:

Last Chance Books

A Disaster in Three Acts

+Plus One

KELSEY RODKEY

HARPER TEEN
An Imprint of HarperCollins Publishers

HarperTeen is an imprint of HarperCollins Publishers.

Plus One

Library of Congress Cataloging-in-Publication Data

Names: Rodkey, Kelsey, author.

Title: Plus one / Kelsey Rodkey.

Description: First edition. | New York : HarperTeen, [2023] | Audience: Ages 13 up. | Audience: Grades 10-12. | Summary: Teen matchmaker, Lahey, has two days to find herself a date for her rival cousin Summer's sweet sixteen.

Identifiers: LCCN 2022031706 | ISBN 9780063243729 (hardcover)

Subjects: CYAC: Dating—Fiction. | Cousins—Fiction. | Interpersonal relations—Fiction.

Classification: LCC PZ7.1.R639526 Pl 2023 | DDC [Fic]—dc23

LC record available at https://lccn.loc.gov/2022031706

Typography by Jessie Gang

23 24 25 26 27 LBC 5 4 3 2 1

First Edition

+1

To Sonia Hartl,
For being more than my mentor

Sunday

One

When I tell Noah it's time to sink or swim, I mean it quite literally.

After all, it's an unspoken rule of meet-cutes that if one of the people can't swim, the other has to save them. It's dramatic and romantic, and it doesn't matter that this particular meeting isn't taking place in the ocean or at an engagement party, but instead at the local pool surrounded by little kids with sticky Popsicle fingers trying to out-splash each other with subpar cannonballs.

The location may not be ideal, but the meet-cute is. I made sure of it.

I've known Noah Chen since kindergarten, when we'd play spies on the playground and footsie in class, and though we grew apart eventually, we've always been there for the other when absolutely needed. And Noah absolutely needs me.

Next to me, he sits on a rickety rental chair, crossing his tan arms and legs tightly like I do when I'm warding off menstrual cramps. If he's attempting to melt out of existence in this early-morning sun, he better try harder. We've been at the pool since it opened at eight o'clock, waiting for Justin Carroll to mount his lifeguard stand for his shift—typically eight in the morning to four in the afternoon—but he's apparently running late. Not part of my carefully crafted plan, but nothing to worry about yet. Noah, however, takes this to mean the day is doomed, because Noah is a pessimist. He takes even a hint of rain as a personal attack against him.

"This was silly," he says, scuffing his leather flip-flop against the grass. "He probably heard I had a crush on him and knew he shouldn't show up. He probably called the police."

"No one but you and I know this plan; I'm discreet."

"As discreet as your outfit maybe," he mutters from the side of his mouth. "Why aren't you wearing a bathing suit?"

I dip my head to glare at him over the top of my round retro prescription sunglasses my parents gave me for my birthday. Despite the other things I could have gotten for the same amount of money, I have no regrets about begging for these nonstop for two weeks. I had grown embarrassed by the dorky clip-on sunglasses I had to wear over my everyday glasses. The fact is, no one with clip-on sunglasses has a summer fling. There are no meet-cutes or romances or even Instagrammable moments for those people. I couldn't let my eyewear be the reason I remained dateless and alone for one more day.

"I'm sorry," he says. "You know I get snippy when I'm nervous."

I smooth down the front of my floral dress and cross my legs at the ankles to highlight my chunky sandals. With a full face of makeup on top of the outfit, yes, I'm overdressed, but it's my battle armor. "I'm going to brunch after this."

"With the Queen of England?"

Don't give her any ideas. "With my family, for Summer's birthday."

He grimaces, because it's no secret that my cousin and I don't get along. He's witnessed the minor spats in the school hallway more than once this past year. "Well, I sure hope me ruining my romantic life forever doesn't make you late." Before I can even react, he says, "*Sorry.* Nervous."

I grab his sweaty hand in mine. "Don't be nervous. I planned this well."

"I know, I know," he says with a sigh. "I've seen you work your magic."

I beam. They say middle children crave attention, but not me. I crave appreciation. *Validation.* And my favorite way of getting it is matchmaking. Couples I've set up, like Noah and Justin, sometimes have next to nothing in common until I make some adjustments. All it takes is a bit of internet sleuthing, some harmless stalking, and occasionally a makeover montage. Noah would not let me have the last one even though I know he has a closet full of heinous Nintendo T-shirts that I feel ideologically clashes with his vanity bursting with makeup and skin care products.

"I try my best." Some people, pleased with their own meet-cute matchups, have insisted I start charging for this service, but I'm honestly just in it for the feels. I love love. "There's Justin."

"Where?" Noah's neck cracks whipping his head toward the pool entrance. Justin strolls inside, looking every bit the Ken doll. Lifeguard Ken, one might say, equipped with the following accessories: tiny swim trunks, a whistle, sunblock, and a set of four-pack abs.

"So, we'll give him a moment to settle in. He's going to put his cell phone on the arm of the chair, like he does every day, and when he's looking the other way, I'll snatch it and drop it underneath the stand. You'll walk by and do that stretchy thing that shows off your arm muscles, and then you'll ask him what time it is. He'll realize his phone is gone and panic because—well, obviously; it's his phone. He'll be so grateful when you find it for him, and it'll give you a chance to tell him that story about when you lost your phone."

Noah chews on his lip. "The fake one?"

"It's not fake, it's exaggerated," I say, pushing my glasses to the top of my head. If Noah doesn't know which fake-not-fake story I mean by now, we're in trouble. "We didn't come up with a story about you losing your phone on the subway in New York just for you to not use it. He's going to NYU this year. Keep up." I take a breath. "Sorry. *I* get snippy when I don't have breakfast."

He wipes his palms against his swimming trunks, eyes tracking Justin's movements as he climbs onto his chair to oversee the deep end. I'm not even sure he heard me.

"Noah?"

"Yeah?"

"Do you still want to do this?"

He turns to me, and what had once been a faraway expression on his face has now cracked to panic, his cheeks filling with red. "I don't know."

I soften. "He's a nice guy. But I don't have to tell you that."

I start ticking things off on my fingers to remind Noah of the list of reasons he gave me for why Justin Carroll is not only a babe, but *the* babe for him. "He doesn't overshare on social media, he recycles, he's part of a book club—oh, maybe you should maneuver the conversation from the phone story to his book club by saying searching for your phone made you late for your book club."

"And what book was this fake book club reading?"

"What books have you read recently?"

He blinks.

"What books have you read ever?" I correct quickly. "For school?"

A blank face, again. "Why would I be part of a book club in a state I don't live in?"

"You spent a summer in New York visiting your grandparents." This is actually true. The best way to exaggerate—read: not lie—is to start with an undeniable truth. "You had a ton of free time and needed to be around like minds." Sort of true. He did have a ton of free time, but he spent most of the summer playing video games in his grandparents' brownstone. But Justin doesn't appear to like video games. He likes books.

"Okay. . . . What sort of things did you do outside the apartment when you were there?"

"I walked my grandparents' dog, Bunny."

"Perfect. Forget the book club, say you were late for a volunteer gig. You walked dogs for the elderly." Who wouldn't like that?

His face brightens. "Okay, yeah." He takes a deep breath and nods. "I'm ready."

I stand up, put my shades back down, and walk slowly toward the lifeguard chair. A little girl in pigtails and swimmies runs past me. I lean into the chair to avoid her and snatch Justin's phone while he's too busy tracking the girl. He blows his whistle lightly and says, "No running!" His orders sound like suggestions; his tone is too sweet to be intimidating. Noah's a lucky guy to (soon) have a boyfriend who doesn't yell and cares about the environment and looks illegally hot shirtless. To think, Noah and I once got married in a very classy ceremony held between the swings and the merry-go-round during recess. Now he's about to spread his wings and fly away from me, right into Justin's toned arms.

I plant the phone beneath the chair and walk until I've reached the closed snack bar. It won't open until eleven, but despite that, my traitorous stomach growls as I skim the menu. Normally, I schedule my meet-cutes in the afternoon, ensuring I'm rested and nourished, but today was an exception. Starting tomorrow, Justin will no longer be working at the pool. He signed up to be a camp counselor, and it'd be pretty hard—not to mention quite weird—to sneak Noah into a children's camp for the purpose of flirting (or, in all honesty, probably just open-mouthed staring). So many questions would be raised, and none of them would be Justin asking, "Would you like to go out with me?"

Noah makes his move, doing a slow stretch, but Justin's not looking. By the time Noah awkwardly moves to the other side of the chair—still stretching—Justin is having a conversation with another lifeguard in the opposite direction. It's the type of idiocy you'd expect on a sitcom still airing long past its expiration date, but this is very clearly a *rom-com* and, therefore, this is unacceptable!

Objectively, one of Justin's best personality traits is that he's kind. It's also his biggest flaw. He needs to brush off the leggy coworker with shiny brown hair and notice Noah in his green swim trunks that I made him buy because it's Justin's favorite color.

If I'm late for brunch, that opens the floor for Summer to start shit-talking me before I even get there, so I need to speed things up. I never told Noah about plan B—there's always a plan B—because he would have been very, very against it.

Shoes clacking against the pavement, wind blowing my dress cinematically, I dash up to Noah and push him toward the pool.

His flip-flops scrape the concrete as he struggles against me. "Hey, wait, Lahey, I can't swim," he says, hands clenched on my shoulders. He may have been working out his arms the last few weeks, but I've had years of evolving into a strangely strong human being courtesy of my jock older sister who likes to wrestle as a means of settling arguments.

"I know. Sink or swim time." I give him one last shove and things move in slow motion.

Plan B:

He'll fall into the water.

I'll scream for Justin to save him.

CPR Ken to the rescue.

The thing is, I should have prepared a plan C. Or at least a plan B-and-a-half, because Noah never unclenches. He pulls me and my brunch-ready body into the water with him. It's cold and jarring, and my makeup and brand-new dress are not waterproof. I hate to admit that my first concern when I surface is my sunglasses. My second is that Noah does not know how to swim.

"Help!" I say, swimming to the edge, my dress clinging to my legs as I tread. "My friend can't swim!"

Now, normally, I'm one of those people questioning why someone who can't swim is at a pool, but today, there's no question about it: he's at a pool for *romance*.

Justin grabs his red life floaty thing and jumps into the pool without a second thought. Of all the days I've watched him lifeguarding, this is the first he's actually done any life*saving*. He cuts through the water and wraps his arms around Noah's flailing body and hauls him to the edge beside me. Justin, busy tossing his float onto the asphalt, doesn't hear me whisper to Noah, "Play dead."

Noah forces himself to stop coughing and, after glaring at me, goes as limp as possible. His eyes shut last, but he couldn't hide that familiar glimmer of hope from me, even without my glasses. Justin pulls him over the edge and I follow.

"Hey," Justin says, suddenly smacking Noah on the face. Not the peck on the cheek Noah and I discussed might happen today, but, hey, it's physical contact. "Wake up, Noah."

"Oh my god," I say frantically and most definitely too over

the top. I never claimed to be an actress. I'm the director, if anything. "Do CPR!"

A crowd forms around us, but Justin's oblivious. He takes his job very seriously, even though he only earns about twelve dollars an hour. That doesn't seem like enough if he's supposed to be keeping people alive. He leans over Noah to start what looks like very painful chest compressions. Noah has crushed on Justin for a year, though, so he's taking it like a champ. All for love. All for the chance of lip-to-lip action, even if it's not the kind he was hoping for. It's a start, and I don't do failure.

Justin's mouth hovers over Noah's for o n e a g o n i z i n g s e c o n d before making contact.

It's not a kiss, no, but it does make me tear up. The hopeless romantic in me ignores the rational part of me that says my eyes are just watering from the chlorine. Noah fake-chokes himself miraculously to life and I leave the two of them engaged in conversation as the crowd disperses. Noah manages to rip away from Justin's gaze long enough to raise one thumb in my direction.

Justin says to him, "I think we had chemistry together last year."

Noah nods, dazed in the dreaminess of Justin, and says, "Yeah, we definitely have chemistry—*had* chemistry together."

Two

"Didn't you already shower? You're really pushing it with the time, Lahey," Liberty calls after me when I run upstairs and into our small shared bathroom. My older sister didn't see that I'm drenched and, therefore, doesn't know the driver's seat of her car, which I borrow out of the kindness of her heart, is also drenched. It's something we'll just have to deal with when the time comes . . . in about fifteen minutes.

"I'll be quick!" I yell back, shutting myself in.

I place my sunglasses on the counter—I took it upon myself to use the pool skimmer to rescue them from the depths of the most epic meet-cute I've ever concocted, since Justin was a little too busy to do so himself—and turn the shower on, praying Lily hasn't wasted all the hot water with her typical morning soak. She claims it's the only way she can properly wake up.

I peel my chlorine-soaked dress off my body and let it rest over the shower curtain rod. I was really excited to show it off today, especially to my aunt, because she always, *always* compliments my outfit choices and my cheap finds from the thrift store, but I guess it'll have to shine another day. Maybe at Summer's birthday party. I envision her jaw dropping when I walk in. It hits the ground and doesn't stop lowering until it pops out of Australia or wherever. I imagine her accidentally swallowing a kangaroo.

It's not until I'm rinsing shampoo from my hair and reaching for the conditioner that I realize someone truly evil used the last of it and didn't replace it. I'm a hundred percent sure it wasn't me—I would have set it aside for a deep cleaning before recycling it like the little green Democrat my parents are raising me to be. I go through the process of wringing out my hair and lathering bodywash in every reachable place, trying to stall until I absolutely need to call for help, but then the door creaks open.

"Hey!" I say, whipping my head toward it. "Can you get me a bottle of conditioner, please?" I refrain from accusing whoever entered of finishing it, because that's one surefire way not to get what I want. Lily, since turning thirteen, has become especially petty and would revel in my tangled, dull hair if I pissed her off.

Whoever walked in doesn't respond to my question, though. All I hear is the overworked fan and the water splattering on the tub floor below me.

"Uh, hello?" Goose bumps prickle over my skin because I swear I heard the door open, but now I'm feeling very alone.

"Here." The voice startles me first, then the sight of a hand that very much doesn't belong to either of my sisters does next.

It's holding the conditioner and has something black caked under a few fingernails and that's how I know it's—

"Adler!" It's just his grease-and-dirt-stained hand from working on cars, but it feels like a thousand eyes he's just shoved in here. My entire body gets hot, even as the water starts fading to a lukewarm temperature. I try to cover the front of myself even though I rationally know that he's not a pervert I need to worry about, just Liberty's best friend with a lack of boundaries. "Get out!"

"How about a thank-you?" He waves the bottle around blindly until it accidentally makes contact with my slick shoulder and topples to my feet with a clatter.

"I thought you were my sister." This is certainly not the situation I expected to be in when Adler and I would finally have a one-on-one chat after the disastrous matchmaking incident. He's been avoiding me since his graduation party over two months ago, when my attempt to meet-cute him and this really sweet girl, Brighton, went sour. Adler very much did not appreciate my help like Brighton had—until Adler kindly, but wrongly, turned her down, that is.

"Which one?"

I pull a face I'm lucky he can't see. "Does it matter? Get out!"

"I have to brush my teeth."

"I'm *naked* in here." I hate how my voice shakes on the word. It feels too intimate to be used between the two of us.

"I would hope so; it's a shower."

I hear the sink running. "Are you really brushing your teeth right now?"

"Well, I'm not here for this great conversation. Mom and

Pop are using the bathrooms, and I have to get to work."

I peek through the crack between the wall and the curtain, making sure nothing of mine is showing. This is not the first time Adler Altman has wandered in from next door to use the bathroom, cook some food, or spend the night. He's been Liberty's built-in best friend since he moved here the summer before their sixth-grade year and it's usually fine that he's around—one could even get used to his teasing if exposed to it enough, because he has redeeming qualities like his unparalleled comedic timing and perfectly baked Pizza Rolls—but right now, as he hunches over the sink, toothpaste foam dripping from his mouth, he needs to disappear. He puts the toothbrush into his mouth again. *My toothbrush.*

"Oh, come on," I groan.

"What?" He swings toward me, some of his chin-length, wavy brown hair getting stuck in the toothpaste around his mouth. His eyes shine in the overhead lighting, but there's no hint of laughter to be found there, none of his typical openness or warmth. He's usually such a smiley person that it must take a great effort to refuse me that kindness lately; he hasn't even slipped up once to accidentally greet me with his go-to "Lay-*hey*, Lahey." And that's his favorite way to get an eye roll from me.

I hold the shower curtain tight against me before realizing that just makes it even easier to see me. My face truly cannot get any hotter. If I had a crush on Adler, or was even remotely attracted to him, this incident might mean everything to me. I'd replay it in my head at night, wondering what he thought of me in this moment. Did I look like a drowned rat, or was the water dripping down my face appealing to him?

But that doesn't matter because I don't feel that way about him and he definitely doesn't feel that way about me. I'm kind of offended that I've never even been a small sexual threat to him. I'm just one of Liberty's little sisters who overstepped and pissed him off.

Liberty yells from somewhere outside the door about how we still need to pick up Sophia before brunch and I'm wasting my time heckling Adler. Imagine, *me* bothering *him* right now.

Water drips into my open mouth as I struggle to find the words. "That's my toothbrush." In his *mouth*.

"Berty said you wouldn't mind," he says, biting the words around the toothbrush handle. He goes back to brushing his teeth with vigor.

"Don't you have a kitchen sink *and your own toothbrush* you could have used?"

"Yes, but the toothbrush is behind locked doors." He makes a gesture like, *So now I'm here.*

I roll my eyes, picking up the bottle of conditioner and applying too much to my hair. It takes a lot of effort for me to stand here, stretched out and uncovered—even behind a shower curtain—with him so close. I want to curve into myself and disappear. "Just throw it out when you're done. I don't know where that mouth has been."

"And it's better if you don't know," he says without missing a beat.

"Please *go*."

I hear him wind up and spit before flooding the sink with

water. "Your wish is my command," he says without a hint of the sarcasm I know lingers right beneath his words.

"Then, while you're granting wishes, could you get me a new toothbrush and never interrupt me in the bathroom again?"

"What was I *interrupting*?"

"GOODBYE," I say pointedly, combing my fingers through my hair. I keep telling myself to just keep showering, because Liberty will literally drag me out of here, ready or not, when the time comes, and I'd rather be ready. She won't take Adler coming in to brush his teeth as a good excuse.

"Liberty said you need to hurry up. This might help," he says.

The toilet flushes without warning, and the shower water runs freezing cold. "What the hell, Adler!"

The door shuts loudly behind him as he makes a quick exit. I miss the days before he declared me public enemy number one—no, I miss the days before he even moved here. Our old neighbor, Mrs. Winthrop, was so nice and kept to herself except to deliver bouquets from her garden and ask my dad to shovel her driveway in the winter.

I finish my shower and tiptoe out of the bathroom, my pale pink towel clinging to my body.

"Adler left" comes Lily's monotone voice from her bedroom.

From the hallway, I see her on the bed, blank face pointed toward the ceiling. She's had high highs and low lows since one of her best friends, Rohan, moved to Missouri last month. Lots of wallowing, lots of laughing until she cried. She's really been going through it.

"What's wrong?" I dare to ask.

"Life's meaningless."

"Jesus."

She points one finger toward her window. "Catthew the fourteenth died, and so have my dreams."

I take in the most recently deceased plant in a long line of dead plants—brown, shriveled, and sad on the windowsill. "RIP."

Since Rohan's departure, Lily's been on a quest to get Mom and Dad to let her adopt a cat, which she will name Catthew (Catt for short); it was some inside joke between them and Lily's other best friend. Our parents said she needed to show that she could care for something—they have always been very anti-pet, probably because having three daughters is fun and expensive enough. Fast-forward to fourteen dead plants. It's for the best (for the cat).

"Did you overwater it or underwater it?" I ask, taking in its appearance. She and I were quite surprised to learn that either action could result in immediate and dramatic deaths in plants.

"I don't even know. Maybe it got too much sun." She sits up and turns toward me. "That's a thing, too."

"Yeah."

"Not a thing I'd have to deal with if I had a cat. Honestly, having a plant is way harder."

"I don't know. I think you can bring dead plants back to life, but the same can't be said about cats."

She quirks her eyebrow at me in such a creepy imitation of Liberty. "They have nine lives; of course you can," she says in a bouncy, sarcastic tone.

"Let's go!" Liberty calls from downstairs.

My little sister huffs and slides off her bed, literally. "Brunch? At a time like this?"

I push her toward the stairs, trying not to laugh at her anguish, and zoom into my and Liberty's bedroom when Liberty literally starts *counting down from sixty.* I'll have to go with wet hair, which will leave me vulnerable to snide remarks from Summer, but I have no other choice if I want to reapply some makeup. Wet hair will dry on its own and is therefore a self-solving problem. A bare face is not. I won't just suddenly get more attractive the longer I sit there.

With my new favorite dress out of the picture, I search my side of the closet for something that says "easy, breezy, covering up the fact that I don't want to be here." Despite our similar noses and blond hair, I'm not of the same slender physique as Liberty and Lily, so I have to consider my options more carefully than they would in a pinch. I have to avoid outfits that are too clingy to sit down in because my rolls would be exposed, so that rules out most of my favorite shirts and jean shorts. Even though dresses give me chub rub, I'll be sitting down for the majority of the meal. So, a dress it is again. No stripes, though. Nothing black, because it's not summery. I have a beautiful green A-line dress, but it's made from anything-but-cotton and makes me sweat just looking at it. I pass dress after dress until suddenly the wardrobe devolves into Liberty's side full of T-shirts, tanks, and crop tops—the natural devolution of her clothes as they get worn out over the years.

Liberty starts racing up the stairs to knock me out and haul my unconscious body into the car, so I pull a flowy blue dress from its hanger and slide it over my frame. As I'm fixing my capped sleeves into place, she leans into our room through the cracked door.

"We're officially late. Hope you're happy. Now we get to have a big dramatic entrance like you probably wanted." Sunlight glints off her nose piercing, and the twinkling feels condescending, too.

"Just because I don't like Summer doesn't mean I want to take attention away from her." Though she's never had an issue doing the same to me—on the last day of school, she trailed behind me so she could interrupt every single time I asked someone to sign my yearbook, to prove that she was more important to that person or something. I have like fifty unfinished HAGS, so, just . . . HA HA HA all over my junior yearbook.

She starts laughing and then harshly cuts herself off. "Sure."

She pinches a hand around my wrist and pulls me from the room, not even slowing down when I stumble over a pair of her cleats I've asked her to put away three times a week for the last four weeks.

To be honest, I've just never gotten along with my cousin—and it's not for lack of trying! Any time in the past that I've tried to get to know her, to be friends with her like our mothers want us to be, she's pushed me away or said something ridiculously rude that I have a hard time forgetting and forgiving. Summer's always critical, cruel, and calculated. It's like there's some competition between us that she wants so desperately to win, but I simply don't know the rules of the game. So, whenever I see her, I come to play.

From the back seat of the car, Lily leans out the open window. "Mom and Dad want to know where we are."

"Did you tell them?" Liberty asks, locking the door behind us. I walk down the driveway and she quickly catches up, moving her legs at the same brisk pace she does everything else.

"You want me to tell them we're still at home? Mom will lose it."

"No, she probably has at least one mimosa in her system. I think it's safe to tell her the truth."

Lily starts muttering to herself as she types back a reply to our parents. "Lahey . . . made us . . . late. . . . This is why . . . you two . . . drive separate."

"Hilarious." I try to wrench open the passenger door, but it's locked.

Liberty stands on the other side, just outside the driver's door. "Sophia's getting the front, obviously."

I scoff but move back one door and force Lily to scoot over. Liberty yanks open her door and sits down, a small squelching sound filling the car. Her body tenses, and I sit there, just as frozen, as I remember I didn't deal with the wet seat thing.

She should thank me, honestly. Her overalls clashed with her shoe choice.

Lily starts texting aloud again. "Gonna . . . be . . . even . . . later."

Three

It's not that I'm putting off walking into Feather for chocolate chip pancakes with a side of passive-aggressive comments; it's that I spy someone outside the restaurant in desperate need of my help and, therefore, I can't go in just yet. It's my duty, and my honor, to assist whenever possible.

Liberty and Sophia walk inside hand in hand to join my family, Lily reluctantly trailing behind with her nose half a foot from her phone screen, but I stall near the entrance, where a twentysomething girl tries to take stealthy selfies in front of my best friend Poppy's latest art installation. A metal man with flowers and moss covering his body holds out two bird feeders like lanterns fending off the dark. Poppy's parents, the owners of Feather, gifted her this outdoor space to showcase her art, but they're still hesitant to let her work bloom inside. Her art isn't always this enjoyable or understandable, and they're reluctant to lose customers solely for aesthetic reasons. I think they're still haunted by that time Poppy submitted a painted mason jar full of dirt and worms for her mixed media final at school.

"Do you want me to take your picture?" I ask the girl.

"Oh, no, I was just . . ." She shrugs, red exploding on her freckled cheeks.

"It's a really cool statue." I step forward and hold out my hand. "My best friend made it, so I've taken tons of pictures in front of it."

I might be in the minority, but I l o o o o v e being approached to take stranger's photos—so much so that I do the asking a lot more than people ask me. It's such an exhilarating feeling to see the joy spread across their faces when they realize they got exactly the photo they were hoping for when they opened their camera app. I can't count how many times I've tried to get Liberty or Lily to take my photo somewhere and end up with an off-center photo—and not in an artistic way. Not even me looking *very* cute can save it. I used to joke that I needed an Instagram Boyfriend to do photo shoots with, but then it turned into a game my sisters would team up against me to play: ask random guys to take pictures of us as an audition for Lahey's Instagram Boyfriend. It *would* be a great meet-cute, but the added unpredictable factors (read: my sisters and their mouths) meant I would undoubtedly stay single.

She hands me her phone. "Thanks," she says, tucking a long strand of brown hair behind her ear. "I'm—well, my boyfriend just broke up with me—ex-boyfriend, I guess—and I want to look like I'm having fun." She gestures lamely toward the statue, and I notice the darkness under her eyes. "Maybe that's pathetic."

"Not at all. I hear the best revenge is moving on, and"—I view her and the statue through the phone screen—"this hunk will surely make your ex remember what he's missing out on. How about you lean into this guy like you're telling him a secret? And put some of your hair over your shoulder?"

I squat, despite my dress, and take some photos from below. It's not the angle for everyone, but for this girl, it's gorgeous. I even manage to get some sun flare in the corner, and it makes the picture seem very summery and high fashion. It helps that she's beautiful to start with, but I *know* I'm helping the pictures shine, too. I hate to think about what these would look like in the hands of someone less experienced.

"Yes, these are perfect. Look over there and smile."

She bursts into laughter, and I fire off a few shots. "Do you do this professionally or something?" she asks.

"I just believe in a strong social media presence. It's how the world views people these days." I hand her phone back to her. "Good luck."

She cradles the phone to her chest with a big smile. "Thanks."

And when she goes into the restaurant, I no longer have a reason not to follow.

I bypass the hostess and make a beeline to the table my family rules over in the corner with the good natural lighting. I try to be discreet when I approach, but Aunt Madison shrieks like she's at a Harry Styles concert and he's just thrown water on her. She acts like it, too. If anyone's ever thought that I was the dramatic one in my family, it's because they haven't met my aunt.

She leaps from her chair, the mauve fanny pack at her waist

jingling with loose change. I've told her several times that it's actually meant to be worn like a cross-body bag, but she claims her boobs are too big. She's not lying; she and I have such similar body types that many people have assumed she's my mother. "Come here, Lahey, I've missed you so much."

She suffocates me against her, and I choke out, "I saw you last week."

"It's been too long." She pulls away just far enough to take in my outfit. "This is so stylish."

"I wish you could have seen the dress I originally wanted to—"

"She's worn that before, Mom" comes the petulant voice of Summer somewhere behind Aunt Madison. "Relax."

Aunt Madison glances over her shoulder. "Well, it works for her." She turns back to me and winks. "Join the table, honey."

I slide into one of the two empty seats between Lily and my mom. It's directly across from the sour birthday girl. "Happy birthday," I say dully.

"Thanks," she says before raising an eyebrow at her mom. "I told you Lahey wouldn't bring anyone. We didn't need the extra chair."

It's been one minute and I'm already the target of her nastiness.

"That seat isn't for your boyfriend?" I ask.

"He's working."

"Convenient excuse to get away from you," I mumble, shaking out my utensils and placing the cloth napkin in my lap.

My mom laughs, cutting the tension building at the center

of the table, and then bends over to hoist her massive purse—full of everything and anything in case of emergencies that never occur—onto the empty chair. "We can use it for storage. No worries." She takes my bag from the shoulder of my chair and places it beside hers as if to nail home the necessity of the extra chair.

"Your mom ordered you waffles" is Summer's stiff retort.

It comes out like an insult, and it kind of is one. My mom knows I *hate* waffles.

"Mom," I whine. "Pancakes."

My mom sets down her mimosa and swallows. "Maybe if you got here on time, I wouldn't have had to improvise."

"It's not improvising. I literally only ever get the pancakes." They are the superior breakfast food, and I'm exhausted by having to drive this point home. "Waffles scratch the roof of my mouth."

"I thought you hated pancakes," she says. "They're soggy."

"That's Liberty." Nice to know she remembers *her* quirks, though.

"Well, I got one thing right: I made sure they're plain, everything on the side." She seems so proud of herself.

"That's *Lily*." My younger sister thinks that all food should start plain so you can build onto it as desired. She doesn't trust anyone, not even a world-class chef, to decide how her meal should taste.

One day my mother will be able to keep our idiosyncrasies straight. It's bad enough she insisted on having three daughters and giving them all weird *L* names, but then not remembering when one is the biggest pancake fan in the world? Kind of hard to forget.

My dad interjects with a laugh. "At least we have an in with the kitchen. I'll go see if they can change the order."

He gets out of his seat and heads to the back, most likely just trying to avoid my wrath. I watch him with a longing I'm unsure I can keep from my face. I'd much rather spend my morning cleaning pots and pans for free with Poppy than sitting here mentally and emotionally alone.

I revert to silence, giving Summer a once-over while everyone—except Lily, who is reading an article on plant care on her phone—talks in small groups. Summer's blond hair has always been a shade lighter than mine—platinum while the rest of us girls have honey-blond hair—and today it's practically glowing in the sun. She's lamented before about how she hates sticking out, but I know she actually relishes being different. If she hated it so much, she'd dye it. Her mother is a *hairstylist*.

Summer picks at the pastel-pink nail polish on her right hand, nodding an answer to some question Sophia asked her. She's far from nonchalant, though. Her tightly coiled energy threatens to spring free and whack me in the face any moment now. She's just waiting. For what, I don't know, but I prepare my nerves in case there's a fight.

My dad comes back and takes his spot on the other side of Mom. "Funny, they already knew the waffle order was wrong. I guess Poppy said something."

I smile. Maybe my mom didn't get the order right, but Poppy never lets me down.

"Now that everyone is here, I wanted to give you your formal invites to my party this Saturday." Summer pulls a stack of envelopes the exact same color of her nail polish from her bag. I don't know what work or money goes into color matching nail polish to an envelope, but I think it's all just a bit much for me.

I hold in my groan, because my mother is not afraid, even in public, to smack me upside the head for such a thing.

"She insisted on doing this in person." Aunt Madison says this to my parents, but Summer responds.

"It's my sweet sixteen. It's important." Summer's head snaps in my direction. "Remind me again, Lahey; what did you do for yours?"

I hold back my initial response—which would have been *Shouldn't you already know that, since you're so obsessed with me?*—and smile. "I had an all-nighter with my best friend. Perfect birthday."

"No party? So sad," Summer says with fake sympathy. No one calls her out for this, or the fact that, you know, it's not sad. It's how I *chose* to celebrate. "But, yeah, I just wanted to do a big thing and celebrate. My dad insisted."

Our waitress brings our orders over, with the help of Poppy. I lock wide eyes with her and mouth, "Help me." She leans over my shoulder when she places my perfectly chocolatey pancakes in front of me and mutters, "Do you want me to spill her oatmeal on her?"

Who orders oatmeal for brunch? On their birthday? Psychopaths, that's who.

"It would be too obvious, but thank you."

"It's such a shame Feather couldn't cater Summer's party," Aunt Madison says to Poppy when she places her fruit bowl down. My best friend stiffens at the attention on her. "But I'm so excited to hear your folks got that fundraiser locked down."

"Thanks. We're really excited." The thinness of her voice gives away her discomfort like it always does—at least to me. The rest of my family continues on, all their googly eyes trained on Poppy, even though she's visibly shrinking in front of them.

"You're more than welcome to come to my party if you're able to sneak away," Summer says. The worst thing about the invite is that it's so sincere—Summer, like everyone else in the world, adores Poppy. When Summer turns back to the table, Poppy's forced smile drops. "Did you hear, Mom? The fundraiser is actually being held at the Hilton, too."

Aunt Madison releases an impressive combination groan and wail. "What are the chances! You'll literally be *right there*! You have to sneak away for a second on your break."

Feather, and thus Poppy's parents, recently secured the honor of catering Juanita González's first official campaign fundraiser on her way to the Senate. Poppy's mom, this kind, tiny Vietnamese woman, became a US citizen a few years ago and, as a result, turned into an avid fan of politics. It's all great except for the fact that Poppy's now expected to become the first female Vietnamese American president.

"Go on," Summer says when it's just the family again. "Open your invites."

I narrowly avoid rolling my eyes as I pick up the envelope in front of me. The expensive card stock is thick enough, and yet still sharp enough, to cut through all three of my massive pancakes.

My parents and Liberty and Sophia share two invites between them, but Lily and I get our own. I break the golden wax seal on the envelope and pull the invite out so I can pretend to read the words until the conversation turns to something else.

"Hey, what does *plus one* mean?" Lily asks the table, putting her invite back into the envelope. Lily's always been the type to keep cards. She likes to preserve things, plants not included.

"It means you can invite one other person to come with you. Some people would use it for a date, but you can bring a friend if you want," Summer says before sipping her fresh-squeezed orange juice. Of course Summer gave everyone a plus one. She wants more gifts and more attention and more people there so she can rub it in my face that I only had one person with me on my sixteenth birthday.

"I assumed Liberty would bring you, Sophia, so I hope it's okay that I don't have an invite for you . . ." God forbid Summer offend anyone but me.

"Of course. I'm really excited." Sophia's red hair shines in the sunlight when she reaches across the table for some salt. "I've actually never been to a real sweet sixteen before. I just hear stories."

"Yeah, I don't think I have, either," Liberty tells her. "The wildest party I ever went to was Adler's bar mitzvah. There were fire jugglers."

"How does one juggle fire?" Sophia asks, a drenched piece of French toast paused before her lips.

"Maybe you'll see at my party," Summer interjects with a wicked smile.

I glance at my invite, heart racing at the thought of inviting a date to the party, but I don't see a plus one anywhere among the gold, shiny script.

I slide my glasses up my nose and lean into Lily, keeping my voice low when I ask, "Where did you see a plus one?"

It's clearly not something Lily made up or else Summer would have shut it down. Undesirables? At her party? No thank you.

"Right here." Lily goes to point at a spot on my invite, but it's blank. She curls her finger back toward her palm. "Weird."

She pulls out her own invite and compares it to mine. There it is in fancy type: *+1*. But it's not on mine. It has to be a misprint.

I glance up from the two invites and find Summer smiling at me with such acid that I know the omission is not a misprint.

I clear my throat and give her what she so desperately wants. It's her birthday, after all. "I don't have a plus one."

Summer stretches her hand across the table to reach mine; it's freezing. "I didn't want to make it difficult for you. I know you've never had a boyfriend, and since Poppy is already invited . . . Who else do you even know?"

I exhale slowly out of my nose, a last whiff of chlorine expelling from my body. And you know what, that's what emboldens me—the reminder that I get people dates all the time. I can certainly get myself one. I've just never really tried.

"What makes you think I wouldn't want a plus one?"

"Who would you ask?" she says with a laugh. People around us being treated to minor blips of our conversation might mistake it for a lighthearted one.

"There are a ton of guys I could ask—who would *accept*—but I don't need to flaunt it like you do. I'm not that insecure."

Summer's jaw clenches.

Liberty and Sophia glance at me and then exchange a pointed look with each other. They should be on *my* side, and the least they could do is not make it so obvious that I'm lying.

"Those who can't, teach," Summer says with fake gentleness. "That little matchmaking thing you do. I understand."

"Last time I checked, my 'little matchmaking thing' is what got you your boyfriend because you couldn't do it on your own." If there was a mic for me to drop, it would have crashed through the floor.

Sophia gasps, partially in delight and partially in horror. I guess she's never heard this story.

In a bout of misguided sympathy last year, I saw Summer crushing on her now-boyfriend, Tommy, pretty hard at school and decided to intervene like a fairy freaking godmother. It was as close to a cease-fire as we've ever gotten, and we almost had a good time together trying to figure out what made Tommy tick. But eventually our truce fell apart the way it always does. She did something cruel, as she's known to do, and I snapped back to reality and realized that she was just using me for my skills and would turn into a cackling supervillain as soon as she got what she wanted, and we went back to our rival barracks to rest up for another day of war.

Lily stuffs an entire piece of bacon into her mouth and chews loudly. "Ladies, calm down. Lahey can have my plus one."

"No," Summer snaps at Lily. "It's nontransferable." She softens. "Plus, don't you want to bring a friend? Everyone else there will be older than you."

"I mean, you guys don't really act it," Lily says. Liberty snorts into her coffee. "Anyway, I don't think Cecily's parents will let her go to a high school party, and Rohan . . ." Her mouth falls into a frown. No more words necessary.

"Look," Summer says to me, rolling out a crick in her neck. "I didn't want to give you a plus one and then make you feel obligated to try to get a date on such little notice. I know how you struggle with romance—for *yourself*," she adds before I can correct her. "I was doing you a favor."

"I'm bringing a date." The words slip out, but they are strong, sturdy, serious. They are far more dangerous than *"maybe* I'm bringing a date." There's no doubt there. "A good one."

"'A good one'?" She smooths her hand over her mouth to hide the grin.

"Yes. I practically have a whole secret roster of guys to choose from; it's just a matter of picking the perfect one." I point to Liberty. "Berty didn't even know."

"This is true," Liberty says before another conspiratorial glance with Sophia. "I thought all of the guys Lahey knew were gay or on a TV show."

"*Unhelpful*," I cough at my sister.

"Well, you're more than welcome to invite someone, then," Summer says, folding her hands in front of her. "It shouldn't be a problem at all for you and your . . . secret roster of guys. There's bound to be at least one of them who can spare the night for some charity work."

"*Girls*," my mom interjects. She must have finally tuned into our conversation. The magical mimosa has worn off, and my confidence is crashing. "Your aunt was just saying how she'll be doing Summer's hair before the party. Did any of you want to stop by the house to get yours done, too?"

Liberty and Lily reject this offer before I can even blink . . . but my aunt takes my tiny moment of silence as a yes.

"Awesome!" Aunt Madison says, biting into an unbuttered piece of toast. "Girl time with our favorite fashionista."

Summer's face falls further than I thought possible. The thought of spending extra time with her doesn't bring me any joy, either.

Four

"The *audacity*," I tell Poppy between bites of a burnt cinnamon roll. With enough icing, I can barely even tell there are charred bits I couldn't properly scrape off. Wasted free food? Not on my watch. "I didn't like her before, but now I think I really hate her."

I'm sitting on the counter in the Feather kitchen while Poppy washes a frying pan with something caked onto it. After the completion of the awkward brunch, my family dispersed in various directions. I begged off to "help Poppy so she can leave work early," but it was really to bitch and moan about Summer setting me up for public failure. She practically ripped that lie out of my mouth. She made me do it, and now I have to deal with the consequences.

"I don't get what the deal is between you two. It's like she's always trying to one-up you."

"Which is sad for her since I'm literally *never* trying to! I'm just reacting to the negativity *she* puts out in the world." I lick some icing off my finger. "What do I do? Everyone knew I was lying about being able to get a date. A guy hasn't looked twice at me in my entire life, except for the doctor who delivered me, and that was only because I was turning blue."

"Maybe just don't do anything?" She sprays some water onto the pan, and it splashes onto her black work shirt. A line drawing of a feather, the restaurant's logo, sits on the fabric against her chest. "It might end up being more embarrassing to try to find a date than to show up alone."

"Wow. Thanks. And here I thought you'd believe in me the most out of everyone." My stomach has felt sour since pulling into the Feather parking lot, but now I'm downright nauseous.

"You know that's not what I meant. Just, finding a decent one to bring on such short notice is going to be hard."

I throw the final bit of roll into my mouth and chew. "No, it's more embarrassing to show up alone. I said I had a *roster* on standby, Poppy. Do you know what a roster is? Because I googled it to make sure and it's like a whole basketball team. So, I *have* to find a date."

There's no time like the present to finally fill my romantic void. No, I've never had a boyfriend—despite the fact that I'm great, and I'm very good at setting up romances for others—but Summer's *wrong*. I don't help people find the perfect relationships because I can't do it for myself. I've just been so busy doing it for others that I haven't had time for myself. This is my chance to change that.

"In just a few days?" Poppy's voice slides into a higher octave. "Do you even know any guys well enough to ask them on a date?"

Why does everyone assume I don't know eligible boys? I try to think of some, but all I can come up with are guys I've matchmade with someone else, or, fine . . . those who are gay or fictional.

"Not off the top of my head, but they exist. They have to." I jump down from the counter and grab my bag, rummaging through it for my phone. I bump into a bottle of hand sanitizer instead and use it to dissolve any lingering bits of cinnamon roll. "I do this for people all the time, so I can definitely do it for myself. I already know me better than anyone, so it cuts down the work by half."

She gives me an offensively skeptical look, and her pierced eyebrow rises. She and Liberty actually got their piercings together. I was supposed to get one—well, two: my ears—but I chickened out when I saw the metal go through Liberty's nostril.

I free my phone and wiggle it excitedly. "I can use the school directory."

"But it's summer. No one's using that right now."

The school directory is this basic app made by our school district to help students stay in contact with those in their classes for assignments and things. It cuts down on needing to swap contact information with people most likely to be serial killers because it doesn't show your email address or phone number, and the school claims to monitor it.

"Yeah, but just because people aren't using it, doesn't mean it doesn't work. The messages still pop up on our phones. I keep getting one about how it's not too late to sign up for AP History, as if I'd willingly want to memorize the shitty propaganda this country is force-feeding us."

She stops scrubbing. "Don't let my mom hear you say that."

"I mean, God bless America," I say loudly. I bring up the app and clear away unwanted notifications. "I can even use the app settings to streamline the process."

"Oh, is there some kind of fuckboy filter on there that I've been missing the last three years? Would have helped me out with Xander Ashbury."

"Unfortunately not." I take a moment at the memory of Xander and his incessant staring at lunch, like he was undressing us with his eyes while he skinned an apple with his two front teeth. He messaged Poppy every night for a week to tell her to have sweet dreams. She, unsurprisingly, did not. "I can still sort by sports, clubs, and classes, though."

She huffs out a laugh. "You don't do sports or clubs."

"The app doesn't care." I start selecting what I think I can work with to find the perfect date: my favorite classes from last year, lacrosse team, debate club, book club, tennis team, Poppy's advanced art and sculptures class, the tech club . . .

She scoffs as she watches me tick boxes on the app. "None of those things add up to you."

"Meaning?"

"You have no interest in that stuff. How are you going to find a real connection with someone?"

"I'm not looking for a real connection, just someone I can have a good time with on Saturday. I'll search the groups, find interesting people who I've had literally *any* positive interactions with, do my usual social media stuff, and private message the promising ones." Never mind the fact that I haven't even been asked on a date before and I'm going on year four of school with most of these guys. They've had all the time in the world to make a move, and for some reason, they haven't. I've almost started believing it's because of me and not them.

"Isn't there a limit to how many people you can message in a day?"

"There is, but it's not like I'm going to message more than five different people anyway." I watch her expression turn as she rinses off a bowl. "You think I'll need more than that?"

"No," she says in that low voice that tells me right away she's lying. She holds all her emotions and deceptions in her voice, always. "Not more than that in one day, at least."

"Poppy!"

"I'm just saying that they're high school boys and you're trying to force some kind of relationship in like six days!"

"It's not a relationship! It's a desperation date."

I frown at my phone when she looks away. My selections populated a list of one hundred people. I'll have to go through it later to weed out anyone who isn't a guy, but the list will still be so long. And even worse, I have to sort through that long list to find a guy on short notice who's free, or into me enough to cancel plans he already has for this Saturday, to make Summer shut her mouth for the rest of eternity. We can hook her up with one of those feeding tubes just to make sure.

I release one long-suffering sigh and inspect the mountain of dishes waiting for Poppy's magic touch. "This is going to take you forever."

"Unless you help me. . . ."

I put on a pair of rubber gloves and dive into the bubbles overflowing the sink. The things I do for love . . . and for putting off my own problems.

She swipes away an errant strand of black hair. "In unrelated life news, so many people have had nice things to say about my art in the restaurant lately that I was able to wear down my parents and—drumroll, please."

I grab a spoon from the bottom of the sink and start smacking it against the side, water flicking into the air.

"I asked them if I could take the lead on the decor for Juanita's fundraiser, and they said maybe."

"Maybe?" I shriek, tossing the spoon aside and hugging her tightly. "That's practically a yes!"

We rock in place to release our energy.

"I already have so many ideas for centerpieces and wall art," she says, turning back to the sink, "but not really a lot of time. We're short-staffed this week because of vacations—"

"Yes, got it." I return to the sink and start scrubbing furiously. "Dishes first, ideas and dates second. We've got a lot of work to do."

Poppy drives me home on her lunch break. It was supposed to be the end of her shift, but someone called off, which means Poppy, as the always-on-call employee (read: daughter of the owners), had to pick up their slack. At least she gets paid well when she's guilt-tripped into working.

It was probably for the best that I do this alone, anyway. I started getting shier by the minute, imagining reaching out to these guys and getting ghosted—or *worse*: rejected—in front of Poppy. She'd never rub it in my face that she was right that high school boys are awful, but I'd have to acknowledge that she was right about high school boys being awful, and that would be like admitting defeat. The selection process will just have to be something kept between me and my electronics.

I take my phone out to the backyard with a container of cut-up cantaloupe and sit at the massive picnic table my parents proudly built last year. There's something fancy about it, according to my dad, maybe the wood type, but it seems like just a picnic table to me.

Instead of removing the people I won't be considering for dates, I make a list of the ones I will be considering. It's less work, and time is of the essence. I am nothing if not efficient.

I'm sure it's because my heart is racing at just the thought of randomly interacting with these guys, but the list I end up with is much smaller than I thought it would be. Only six guys. But I don't have a lot of time to work my magic anyway, so six is more than enough. I only need one in the end. The top contenders are:

- Cameron Tamburello
- Wilson Hammond
- Jackson Keller
- Kabir Khan
- Brad Tamburello (brother of Cameron, but they run in different circles, so I doubt they'll know I'm pursuing them both)
- Tyson Garcia

A first impression is important, yes, but I know it's not the only important thing. So, I don't go through the whole process of typing and deleting greetings to try to find the perfect one, and instead type hi :) to five of them while holding my breath. It's true that I can only message five people a day through the app—to avoid someone spamming the entire school—but, lucky me, I already have Tyson Garcia's phone number from when we worked on a group project freshman year. I text him the same thing.

A moment passes, and I really hope the Tamburello brothers aren't sitting next to each other.

I don't have to hold my breath long, which is great because I've never had the best lung capacity—I was always the kid who had to blow twice on birthday candles, and not just the ones that reignite to frustrate you, but the normal ones—because Tyson messages back instantly.

Tyson
Hey. Long time no see

Last year, we had a good time messing with our World Lit teacher, Mrs. Phillips, who was chaos embodied. She took so long to cover each of our reading assignments, with long, passionate rants and rambling, that we never actually completed one. As a running joke, Tyson and I bet on which we'd finish first: the syllabus or an actual assignment. I use this to start my flirting.

Lahey
Yeah sorry, I've been so busy finishing all
those books mrs Phillips made us start

Tyson

Oh yeah? How far did you get?

Lahey

Did you know that Frankenstein is the doctor???

And not the monster???

Tyson

Lol. Yeah

Lahey

Why did no one ever tell me?

Tyson

Probably bc you're so cute and they

didn't want to upset you :)

Lahey

Oh. Well in that case. I appreciate not having known

God, are those butterflies in my stomach? This is going so well so far. I don't know what I was so worried about. I could probably focus all my efforts on just Tyson, but then Cameron messages next. I can hear the imaginary crowd cheering for my imaginary basketball team.

Cameron

More like hiiiiigh

Cameron and I didn't have class together, but he had art class with Poppy, which is basically like having class with me because I was always there before and after the bell rang, and even sometimes in the middle—I had a free study period and would often spend entire classes sitting with Poppy while she worked on her latest art project. Cameron did a lot of experimental things like destroying dictionaries with paint. One day, we bonded over accidentally getting high off the rubber cement he was using for a spiderweb sculpture. The fumes got trapped in his preferred creative space, a small closet in the art room that people would use to text without getting in trouble, and we spent the next thirty minutes with the nurse while we giggled ourselves sober. I remember that he said my hair was shiny that day. I said his was brown. He loved it.

Lahey

Will you ever not associate me with glue?

Cameron

Never. Get used to it.

Lahey

There are worse things I guess

Cameron

Like what?

I'm feeling bold and go for it, saying, Like not having your number to text you when I was thinking about you. I think back to Cameron's dating history. In the past, he's shown a preference for "attentive" girls—like Zoey Dugan, who's infamous at our school for stick-and-poking the initials of her previous boyfriends on her body—and he proves that my aggressive approach is working by sending me his number with a bunch of winking emoji faces. I force my body not to react. I know that Cameron is a flirt; I'm not anything special to him—yet.

Lahey
Hi again

Cameron
So what's up? Why are you thinking of me?

Lahey
Oh, I just saw Poppy's latest creation this morning and it got me wondering how you're doing

Cameron
I'm great. How's your summer?

I hate even when her *name* comes up innocently in conversation.

Lahey
Kind of boring tbh. Have you done anything fun?

Cameron
Not yet, but there's still time

You're right . . . maybe we could do something this week

I don't phrase it as a question so there will be less of a chance he'll reject me. Out of my prospects, he's probably the most likely to give me an easy yes, but if I'm proven wrong, I'm in for a hell of a week.

Cameron

I work but I'd really like that. Let me get my schedule and I'll get back to you

It's a start, and I feel pretty confident that he's not trying to let me down gently. It's what I tell myself, at least, to avoid premature panic. I keep this conversation going while engaging Tyson about something completely different. He won't be as receptive as Cameron to my blatant flirting—I've never seen him date anyone—but he's definitely worth the effort. If I could score Tyson, the guy who's never seemed interested in anyone, Summer might simply implode.

More messages—from ALL OF THEM, thankfully—come in and change into text messages as I gather their numbers like strawberries from a field, just *pluck pluck pluck*, and into my little basket they go. It's surprising how easy it is to keep track of each conversation I'm having. They all get a slightly different version of me than the others, tailored to their needs, but I have a singular mission, and I keep it front of mind.

I comb through their socials for conversation starters, hints

of the kind of girls they like, and more, while trying to schedule plans for the week around their availability. Wilson, a guy
I know from Liberty's very short stint on the student council,
suggests lunch tomorrow, so I focus on him first. He gets points
for eagerness. There is no time to waste.

WILSON HAMMOND, 18, through the eyes of Lahey Johnson, who has unblinkingly stalked his online presence for the last two hours

How I know him: was secretary-treasurer for the senior student council with Liberty; graduated a year before me; once offered to throw out my empty water bottle after a pep rally but I declined because you don't throw out plastic

He likes: the smell of manure in the morning (possibly a joke but TBD); spring rolls from Ho Wah; ventriloquists; wearing jeans year-round; PDA, as evidenced by his many IG photos from previous relationships

He dislikes: proper punctuation; a fully cooked burger; wet socks; plastic utensils; wooden pencils; being single

Dating history: two long-term relationships, one starting in eighth grade and then one sophomore year, basically back-to-back, and he's willing to go on a date with me even though he only broke up with the latest girlfriend two months ago

Bio: Wilson grew up with two sisters in Camp Hill. They were raised by their single dad after his mother died in a car accident when he was two. He gets told that he looks like her all the time, and to make light of the situation, he tells people to stop insulting his dead mother. He made a TikTok of one of these exchanges and it went viral. None of his other content has reached that level, but he has a steady fan base of girls who like his dimples.

Monday

Five

Wilson Hammond is a country boy, if you ignore the fact that he was born and raised right here in central Pennsylvania.

When he swaggers into the LongHorn Steakhouse on the Carlisle Pike—his pick—I recognize him instantly, even though it's been a while since I saw him outside of my phone screen. He's even wearing the same shirt as his casual senior photo, a collared denim number with the sleeves rolled up, as if he'd been working on the farm this morning. He, very unfortunately, pairs his top with the same color wash of jeans and weathered cowboy boots.

I remind myself that it doesn't have to be forever, or even love; he just has to be willing to go with me on Saturday. This is nothing a makeover montage can't fix.

"Wilson," I call, signaling to the front of the restaurant from my seated position. Here's the moment I think everyone must dread on a first date: the moment when it's still possible for the other person to pretend they didn't see you, bail, and then mysteriously lose your number.

Instead of racing away to jump on his horse and win the Kentucky Derby, he shows me practically all the teeth in his mouth. "Hey!"

I worry he'll butcher my name when faced with saying it out loud, so I offer it like I'm introducing myself formally. I typically don't tell people that I was named after my dad's first dog, a three-legged mutt with bald spots and a heart of gold, but something tells me Wilson would find it funny if I decided to do it today.

"Lay-hee." I offer my hand as he sits down and he . . . twists it so he can kiss my knuckles. Okay. I need to decide if this is gentlemanly or outdated or sexist. I settle on . . . almost cute. No, actually, it *is* cute. I'm choosing to believe it's a conscious brand decision on his part and I'm here for it.

"Sorry I'm late." He takes the seat opposite me and fidgets with a crease in his hair—the result of eating, sleeping, breathing in hats. I wasn't sure he even had a fully formed head before today because I've never seen the top of it.

"No worries. The waiter hasn't even come by yet." I glance around to see if there's someone I can signal to, and Wilson seems to be doing the same. I wonder if he's doing it out of nerves, like me, or because he's starving. I was hungry until he sat down. Stress and his presence have stolen my appetite now.

"Those are some boots," I say enthusiastically. Not technically a lie. "Where'd you get them?"

"Oh, thank you. They were my grandfather's actually." He kicks his leg up in the air and gives the lady at the table next to us a heart attack. She clutches her imaginary pearls and then laughs when she meets my eyes, because I'm just as stunned. "I only break them out for special occasions."

"Thanks for considering this special," I say. "Unless . . . are you going somewhere after this?"

He breaks into laughter, putting all those teeth on display again. "That's funny. You're funny. Liberty was always funny, too. It must run in your family."

"Yeah, I steal a lot of jokes from her, but I have a few originals up my sleeve."

His brown eyes twinkle. "That's better than me. I steal from a famous person and then everyone knows it."

Something sinks in my gut.

Oh no.

Please don't bring up the puppet guy.

"Do you like Jeff Dunham?" he asks, bringing up the puppet guy. "I've never met a girl who's even heard of him."

It's true that I didn't know who Jeff Dunham the ventriloquist was before an hour ago. I only learned because Wilson makes a lot of TikToks dubbing his skits. I couldn't even watch for research purposes because it freaked me out too much, but a simple Google search taught me that his work is sexist, racist boomer humor. Stuff about hating your wife and terrorism. It's a real "product of the times," as my parents would say—I'd be lying if I didn't admit to showing up today with the hopes of finding out exactly why Wilson likes him.

If things were to ever evolve between us, I would find a way to scour Wilson's flawed interests from the internet. I *know* Summer would find it otherwise, especially if he's going to insist on bringing it up as the first topic of conversation. It's not exactly a red flag, but maybe a maroon one.

"My dad is a fan," I say. Translation: I asked my dad if he ever heard of him before he left for work this morning and he said, "I think so."

"Your dad sounds pretty cool."

"Yeah, he is. I'm a daddy's girl." Excuse me while I vomit into my napkin. I don't know why those words just came out of my mouth.

"Hi, sorry, I'm here."

The appearance of our waiter, which should make me happy, is accompanied by Adler's voice and body, so instead it makes me want to implode. Or, actually, explode. That way, I have the chance to take Adler out with me and be remembered as a hero.

"Oh, this will be good," he says quietly when his green eyes land on me.

"Why are you here?" I'm proud of how soft and calm my question comes out when I want to shriek it. As if this whole situation isn't awkward enough, Adler is going to witness it?

"I work here." He gestures to his all-black attire and notepad with a stupid flourish that might make another girl laugh. He's so annoying; he's never cared about his body, never outwardly shown that he's felt uncomfortable in his skin or with his gangly limbs all over the place. It's not natural. It's un-American. "Why are *you* here? Don't you have a bog to haunt?"

"Excuse me," Wilson cuts in sharply, glancing between us. His brow sags down. "Is there a problem?"

"How much time do you have?" Adler asks.

Now the brow goes sky-high. "Excuse me?"

"Oh, nothing," he says with a fake chuckle. He continues in his sugary-sweet server voice, "What can I get you two for drinks? Lahey? Some blood of the innocent?"

He jots it down on his notepad and turns to Wilson before I can even process it. "And you?"

"I'm sorry," Wilson says slowly. "You know each other?"

"Unfortunately," Adler says. "We have Coke products."

"Yeah, Coke is fine." Wilson flips his hand toward me. "What would you like?"

"I'd like a new waiter." I glance at Wilson before adding, "Please."

Adler smirks, or maybe it's a grimace. "Anything else?"

"A Diet Coke—"

"Oh, look," he says, pointing to his right, "an excuse for me to walk away." And he does.

It's for the best. I was going to ask him to jump off a cliff next if he kept on embarrassing me like that. I can only imagine how poorly the rest of this date would go if Adler was around; I wouldn't be able to let my guard down. I'll be looking for him out of the corner of my eye, waiting for ice water to be "accidentally" poured down my back. One of his favorite pastimes when we were younger was to sneak up on me and make me think bugs were crawling down my neck.

I swat at a strand of hair that tickles me now, goose bumps pebbling my arms.

"What just happened?" Wilson asks, leaning in like we're sharing gossip. His concern is actually really endearing.

"I'm so sorry. That's—do you not know Adler? He's Liberty's best friend. He's . . . an ass—" I end up drawing out the word accidentally as I search for another one, then just stop. He's an ass.

Wilson chuckles. "No need to say any more. I get it. I have sisters. I'm really protective, too."

"No, that's not what this is." Adler's favorite game since the day we met has been to get a rise out of me. I'll never admit it, but it ranks somewhere in the top twenty of my favorite games, nestled cozily between laser tag and Connect 4.

"I don't know, I see the signs." Wilson pointedly looks over my shoulder and I follow his direction to spot Adler quickly turning away from us at the drink machine. "He's keeping an eye on you. I promise him, I'll be sweet."

I use all my willpower not to cringe, because he means well.

"Thanks. I'm pretty certain he was just making sure I wasn't looking as he spit into my drink, though."

Wilson laughs again, not knowing me well enough yet to understand that I'm serious.

Adler approaches the table with a drink in each hand and a cute redhead in tow. There are more freckles on her face than there are people here for the half-priced lunch special that I'm convinced is just leftovers from the previous day.

"This is Daphne, and she'll be your waitress today." He sets down our drinks and a bit of Wilson's Coke splashes onto his lap because of the force Adler uses. He grins in apology and then unrolls my napkin to steal my fork. "She won't need this. Forked tongue and all."

"*Adler Altman.*" It's times like this that I wish he had a middle name. Instead, his parents wanted to honor both their Jewish families by giving him his mother's last name as his first and his father's last name as his last. At least I can soak my rage in the alliteration, if not the dreaded three-name combo. "*Stop*," I hiss.

Daphne laughs a bit awkwardly and then starts listing some of her favorite meals to an overly attentive Wilson, both of them ignoring my existence right now as I'm straight-up harassed by our former waiter.

Adler moves in so only I can hear him. "It sucks to have someone get in your business, huh?"

He walks away after a playful shrug. The satisfaction coming off him is palpable—he's clearly been waiting for a chance to get back at me for the matchmake.

This is probably the moment I should mention that I did not have entirely selfless reasons for trying to match him with Brighton. I didn't really do it for Adler, or even for Brighton. My sister and Sophia had started dating, and Adler was suddenly a third wheel. I didn't want him to ruin the good thing Liberty had going on. It had been a while since Adler had a girlfriend, so I thought maybe he merely needed my assistance. In the end, even though I was just trying to *help* my *sister*, both she and Adler were pretty mad at me. Liberty has since forgiven me, though, and Liberty doesn't just hold grudges; she hugs them tight. She's still hugging a grudge against our parents for conceiving her in early summer, thus giving her a winter birthday. So, I feel like Adler should just forgive me. My intentions were good.

"Lahey?" Wilson shakes me out of my stupor.

"Yeah?"

Daphne and Wilson stare at me with matching bemused smiles on their faces.

"Do you need more time?" His tone is patient and playful, even though he shoots Daphne an apologetic wince.

"For?"

"Ordering?"

Damn Adler for making me look like a space case.

"Oh. Food. Yes. I'll take the—" I glance at the menu and resist ordering a burger the size of my ego because I know I'll barely eat it. "Salmon with rice?"

"You get a side and a salad with that," Daphne says, waiting.

"How about a chocolate milkshake instead?" I joke, but I'm not really joking.

Daphne, to her credit, and probably because she wants a tip, laughs. "I wish, but we don't have those here."

"You know, I'm more of a vanilla guy myself," Wilson says, crushing me underneath his boots. He smiles at Daphne.

"Me too," she says, blushing. "Girl! Vanilla *girl*."

She turns back to me. "So . . . ?"

"Uh, the house salad and broccoli, I guess."

"Got it," she says with a nod, jotting it down on her notepad. "I'll be bread with some back shortly."

"I think you meant back with some bread," Wilson teases.

She tries to hide her face, but he says, "I was just joking. You're fine. It was cute."

When she walks away, biting back a grin, his eyes follow.

Oh. He has a type.

I knew I was being naive when I looked at his Instagram and decided it was normal for a guy to follow that many hot red-haired celebrities. True, the list isn't that long, but he follows *all* of them.

"Do you know her?"

"Oh, yeah. Sort of. We went to school together. I guess that means you went to school with her, too." He's not meeting my eyes when he speaks, alternating between staring into his Coke and gazing over my shoulder.

"So, completely random question," I say, playing with the loose napkin in front of me, "but do you like yellow or red more?"

"What?"

Daphne's not back with the bread soon enough. I need carbs for courage, or at least compensation—I'm about to blow up this date, and I've gotten nothing out of it. Maybe Wilson will surprise me, select correctly, and I'll get to stay here and enjoy it fully. Yellow equals blond, which equals me. Red equals Daphne. "If you had to pick a color."

He finally realizes Daphne won't be returning any time soon and grins at me. Only half his teeth are showing this time. "Red. What about you?"

Damn. "Green."

He laughs. "But that wasn't an option."

"Would you have picked it if it was?"

"Well. No."

"That's what I thought." This poor boy doesn't know himself as well as I know him right now. "Wilson, this isn't going to work out, but I appreciate the attempt."

I can't show up to Summer's party with a date who has his eye on someone else—that would be worse than going solo. Even if I *could* chance it, it goes against every fiber of my being to stand in the way of love.

"What?" He sits up straighter. I wonder if he's ever been rejected before—not that I'm really rejecting him; imagine, me rejecting a boy when I so desperately need one. A ludicrous concept. "Why's that?"

"Because you have a type, and I'm not it." I wish it could have been this easy. A cute sweet boy who only needs some minor fixing . . . but it's never that easy.

He puts his hands up. "Wait, no, I'm okay with—" He looks around before leaning in and whispering, "*Fat girls*." In a louder voice, he continues. "I agreed to the date. You have a really pretty face, and you're funny."

I swear I start vibrating with annoyance. I'm surprised the wobbly chair beneath me doesn't start clattering around the dining room. "Not what I meant, but it's nice to know how *open-minded* you are."

Just for that comment, I should have ordered the burger so I could take it to go.

"I'm sorry. I thought that was PC now. Am I not allowed to say that word?"

The only reason I haven't left already is because I just can't waste this easy setup in front of me. I know there will be the sweet feeling of victory in just a few minutes, plus it will feel like closure on this date prospect. "Let's forget that for now. If I could help you get with Daphne, would you want that?"

He frowns. "No . . ."

"You don't have to lie. I want to help you." I literally can't help myself, even when it's to my own detriment.

"Are you—I heard you do this thing . . . You pair people up?"

"Yeah, I'm kind of good at it." Just not for myself. I hate when Summer is right. *No, she's not right. Wilson* is not right, for me. That's why it doesn't work. I'm simply crossing him off my metaphorical list.

"Daphne's nice," he says after a moment of silent thought, his shiny white teeth nibbling at his bottom lip. I'd be lying if I said it didn't hurt to have confirmation that he'd rather be set up with our waitress than sit here for the rest of the meal with me. "She was in the grade above me, so I always felt like I couldn't talk to her."

"A hot older woman." I nod approvingly, just to help him get more comfortable with the thought of discussing romantic options with one girl while on a date with a different one. It's not his fault. I appreciate his honesty. There are other guys I can work with for the party, and honestly, Wilson would not have been my first choice if others were available anyway.

"We both ended up doing trash pickup as a volunteer project two years ago, and she would listen to music and zone out—she would start singing to herself. It was—" He bites his lip. "It was really charming. She's a good singer."

"What else?"

"What do you mean?"

"What else do you like about her?" ~~And what's so wrong with me that you didn't want to find more things you could like about me?~~ *No. Think of the puppets.*

He leans in, both elbows on the table as he starts spewing a long list of what makes Daphne so special. He really likes her. Her brains, her humor, her dedication to work and education.

"Okay, I'm going to give it a shot." I stand from the table and grab my bag.

"What are you going to do?"

"Probably just talk, I don't know yet, but just go with it when it happens."

"You're an actual saint, Lahey."

I beam at him over my shoulder, give him one last look at what he's missing out on.

He tracks my progress to where Daphne is taking another table's order, everyone sharing a laugh. When she's done, she pushes her hair over her shoulder and comes over to me, eyes wide.

"Did you need something?" Her voice is caring, sweet, concerned. Probably too good for Wilson.

"Yes, actually. My friend over there—" I point to Wilson, who awkwardly waves. "He knows you from school, I think?"

"Yeah. Wilson. He's your . . . *friend*?"

"Yeah, the only guy my boyfriend trusts me to hang out with one-on-one, you know?" I roll my eyes like *Men*. "He's just such a dorky gentleman, and he's—oh, look at him, he's blushing—he thinks you're really sweet, and he will probably kick my butt for saying all this to you, but he deserves a great girl and—"

"I never thought he saw me like that." She glances at him from the corner of her eye. "I've embarrassed myself around him a lot."

"No way! He gets really nervous around girls he likes usually, but he was so smooth with you earlier. Talking about how he's a vanilla guy and joking around. Adorable. Anyway, I'm going to leave so you two can, you know, have a real conversation. Do you have a break soon? Maybe Adler could take over for you."

Her mouth drops open, and she starts smoothing down her black shirt. "I'm not really dressed for a date."

I appreciate fashion as much as the next person, but this is LongHorn, not *Vogue*.

"Are you kidding me? You could be walking down a red carpet right now. Super chic."

"If you . . . say so . . ." She nods to herself. "Yeah, I have a lunch break I could take."

"Amazing. I'll tell Adler on the way out."

Another success.

Except, not for me. I just . . . wasn't enough.

Refusing to fully deflate, I head for the host stand, where Adler hunches over his phone, distracted. I tap him on the shoulder and his muscles tense. "You need to cover for Daphne."

"Scare her away, too?" He looks between my table, where Daphne now sits and nervously unclips her name tag, and me. "What's happening?"

"True love." I consider the pair for a moment. "Or a year-long relationship destined for failure. That part's not up to me; it's out of my control now."

"So, you're just leaving? Leaving your date with another girl?"

"There was no chemistry between us, just some niceties and subtle condescension. On to the next one, I say!" I don't really have a choice.

"Next one? What are you doing, Lahey?" His words stop me as I've clasped a hand around the door handle. I guess I could consider myself lucky he finally wants to have a conversation with me, but after the way he behaved at the table, I'm cautious.

"I'm surprised Berty didn't tell you. She wouldn't stop laughing about it last night." I cross my arms and move away from the door so a family of four can come inside. "I told Summer I could get a date to her party without a problem, which is . . . a problem, because I'm me. So now I have to find one in six—*five*—days and make her admit she was wrong." Finger guns. "Or just make her screw off eternally."

He bites his lip to hold back a smile that I'm sure would decimate me and my self-esteem. "Wow. Good luck out there."

"Thanks." I'm not even ashamed to admit this to him. He's seen me lower. Like that time I crawled on the floor to grab a chocolate-covered strawberry he dropped, from his mouth, just because it was the last one.

"Oh, no, that was meant for all the guys you'll be bothering this week." He shifts to the side as the actual host comes to the stand and welcomes the family.

"Oh, aren't you charming?" I turn on my heel and relish in the way my dress spins in the breeze. "Now, if you'll excuse me, I have a bog that needs some haunting."

This time, there's no holding back the smile that grows on his face. I have to say, it's a relief. I've gone too long without it. But, speaking of things I've gone too long without, I need to focus on finding a date. Getting Adler's forgiveness will come in due time, and it seems like we're making quick progress back to the days of casually dunking on each other, but the clock is ticking on the search for a date to put Summer in her place once and for all.

This is certainly going to be a much harder week than anticipated if I can't get out of my own way. I wasn't Wilson's type, and I can deduce based on my lack of dates the last seventeen years of my life that maybe I'm just . . . not *anyone's* type. So, I need to change types.

Maybe I need to reframe this from match*making* myself into match*faking* myself.

Six

When I return Liberty's car, driver's seat perfectly dry this time, I find her buried under four feet of fabric in our bedroom. It looks like a bath bomb went off in here. Makeup, clothes, and shoes line most surfaces. I wouldn't have even known she was in here if I hadn't heard her frustrated whine when the top step groaned, announcing my presence. I would take tripping on her cleats over not being able to see the floor when I walk any day. She better clean up her stuff before she leaves for school or else I'm donating all of it while she's gone—or better yet, selling it.

"Hey," I say cautiously, peeking into our room. "Whatcha doing?"

Her head pops free from a lacy top I've never seen her wear, her short golden waves scattered across her face. "Oh, nothing. What's up?"

I hold out the car keys, too afraid to step closer.

"How did your date go? You're home early." She smooths

her hair into each strand's rightful place. "You're early, right? Or am I *late*?"

"I'm early," I sigh, dropping myself to the bed next to her. She pushes off a few pieces of clothing and sits up. "I helped my date get a date with our waitress."

Liberty blinks. "Why?"

"Because I'm self-destructive? Too nice? I don't know!" I fling myself backward and land on the heel of a comically sparkly silver shoe. If I keep digging, I'm sure I'll find the rest of Disco Barbie's wardrobe here. "It probably would have been a perfectly fine date if I hadn't noticed the suspicious twinkle in his eye when he talked to her. I could have ignored it, I guess. But apparently I like making things difficult."

"That *is* something you do." She watches a pair of jeans slide to the floor at her feet. "So, you have to go on another date now?"

"I have to *find* another date before I can *go* on another one. Unless one of my classmates has been harboring a crush on me and he'd like to admit it today, the rest of the day and probably tomorrow are shot."

"In fairness, you did this to yourself."

"Whose side are you on?" I finally dislodge the shoe from my back and toss it toward her side of the closet, where a shoe rack sits empty. "Since when does Adler work at LongHorn? I thought he was working for his mom this summer."

Liberty tugs her blouse off—revealing a maroon bralette that we compromised on her buying because it wasn't a sports bra (my demand) and didn't try to give her boobs that her body didn't already have (her demand)—and grabs a striped dress next to her that I'm positive usually lives in our mother's closet. Mom's style is about a hundred miles nowhere near Liberty's.

"Yeah, he's working at the shop and some other places now. That cat café, I think. Don't let Lily know."

I wonder if that's why I've seen less of him around lately. Sure, he currently hates me, but he loves Liberty—third wheel status be damned. They've been inseparable since they were kids.

"Why all the jobs?" I ask, methodically searching through the clothes for something that actually belongs to my sister. "He's a little early for a quarter-life crisis."

"Well, he's going to HACC this year to get all his gen eds done, and he wants to pay entirely in cash to avoid death by student loans."

I've tried my best to avoid even overhearing the tedious conversations about college and financial aid that have occurred between my parents and Liberty. It's all too depressing and stressful to fully contemplate. My parents, even if they had stopped having children after Liberty, would not have been able to send her to college without the "help" of several loans. It's just a fact. All the Johnson children will be in debt for a long, long time. Liberty especially so because, while she's gotten a small scholarship for freshman year, she's not going to a state school and she's unable to hold on to a dollar for more than three minutes. Her allowance has never stood a chance against her habits, and our parents have meltdowns when we mention getting jobs—like we're trying to guilt them for being unable to provide us with every little thing that pops into our heads, like Summer's parents do.

I did try to get a job at my dad's work last summer, and avoided the parental meltdown by saying I wanted to spend more time with my father figure. Nepotism seemed like a great way to earn money until I realized he actually expected me to work. He became the manager of his pride and joy, It Takes a Village Daycare, about eleven years ago. He started working there to get free child care for Liberty, then for me, too, and then Lily, but even once Liberty aged out and could watch all of us for free, my dad stayed. My dad has always loved children, and he really enjoys his job. I just couldn't do it. The mess. The noise. I bailed after barely a month and have never questioned my parents' stance on children in the workforce ever since.

Liberty straightens out the dress and twirls into a standing position in front of me. "How's this?"

"Great, if you're going to a business conference all about sharpening pencils. What's the occasion?"

My sister single-handedly keeps every clothing compa-ny's athleisure line in business with her previously mentioned meager allowance, so while I wholeheartedly approve of her wearing a dress—any dress—it doesn't exactly scream Liberty.

"I'm looking for an outfit that says 'I love you, don't break up with me.'" Her bottom lip wobbles. "Because I don't want us to break up."

"Berty," I say, squeezing her hand and pulling her closer. "If you don't want to break up, then don't. You two made up this stupid rule."

Sophia and Liberty knew their relationship would be short-lived because of the schools they were going to attend: Sophia at Pitt for nursing and Liberty at UPenn for engineering. They agreed to end things before classes began—despite my many long-winded conversations with Liberty against it—and then along this path of destruction, they forgot where they were headed and fell head over heels in love.

She yanks her hand away like the truth burned her. "It's for our own good. We won't last long-distance. We've only been together a few months and she'll be going to school five hours away from me."

"What are you so afraid of?" My internal romanticism shows me a highlight reel of them falling asleep together over Face-Time, spending a long weekend in the other's dorm, mailing handwritten letters, and planning to meet in the middle—read: home—during breaks from school. "It's not like Sophia would ever cheat."

"And I wouldn't, either," Liberty adds. "I just—long distance puts distance between people, like, emotionally."

"They actually say it makes the heart grow fonder. And there are ways to stay close." I pick up Liberty's favorite jeans from the floor and fold them on my lap. "I could give you a whole list of things you could do to keep things fresh and romantic. Care packages you could mail back and forth when you get extra lonely. Stuff like that."

"The shipping costs would add up."

"If you give me time, I could come up with more things."

It's just so ridiculous to break up if you don't want to. Here

I am, searching for someone to keep me company for just one night, to literally just *show up to a party*, and Liberty has someone she loves, who loves her, and wants to be with for the foreseeable future. It feels wasteful and rude to give it up. *Think of the singletons who want to be a twosome but can't, Liberty!*

She huffs in response but says nothing else.

"Fine, then," I say, standing. "If you're so sure there's no way to make it work, why don't you at least make this last week extra special?"

She unearths a strappy red shoe—mine—and stares at it with a blank expression. "How do you mean?"

"Instead of being sad all week, remind each other how much fun it's been. Do things you always meant to and then maybe if you're still feeling like you *have* to break up, at least you went out with a bang."

She sucks her bottom lip in and chews. She looks so much like Lily when she does that—or I guess Lily reminds me of Liberty when she does it. It's actually kind of unfair how much of each other I see in them. It makes me feel like the odd woman out.

"Yeah, I guess."

"If you two end on good terms, you could always get back together anyway."

"Yeah. Yeah, maybe." She nods. "Maybe we break up and then spend a semester apart and get back together. There are a lot of ways it could go."

It doesn't matter how much sense it makes not to start college with a long-distance partner; if you're in love, you're in love. If you're *made for each other*, then you shouldn't let things stand in your way. These two managed to sit next to each other at graduation despite Liberty being in the *J*s and Sophia being in the *W*s. If they can do that, they can do this.

And maybe I'm a romantic, but I'm certainly not hopeless. True love is out there for me, and while I may not find it this week, I can definitely fake it until I make it.

Tuesday

Seven

"Maybe it needs to happen more organically."

I lift an eyebrow at Poppy, my hand stalled over the dress rack in JCPenney—you'd think there would be a ton of cute choices because it's summer, but you'd be wrong.

"Like you want my date to spring from the ground?" I ask skeptically.

"Obviously," she says with a roll of her eyes. "Because that's easier than seeing a boy in real life and asking him out."

I grab another option for Saturday and lay it over my arm. It's a bit on the plainer side when it comes to pattern, but the fit should be flattering. This is the second store we've hit this morning, and nothing is speaking to me or my budget.

"That process is medieval, and I can't believe you of all people would suggest it. You're always warning me about stranger danger."

"Well, what other choice do you have—aside from, you know, showing up without a fake date like I wisely suggested?"

"It's not a fake date. It's a real date, but with a boy I may fake like."

With a sour look, she plucks my most recent option from my grasp and puts it back on the rack. "The chances of your dates getting *better* after the first one failed are barely fifty-fifty."

The stakes send a chill down my spine despite the store's struggling AC. "You've never been good at math, though; maybe you're wrong this time." I glance around, but there's no one but Poppy to hear me. I'm pretty sure I saw a tumbleweed roll by earlier. "I need all the help I can get, but I'm not about to go around cold-asking people on dates. What if I ask a potential serial killer?"

She shrugs, eyes focused on the clothes in front of her as she searches for her size. "Look, I'd also rather be single forever than give a stranger the chance to reject me to my face, but you aren't even entertaining the option."

"Why do you assume I'd be rejected?" I know she doesn't mean to hurt my feelings, but, alas, my feelings are *quite* hurt. I'm starting to feel like there is no one out there who believes I can secure even a single date by the weekend.

"We have to cover all the bases in this hypothetical mess: either you die literally or you die from embarrassment. I don't make the rules."

It never fails to astound me—or turn me into a slightly jealous monster—that Poppy's firsts have all come before mine. This girl who doesn't like waitressing because it's too much interaction with strangers, who sees a person coming a mile down the sidewalk and switches sides to avoid the obligatory head nod and strained smile. This girl has held hands, kissed, and *had sex* all before I've found someone who has even a fraction of the same interest in me as I do them. It just doesn't seem fair. I'm begging for those things, willing and ready, and she stumbles upon them last winter break with her family friend's hot and sensitive son who wanted no commitment, only to give Poppy one hell of a night (it was not, she reported, one hell of a night, but I'd maybe even take a lackluster first time over no time).

"I ask again," she starts with a heavy sigh, "is Summer really worth all this stress?"

"It's not Summer herself; it's the opportunity to get her off my back once and for all, and *yes*, that's worth the stress." I head toward the changing rooms. "You know, when I was thirteen, my mom made me invite her to a Halloween party I had, and she showed up in this gaudy custom thing that cost my parents' mortgage. My amazing costume was *wasted* because no one even looked twice at it."

Poppy opens the nearest changing room and holds the door for me. "Next time someone asks what grudge you're holding on to, don't mention that specific one. It's not doing you any favors."

I slide in, and she follows, locking it. "But I know you're dying to tell me what your costume was, so . . . out with it."

"An egg bodysuit with a red horn headband."

She pauses hanging up her clothes to picture it. "What is—"

"A deviled egg."

She resumes her action with a withering look over her

shoulder. "Maybe Summer did you a favor."

Absolutely *not*. I was so proud of that costume—I came up with the idea, and my mom hand-made it over the three nights prior to the party—but then Summer showed up in her flashy Scarlet Witch costume that her dad hired two cosplayers to make for her. Half the people at the party didn't even know what a deviled egg was and thought I had invented it. The other half gave me a sympathy chuckle before asking if they could wear Summer's intricate headpiece.

We start trying on dresses, but the first is black and doesn't do my complexion any favors. I personally think I'm pretty tan compared to what I look like in the winter, but I'm still several skin tones below what is considered a summer glow for a white person. Poppy's first dress is actually really pretty, but it's not her style (or my size—I checked). The next for me is too clingy around the stomach and not clingy enough around my boobs, the fabric sagging whenever I move my arms. Poppy's, once again, fits her like a tailored glove, but it's hot pink and, therefore, a no-go. I'm not even sure why she picked it up; that dress *screams* "perceive me," and I know that's the opposite of what she wants to happen at the fundraiser. She'll probably end this day with a resigned sigh and go home to press her black slacks or whatever you wear to look very mundane and professional.

"It's okay if you don't find something, you know," she says through the fabric she's pulling over her head. "You have a closet full of great dresses already."

"Yeah, but nothing to be the icing on the cake. I need to be on my A game Saturday night." I take Poppy's next discard because it's too big for her. I've tried to get Poppy comfortable with talking about my fatness, but she's still squeamish—instead of saying it's too big for her, she says something like, "I think it would be prettier on you." As if both couldn't be true. "Do you think you'll be able to get away for a bit? I can delay my grand entrance until you arrive. The more people there to witness my victory, the more idiotic Summer will feel."

"As much as I'd love to—and as much as I'll *try* to—I think I'm going to be pretty swamped helping my parents."

I give up and put my own dress back on; it's a simple green wrap dress with white polka dots that required shaving only three-fourths of my legs this morning since the hem just barely skims the tops of my knees. "Have you nailed down an idea for the decorations yet?"

"I think because Juanita is really green, I'm going to do mini trees made of fully recycled materials and make some art on recycled paper to hang on the walls. Maybe some burlap table covers. I have to get my parents on board, though. They think I should just do something uncontroversial, as if sustainability is controversial."

I hold her hand as she balances on one foot to secure her beat-up pair of Toms onto the other. "So, what are they thinking?"

"Flowers? Mason jars full of pebbles? I don't know, white people stuff. But I could make a different tree for each table made from wine bottles and aluminum cans and plastic bags. I think it would make a statement and be so pretty."

"I'll snag anything good from the recycling at home."

She kisses the top of my head, something she started when she became tall enough to do it. "You're an angel."

We dump everything onto the return rack and decide to take a sustenance break, heading to the quiet mall food court. I'll absolutely perish without some kind of nutrients in my system right now, so I buy a small strawberry smoothie and wait with Poppy for her coffee. The only other people in the food court, besides the workers, are some old ladies taking a break from their mall walking and a group of three guys around our age. Two of them are talking and laughing, nudging the third in his side. Their eyes follow Poppy and me when we take our drinks to a table nearby.

"Are those future billionaires staring at us?" Poppy asks after a sip.

They look more like guys you'd find out have alarmingly large Funko Pop! collections than future billionaires. The one on the left has glasses—*not that that's an indication of anything*, I remind myself from behind my own frames—while the right has a jean jacket with a bunch of pins on the collar. The middle one is . . . Jackson Freaking Keller.

I stop chewing on my straw, my stomach dropping. This is the first time I've seen him in person since I started texting him this week. "Oh god, that's Jackson Keller." I take my glasses off and wipe them clean on my dress.

"Yeah, you're right. I don't know the guys with him."

"It looks like they're trying to coerce him into approaching us. Oh my god." My smoothie threatens to make a reappearance at the thought of him coming over and telling me to stop inundating him with texts, or worse, by bringing up my blatant attempt at flirting with him the past two days. So far, he's responded politely, but he hasn't really initiated or tried to *continue* the conversation—I've been carrying it all. This is extra dissatisfying knowing that he's unemployed, and thus very available during the day to entertain my charming self.

"What's the problem?" she asks, looking between Jackson and me. "Wow, they're definitely talking about you."

"I've been texting Jackson." I deliver a pointed look over my glasses. "For Saturday."

Her mouth falls open. "This is so awkward," she says. "Why don't you just go say hi? You could ask him out in person! Live that organic life!"

My nerves bunch up in my gut. "You say that as if it's easy."

"Is it not?" She grimaces. "Did he already reject you?"

"*No*, I haven't asked yet. And, again, I don't appreciate the assumption that he would reject me. I'm just . . . working up to asking." I've had several conversations with the automated text messaging system at my dentist's office that have been more intimate than mine with Jackson so far. "Stranger danger," I add.

"I'm not sure you have a case there. We've gone to school with him for three years, you have been texting him, and his limp-noodle arms hardly seem suited for strangulation." She pulls my empty smoothie cup from my hands, where I was unconsciously pulverizing the straw again, and takes it to the nearest receptacle. With a look, she cuts off my impending argument about how she should have rinsed out the cup in the bathroom and then recycled it. "Go. It's Tuesday. You need to prescreen him before Saturday and this is literally the perfect opportunity."

"I liked you better when you wanted me to show up to the party with just my honesty." I push my seat out and stand. I hate when she's right. I hate how often she's right.

"Lahey!" Out of nowhere, I see my aunt maneuvering around several empty tables, bags swinging from both her arms. Behind her, Summer follows with eyes pointed to the ceiling. How can she be annoyed when I didn't even do anything yet?

"Hi." I hug my aunt, who then moves aside so I can hug Summer. So that's how Summer and I end up hugging for half an unbearable second, for the first time in years.

"Hey, Poppy." Aunt Madison nudges Summer in the arm. "Look at that lipstick Poppy has on. What do you think of that for Saturday?"

"I don't want to wear lipstick," Summer says, staring at the floor.

"What color is that?" my aunt asks.

Poppy *hmmm*s. "I think it's called Watermelon."

"Well, it looks beautiful on you."

For a hot second, I'm convinced Aunt Madison is going to sit down at our table for more girl talk. I'll lose my nerve to ask Jackson out, or miss him completely, if I get sucked into her gravitational pull.

"What are you girls up to?" she asks.

"Nothing—" I say as Poppy blurts out, "Dress shopping."

"Ah, good call with the coffee, then. That can be exhausting.

Or maybe it's just dress shopping with this one." She scrunches her nose playfully at Summer. "She's so picky."

"Mom," Summer interjects. "You said you had an appointment at one o'clock."

"And? It's barely noon."

My aunt runs her own salon in Mechanicsburg, taking client appointments only when she feels like it. She's a bit of a diva ever since her divorce with Summer's dad, but I'd probably be the same way if I suddenly had access to a bunch of zeros after my settlement amount, too. She likes to play it off jokingly that she married him for his money, but my mom has always reassured me—because, *oh my god, Madison*—that they were actually in love at one point.

"I thought we were going to get lunch, you know, one-on-one. Not here," she quickly adds, looking at me and then the food court offerings.

"All our meals are already one-on-one." Aunt Madison laughs, latching on to my shoulder like she's sharing the joke with me, but I'm stunned into silence.

"Can we go?" Summer asks, staying firm.

Aunt Madison groans dramatically. "Teenagers. First they want to be at the mall and then they want to be somewhere else. I'm just a chauffeur, huh?"

She smiles at me and Poppy before turning on her heel and heading toward the double doors leading to the parking lot. Summer is slow to follow, like she's debating staying behind even though fleeing like a coward was her idea. She spins to face me, a steely glint in her eyes.

"So you're still planning on coming to the party?"

"Yes," I say through clenched teeth. Though I really don't know why I'm putting myself through all of this. The mature thing would be to act unbothered and unoffended.

"Good luck dress shopping, then. It's going to have to be a hell of a dress to distract from your lack of date."

I don't even get to answer before she smiles, waves at Poppy with dainty fingers, and then scurries after her mom.

"Why is she so *mean*?" Poppy wonders aloud.

Oh yeah. This is why I'm putting myself through all of this.

"She will *not* win." I swallow my anxiety and head to Jackson's table without any further nudging necessary. His friends shut up as soon as I'm a few feet away.

"Hi," I say a little shakily. My face heats up, and I'm sure it's the color of Poppy's lipstick by now. "It's good to see you, Jackson. Can we talk? Alone?"

"Yeah," the one on the left says. He pulls off his black cap and attempts to fix his hair, but it's a hopeless, curly mess. "We don't mind."

"She was talking to Jackson, dumbass," the one on the right says in a deep voice. He pats Jackson on the shoulder. "Can you, like, stop staring and answer?"

Jackson shrugs off his friend's hand. "Sorry, we didn't mean to be creepy."

Left Friend laughs. "He can't help it."

"I did say *we*," Jackson tosses at him.

Right Friend hits Left Friend behind Jackson's back. "Don't ruin this for him. You want him to be a virgin forever?" Right Friend looks to me quickly, but not quickly enough that my stomach hasn't already fully dropped. "Sorry, I don't mean any-thing by that. I just mean if he can't even talk to a girl, how is he going to—I'm gonna shut up."

"Yeah," I say, nodding, my heart in my throat, "that would be good."

The friends get up to leave, but what little confidence I managed to squeeze into my brain has dissipated at thoughts of not only a date with Jackson Keller, but touching him. In many different and increasingly sexual ways.

I use the time they take to vacate the table, smacking each other and whispering, to clear my head. There will be no mutual de-virginizing happening this week—definitely not happening *today*—so I need to stop. thinking. about. it. I sit across from Jackson before I can back out and disappear in a cloud of dust like a cartoon character, my face hot. I take a deep breath and drop the most eloquent should-be-a-question-but-isn't ever:

"Let's hang out today."

Jackson chokes on a laugh. "Oh, uh, I already have plans."

"I'm down for whatever." And desperate.

"Uh, wow. You know," he says, rubbing his chin idly, "I never really thought you knew who I was before this week."

Wilson thought the same thing of Daphne, but I tell my brain to stop thinking about other people's relationships and extend my hand to him. "Let's make it official, then. I'm Lahey."

His skin is ice-cold to the touch. "Nice to meet you. I'm Jackson."

"I'm going to be honest." *No, I'm not. I'm done being honest. There's a war to win.*

I glance at his shirt and nearly cry from relief that I actually recognize the movie it's referencing. The universe couldn't make my matchfaking easier if it tried. "That's a great K-2SO shirt."

It's offensive how his eyes bug out of his head. "You like Star Wars?"

What a loaded question to ask a girl.

"I do. My dad got me into it when I was little." Point for a half-truth. My dad *tried*, but from what I've read online, he made the mistake of starting with the prequels. No matter how much better the original and sequel trilogies are, I judge the series by its worst and most boring installments.

"Who's your favorite character? Don't say Rey. Or Kylo Ren."

The innate sexism in that comment causes me to blurt out "Ben Solo" just to feel alive.

He smirks. "Fine. I'll allow it."

Oh, wow, thanks. "So, about that date?"

He blushes, and I hate that I have to come on this strong— I'd be running away if a guy was treating me like this—but I can't show up to Summer's party alone. She'll mock me until I retire early to my grave.

"How about this," he starts, alighting his phone screen. "I'll give you the address and you can decide if you want to join me this afternoon. The—*it*—starts at one thirty."

I nod for him to continue. "I like where this is going, even if you won't tell me what it is."

"Don't worry, it's a public place."

"I appreciate that." More nodding.

He grins. "I couldn't have you thinking I'm some kind of a murderer or something—"

"Sounds like something a murderer would say, but go on."

"Tons of people will be there."

"Love it. I love people." I sandwich my phone between my palms. "Why all the mystery?"

"Mostly I don't want to scare you away. And partly because it's a word-of-mouth kind of thing." He glances around and leans in. "Can't have everyone knowing about it."

I offer him a playful smile. "The suspense is killing me."

He laughs. "Okay, fine. It's—"

My phone starts vibrating against the table. "Ignore that. You were saying?"

"You can answer it." He looks over his shoulder, where his friends have made a point to very clearly eavesdrop.

I make a very unattractive face and sound when I see from the caller ID it's Lily. "It's my little sister; I'm sorry.

"Hello?" I ask in my most polite voice ever. I think the tone surprises Lily so much that she's caught off guard. She says nothing for a moment. "Lily?"

"I need you to come home, right now," she says in big, gasping breaths. "Now, Lahey."

Eight

I don't know what the emergency is until I get home. I'm not even sure what to expect—I picture the house on fire because she tried to microwave something metal, wasps in the attic that have chewed their way directly into her room, or Lily with blunt baby bangs and the offending scissors glued to her hand. She's barely a teenager, so it could be anything, and my imagination is nothing if not limitless and wild. But because of Lily's abrupt ending to the call, and my anxiety spiraling, Poppy dared to break the speed limit to get us to my house as quickly as possible. She never uses her powers of acceleration lightly.

I throw open the front door and yell, "Lily!"

"Bathroom!" Her voice echoes around the shared room, like it's trapped inside and fighting for a way out.

"You better not have called me for your period," I start, stomping up the stairs. "Mom, Liberty, and I have *all* taught you what to do—Poppy?"

Poppy stands paused in the doorframe, one hand on the

doorknob and the other reaching for her throat. "I'm a little . . . scratchy." She takes a deep breath and cuts off suddenly, coughing. "Did you guys get a cat?"

"No—" I spin and shout up the stairs. "Lily, you better not have brought a cat in here! Poppy is—"

Out the door.

Poppy is also severely allergic. One whiff and her body panics. I don't blame her for leaving, but there's no way that Lily actually got a cat. Poppy gives me a thumbs-up from inside her car—either to signal she got her EpiPen or to say she's feeling better, I don't know—and I barge into the bathroom to find my little sister vigorously washing long red scratches on her forearms.

"What did you do?" I reach around her to the medicine cabinet and free the bottle of hydrogen peroxide we've had for who knows how long. I push her arms under the sink faucet to wash off the soap and then douse her arms with peroxide. The wounds fizz up instantly, white and bright. She hisses at me, which just reminds me that she one hundred and fifty thousand percent needs to explain herself.

"What happened?"

"Catthew's just a little scared."

"Where did you get a cat? Where is it? Just. Explain." I glance around the room, like the little devil with knives for nails might be lurking, hoping to slice me open, too. I bet it lives for the thrill. It wakes up every day and chooses not only violence, but also bloodshed.

She pats her arms dry with the hand towel and sighs. "There's just no way to keep these dumb plants alive!"

I blink. "Buy a fake one! Problem solved. What *happened*?"

"I was at the skate park with Cecily when I saw him, all round and orange." Despite the vicious claw marks on her arms, she sounds smitten. There are quite literally hearts in her eyes— is that a sign of rabies? "So I chased him down and scooped him up. He fought me the whole way home, but I figured he just didn't like being on my skateboard."

"And where is he now?"

"That's the problem. I let him go so I could clean my arms, and I don't know where he is." Her eyes dart toward the hall. "I heard him for a while. Sounded like he was running around, but now it's been quiet for a minute."

I pinch the bridge of my nose. "You understand that Mom and Dad are never letting you have a cat now, right?"

"They'll warm up to him!"

"He tore you apart! He could have a disease or something, or *belong to someone else*! You can't just take a cat off the street; this is suburban Pennsylvania—there are a ton of people with cats that go outside." I head into the hallway, not completely sure what I'll do if I find him. Maybe punt him out the door or buy him a ticket to Florida, where other very dangerous animals live. "I'm going to get some oven mitts. Go to your room and try to be quiet so you don't spook him from coming out of hiding."

"We have some tuna in the pantry," she whispers as she flits to her room.

"I'll crack it open when I get the mitts." I pass by my room. The door was shut when I left after Liberty, but now it's ajar.

This could be a coincidence, since my mom badly replaced the doorknobs on the interior doors and now none of them fully close, but it could also be because the orange monster has taken residence in my room. I tiptoe forward and enter.

The bastard tore a hole in my duvet!

I fly forward to inspect the damage done to the coral-pink linen cover I requested for Christmas, but then something moves underneath and I hesitate just long enough to brace myself. Inside the cover, Catthew rolls onto his back, exposing his belly to me as he stretches slowly. Except. I am pretty sure he is biologically a she. Because while I'm fat, this cat . . . is plump in a different way.

Leave it to Lily to find a pregnant stray when she's not supposed to have even one cat.

Catthew makes eye contact with me and wiggles a little, as if tempting me to touch her belly. I'm tempted; I won't lie. Cat belly is sacred and forbidden. Adler's cat, Muffin, constantly lures people in, and just when you think it's safe to pet her belly, she latches on to you with claws and teeth. This is why I prefer dogs: no tricks, only treats.

Catthew meows and, *fine,* I risk it all for the belly.

She wiggles closer and starts purring and, okay, maybe she was just scared and wanted a comfortable place to hide. I'd be terrified if someone abducted me off the street, too. She rolls over, still purring, and starts rubbing against my hand, making it very clear she wants some love. She even wiggles out of the duvet and puts her two front paws up on my chest to better nuzzle my face. *Oh, this is what true love feels like.*

Anything less is an absolute sham.

I dare to pick her up and release a tiny exhale when she allows it. I don't know what to do next, though. We definitely can't keep her, and if I'm right, we can't keep her *and* all her kittens. Lily will be crushed, so I have to let her believe Catthew is a boy who will never be tamed and will always scratch her and, therefore, she cannot keep him. Plus, Poppy would never be able to come over again, and all this Catthew cat hair would cling to my cute clothes and cause me to look like a mess.

I make my way back to the bathroom and set Catthew on the ground. She investigates the tub immediately, hopping inside and smelling. I know nothing of cat gestation cycles, so I can only pray she's not as close to popping as she appears. Liberty is out with Sophia, and Mom and Dad are at work, so I'm carless now that Poppy has, rightfully, fled the scene. I wouldn't have even been able to utilize her or her car for this because of how bad her allergy is. I leave Catthew—Cathy?—in the bathroom and return to my room to look out the window for Adler's car. It sits in front of his house like it usually is when he's home, so I take this as an invitation.

Lily springs from her bed when I dash over to her room. "Did you find him?"

"I have him locked in the bathroom—do *not* go in there. I'm going to see if Adler has a carrier and any clue what we should do. Maybe he can take he—him to the cat café."

It's a truly amazing feat that I can be smack in the middle of a crisis and still have time to stop and think: *Aww, a cat café would be a really cute date place.* I'll have to utilize it for a meet-cute, maybe even one of my own this week—Cameron has always struck me as a cat person.

"No, they'll put him up for adoption there," she says. "I want to keep him. Did you even look in his eyes? He's so cute, and he has an old soul; I can tell. Just look in his eyes."

"He didn't seem to like you very much, or at least, appreciate you bringing him here. He probably has his own home, and if not, he'll find a good one now."

I don't trust her not to set Catthew free, so I drag her over to Adler's house with me. I ring the bell, Lily's wrist in my free hand.

Adler opens the door and raises an eyebrow. "Little Johnson," he says to me with a curt nod.

"Baby Johnson," he says just as seriously to Lily.

"I have an emergency, so please remember that we're Liberty's sisters and not that you hate me." I hold up Lily's scratched arm.

To his credit, Adler adores Lily and is appropriately concerned, inspecting her arm closely. "What happened?"

"I—" Lily starts.

"She brought a stray cat into the house. What do we do?" I ask.

"Did you clean these scratches?" I nod. He rubs his cheek roughly before sighing. "I'll grab a carrier."

"No," Lily whines. It's *so* immature, and honestly pretty grating at this point, but I keep the critique to myself. It wouldn't help anyone right now, most of all me. "Adler, don't take him. I need him."

"I think what's best is to take him to Purrfect Match and

see if he has a microchip. If he has owners, they might be really worried."

"Or maybe they *dumped* him on the streets and I'm doing him a favor!" Lily rips her arm from my grasp. "What if he doesn't have a microchip?"

Adler's eyes shift to mine quickly, and I ever-so-subtly shake my head.

"He might be feral, then, and unable to be homed, but he can stay at the café for a little until I figure it all out. Maybe if he adjusts to people, you can talk your parents into letting you adopt him."

"Fine. But I'm going with you so I can see where he's going to be living. It has to meet my standards."

"Lily. Adler's helping us out; you're not going to bother him more." Lily is too young to have formed the "must not be an inconvenience" reaction. She doesn't yet understand social cues and hints given to indicate she's being entirely too much. It must be freeing.

"It's fine. I respect that," Adler says. "Maybe you can help me with some of the other cats. They never seem to get enough attention and, you know, I'm old, so I get worn out pretty easily when I try to play with them."

She rolls her eyes. "Oh, please. I know what you're doing, and I obviously accept."

Nine

Before we leave, I dash off to change because this emergency has pushed me uncomfortably close to the time I'm supposed to meet Jackson at the secret, yet public, location. I cannot show up in the same outfit, as if I put absolutely no effort into this date I begged him for. I haven't had a chance to do any additional research on him, so all I know is what I learned prior to texting him and during our short conversation at the mall. Being me, I don't have any sci-fi-ish clothing, but Liberty did go to Comic-Con one year with my dad and got a T-shirt. It's a bit too small for me, but I think it hugs my curves in a nice way and looks cute with my high-waisted buttoned shorts and the barely worn high-tops I find deep in my closet. I blow some dust off them and meet Adler, Lily, and a howling Catthew in the car. Lily asks why I'm wearing Liberty's shirt, but Adler, thankfully, keeps his comments to himself.

We arrive at Purrfect Match about fifteen minutes later, which is about twelve minutes after Catthew's crying stopped being cute and tolerable. A space as small as Purrfect Match should not house this many cats, but I guess it's appealing to people who love cats—like Lily. She barely says a "be right back" to Catthew before tracking down a playful calico cat and loving on it against its will.

I lean into Adler so she doesn't overhear me discussing Catthew's possible pregnancy, but then the rest of my sentence drifts away on the same breeze that carries his strong, clean scent to my nostrils. Why does he smell so good? "Huh."

"What?" He turns into me, closing this two-person circle we've created, and now all I can see is him and all I can smell is him . . . but all I can hear is cats.

I blink a few times. "I think Catthew is a she and she may be expecting."

"Expecting what?" He sets Catthew's carrier on the counter with a practiced grace that draws my eyes to his long, slender fingers. They're usually caked with grime from wiggling them into car parts no one else can manage at the garage, but they are pristine today—not that I'm noticing. "A package? A very important phone call?"

He winks and turns to a Black guy behind the register, ringing up a customer for takeaway coffee. *Who gets takeaway coffee at a cat café?* "Hey, Harry. Can you scan for a chip?"

Harry smiles, and the cheek piercings on both sides of his face turn into charming, shiny dimples. "Sure thing, man." He hands the woman her receipt and joins us. "Who do we have here?" he asks me.

I grin, smitten with the small gap between his front teeth. "Lahey."

Adler snorts. "He meant the cat."

"Oh, I don't know. It's a stray, I think." To our side, Lily plays with two cats at once, a gray striped one with a penchant for jumping after my sister's fingers and a black-and-white tuxedo with a cone of shame around its neck. "My sister calls it Catthew."

"*Catthew*," Harry says into the carrier. "Let's get you out of there, buddy."

Harry pulls the cat free despite Catthew digging her claws into his arm and lets us know that there's no microchip. I wonder if I should lie to Lily and say there is. She'll be heartbroken, but better to be heartbroken thinking Catthew has a home than to know that she doesn't and our parents won't give her one.

I tighten the space between Harry, who's loving on a calmer Catthew, and myself. "For the sake of my sister not having a *full* meltdown that traumatizes these innocent kittens, if she asks, can we say that the cat has a home?"

He looks at Lily. The gray cat climbs from her arm to her shoulders.

"Sure thing. There's no crying at the cat café." He holds up the cat. "By the way, Catthew is—"

"We know," Adler and I say in unison. "All the more reason not to tell my sister," I add gently. "She would love nothing more than *multiple* cats."

Harry tucks Catthew against his chest. "Okay, okay. Just had to say it. I'll have the vet check out Catthew, and we'll make sure that no one is looking for *him*."

"Thank you so much. Do I—" I glance at Adler, who's leaning his back against the counter and watching Lily have the time of her life, and then at Harry. He's attentive, and his face is soft like a golden summer afternoon. Some butterflies do the tango in my stomach. "Do I have to pay?"

"No," Adler says.

"Yes, actually," Harry says with big brown eyes. "Policy changed. There's a huge fee."

"What are you talking about? Since when?" Adler sets both his hands on the counter like he might square up to Harry over what's probably a small fee—though it's not like I have a ton of money to blow right now. I still haven't found the perfect outfit to dazzle everyone at Summer's party. Lily will have to repay me for this, with interest.

Harry's face collapses into a wince. "Since right now, sorry. I'm afraid it's going to cost you a whole conversation with me." He flashes a hell of a smile.

My face warms. "Oh, is that all? I'll do you one better—I'll throw in some compliments, too."

Harry continues absolutely *beaming* at me. "How generous."

I lean on the counter with my elbows, propping up my goods a bit. I usually find slouching rather unattractive on people, but it serves a purpose this time. "Your piercings are very cool and distracting."

"Speaking of distracting," Adler says with a low growl under his tone, "we shouldn't bother Harry any more while he's working."

I glance around the café, expecting to see a winding line behind us or even one single soul, but the place is empty, save for the cats and us. "Sorry, am I keeping you?"

Harry's grin sparks to life. "Hopefully."

I resist the urge to cover my flaming cheeks. "He doesn't seem to mind having someone to talk to, Adler." I nod in Lily's direction. "Why don't you show Lily how you . . . whatever you do here."

The look he gives me in return is unreadable. He almost looks chastised or, maybe, hurt. Probably because his job is cleaning litter boxes or drowning fleas. I wouldn't want to do that in my free time, either, and I really should be more grateful that Adler brought us and handled this, but, *excuse me*, he knows I need a date and this boy is clearly flirting with me. This could be an easy and unexpected win!

"That's a great idea," Harry says with a pointed tone.

"Really?" he asks Harry, incredulous. Then he looks at me, his eyes darkening. "*Really?*"

I bite my lip, not wanting to tread any heavier on the already very thin ice. Obviously I can't tell Adler what to do, and he'd have every right to just leave Lily and me here to find a ride home, but Harry and I aren't asking *that* much of him.

We engage in some kind of telepathic war, the silence between us building until Adler suffers a tragic defeat, sighs, and heads over to the corner where Lily and her growing army of cats have made base camp. I hold in my victory cheer. It's not often that I win any kind of fight with Adler.

"How do you like your coffee?" Harry pulls two mugs out from under the counter. One is shaped like a large cat with the tail as the handle, and the other is just plain blue with a chip on the rim.

"Not at all," Adler says loudly from across the room.

Lily watches us with mild interest. Mostly, the cats have her attention. Maybe this place can be a compromise for her feline-loving heart. If it's still in business by the time she's old enough for a job, she'll be set.

Harry very obviously resists rolling his eyes. "I wasn't asking you."

"I wasn't answering for me," Adler responds in the same fake breezy tone.

I offer a shy smile as I take a seat across from Harry at the attached bar. "I don't drink coffee. My average buzz level is already way too high according to everyone who knows me."

He pulls a water bottle from the refrigerator and offers it to me with black-nailed hands. *I love a guy who breaks gender norms.* I accept, and he goes about making a drink for himself. Once he sets it opposite me, he leans against the surface and smiles.

"I'm Harry, by the way."

"I figured when Adler called you Harry." I grin at the rosiness that blooms on his cheeks around his piercings. *I'm* having an effect on *him*. "I'm Lahey."

"I figured when you introduced yourself as Lahey." His cheek piercings twitch. "How do you know Adler?"

He blows on his coffee, and I hold in a gag. It's easy to avoid excess caffeine when coffee smells so repulsive.

"I'm assuming you're not his girlfriend, or maybe you are and you guys have some issues you need to talk through."

I cough on the sip of water I take. "No. I'm his neighbor."

His face opens in surprise. "Liberty's sister? I should have known; you two look a lot alike." I nearly beam—it feels like an honor to be told I look like Liberty. He points to Lily. "Another sister?"

"Not by choice."

He moves his attention back to me. "So we must have overlapped at school for a bit, then."

"Yeah, I'm a year younger than you guys. Go Hawks," I say unenthusiastically.

He raises his mug to toast me. "I only went there for a few semesters, but I feel like that makes us old friends now."

"Practically. I can't wait to be the best man at your wedding." I wish I could shove all those words back into my mouth, but—

"Yeah, best man, or . . . maybe you could snag my coveted third-wife spot," he says.

I laugh in surprise; I can't remember the last time my insides were firing on all cylinders like this. It feels dangerous, but easy, like running on autopilot. "*Third?*"

"Yeah. The first one will die mysteriously, and the second will cheat on me. That way I'm well-rounded and sympathetic by the time I get to number three."

Something clatters to the floor behind us, cutting off my response. Lily chases after a few cats that run at the noise, cooing. Adler swoops down to pick up his phone and then pushes back into his seat, eyes cast down.

"How long have you worked here?" I ask, chasing an itch up my arm with navy-blue-painted fingernails. I'll have to ask what shade Harry's own polish is. We could coordinate on Saturday.

"A little over a year. My friend Logan used to work here and he went away to school, so he knew they needed help. I just kind of slid in to fill his spot." He lifts his mug to his lips and asks, "Are you working this summer?"

The conversation returns to a place where I feel comfortable holding his soft stare.

"Uh, yeah," I lie, choking on a gulp of water. A guy like this, who is obviously charming and evolved and spends his days rehoming cats and smashing the patriarchy and gender rules, seems like he would not take kindly to me sitting on my ass all day.

"Sweet. What do you do?"

"This and that, working with people, kind of like . . . non-profit work." I point at the menu behind the counter quickly. "What's in a cat-ppuccino?"

"Secret recipe. I'd have to kill you if I told you."

"I'm not ready to get married, so . . ."

He snorts into his drink. "I said she'll die mysteriously, not that I had anything to do with it."

I tap at my temple, dragging my finger down through an itch. "I'm reading between the lines."

"So, what's your fandom?"

I blink, caught off guard. "What?"

"Your shirt. Comic-Con."

"Oh, no, this is for—" *My other nerdy date today.* Shit. "Irony."

He nods slowly. "Okay . . ."

"I wear it to bring awareness to . . . capitalism." I try to stealthily glance at my phone to check the time.

He squints, holding back a smile. "By falling victim to capitalism?"

I lock my phone and stare at him for a brief moment of silence, calculating my next move. I didn't bring a shovel and can't stand to dig myself further into this hole. "So you see the irony?"

Adler clears his throat loudly, effectively pushing all the dirt back into my hole. I glance over my shoulder, and a bolt of surprise runs through me when we immediately lock eyes. He looks away quickly, tapping his sneaker against the ground as he pets one of the cats half perched on his lap.

Harry's voice brings me back to the task at hand. "So where did Catthew come from?"

The fizzle from catching Adler watching me fades away. "I think it was just like Matthew, but a cat. I don't know; my sister named him—her."

"I meant physically."

"Oh, obviously. I was"—I think for a second and hope he doesn't notice all my pausing while I try to figure out the best way to spin this story to be about me—"teaching my sister how to skateboard. I actually volunteer for a summer program that teaches neighborhood girls how to skate and skateboard. The cat came up to us." I shrug like it's no BFD.

"Oh, that's really sweet. You know, pregnant stray cats are known to 'adopt' humans," he says in a low voice so Lily doesn't overhear.

"I imagine she was desperate."

"No, I think she chose wisely." He bites his bottom lip, and *oh*, to be that lip. "You got her to a safe place, which is best for her and the kittens. Our vet will make sure they're taken care of and adopted."

"Yeah, I love cats," I say, gently nudging one away with my foot. "And helping out."

I'm not totally lying here. I'm enhancing the truth. I did enjoy my brief cuddle with Catthew, and I *do* like helping people, just maybe not in the ways that Harry does or in the ways I mentioned with my vague summer job.

He bends down below the counter, and I check the time again. Harry's sweet and attractive, but I have to leave in the next fifteen minutes to make it to the date I actually planned on having today. I don't know if I should go for that lukewarm chance, or stay for this hot one. The uncertainty leaves me itchy.

Actually, I've been itchy for a while.

Red bumps have scattered across my arm, scratch lines etched through them like I've been trying to cross them out.

Harry straightens, a white fluffy cat in his arms. "Oh, shit. Are you allergic to cats?"

"No." I don't know what else to say. I can only focus on the itch and the fact that Harry is seeing me in this polka-dotted state. I smooth my hand over my face, which has been hot for a long time, but I assumed it was a blush, and feel some swelling under my fingertips.

"It looks like you're allergic to cats," he insists calmly, putting the cat down on the counter to walk wherever it pleases, and I'm too busy panicking to inform him that allowing that in a *café* is unhygienic.

I shake my head and stand, like if I get far enough away from his accusation, it will go away. "I'm not, though."

Adler comes up behind me and gently places a hand at my elbow. "You've been around Muffin plenty. You're not allergic to cats."

Lily watches us from across the room, a senior cat with one eye lounging in her arms like a drunk baby. "If you're suddenly allergic to cats now that I might get a cat, Lahey, I'm going to flush all your makeup down the toilet."

"Those are definitely hives," Harry says, unhelpfully pointing. His eyes roam to my face. "You've got them on your face, too. Are you having trouble breathing?"

"I'm fine," I say in a high-pitched voice. The only reason I *am* having trouble breathing is because I'm faced with the impossible decision of allowing *another* suitor to see me like this by meeting with Jackson, or going home and hoping the reaction stops. I don't know what caused the hives, or how long they'll stay, but I'm feeling pretty certain that I am doomed to be undatable all my life.

Adler pulls me into the employee break room, and then into the cramped bathroom, as I'm having a near-catastrophic meltdown the likes of which no one has ever witnessed and survived. There could be at least three late-night news documentaries and one Hollywood flop with a "based on true events" tagline made from this moment.

"Oh my god," I say, running a finger over a particularly large hive on the inside of my wrist. It doesn't hurt to touch, just itches unbearably, and it's unsightly. "I'm a monster."

I don't even dare to look at myself in the mirror. I don't have the energy for the cleanup when the thing shatters from reflecting my face.

"You are, but not for this. You're just having a reaction. Calm down. Getting stressed will make it worse."

"How am I supposed to calm down? My body is revolting against me, and it did it in front of an adorable, animal-saving guy."

He grabs a clean rag from a shelf boasting about a hundred clean rags and then turns the small sink faucet on. "Harry's nice," he says quietly, "but he always has coffee breath."

"Tragic, but not a deal breaker. I only need him for one night."

He clears his throat. "Wow."

"You know what I mean. What are you doing?"

"I'm going to clean you off." He pumps some soap onto the washcloth and lathers it.

"Excuse me?" I flash back to the weekend: me, naked and wet in the shower, with Adler in the same room. My face burns more.

He wrings the rag out. "You're not allergic to cats, so maybe you're allergic to something the cat had on her fur. You held her, right?"

"Yes." I think of how that little traitor nuzzled against my face. How she burrowed into my bed. "That *bitch*."

"My dad thought he was allergic to Muffin when we rescued her, but it turns out Muffin just needed a bath." He raises an eyebrow, rag lifted between us. "He got tested, and he's actually allergic to dust mites, so this is worth a shot."

He exposes the worst of the hives with a gentle twist of my arm. Goose bumps travel up my tender skin; I hope he doesn't read into them and taunt me for the rest of my short life (I'll be dying of embarrassment momentarily, I have no doubt).

"It might not work instantly, but it should help." His voice is soft now as he watches the rag's movements instead of my reaction to them. "My dad would wake up with hives and then go to work, and he'd be fine until he came home again."

It's my turn to clear my throat. The only thing that could be blocking it is this unexpected lust. Am I so touch-deprived, so ridiculous, that Adler washing dirt off my hive-infested skin is somehow sexual? The warmth he leaves wherever he touches, wherever the rag slides, causes the rest of me to feel ice-cold in comparison. I want the heat everywhere. This has got to be an aftereffect of Harry. Or a side effect of the reaction. I prefer it be Harry's fault, though.

Not that Harry will prefer *me* now. I'm disgusting.

"Thank you," I manage to say, like a normal human being who is not thinking of the logistics of a full sponge bath suddenly. It would be easier to clear my mind if the smell of Adler's own soap wasn't pressing into every part of my senses.

His eyes lift to mine and he's . . . is Adler cute? Not just subjectively, but objectively?

"Yeah, you're welcome. Had to put this weird knowledge to some use eventually." After running the rag under the water again, he wrings it out and takes a breath. "Are you going to tell me what was with the lies you told Harry out there? You are fully unemployed. And you can't skateboard."

"One: you're nosy. Two: I'm trying to get a date, remember?" I watch as the rag makes slow circles against my forearm, fully aware that I could be doing this myself and flat-out refusing to point it out.

"Have you even tried asking someone?"

"No. I can't just cold-call someone for a date. I need to butter them up, let them get to know me."

"But they're not getting to know you. You're lying. Why not just be yourself?" There's something about his voice. It's rough, annoyed, but like he's trying to hide it—maybe trying, because of my current state, to go easy on me. He can't hide things from me, though, and he's a fool to try.

"Being myself hasn't exactly done me any favors in the past," I say lightly, avoiding his gaze. "I've been horribly single all my life."

"You're only seventeen."

As if he has any authority to talk about age and experience. He's only eighteen.

"And yet my sixteen-year-old cousin has a boyfriend. My best friend who is practically a hermit has had sex. Liberty is in love with Sophia. I feel like I'm falling behind and I'll never catch up and everyone's busy living their own love lives and I'll never even get started with mine."

The silence that rings around the room after my confession hurts my ears. I swallow, and it's difficult. Maybe I'm having a worse reaction than we thought. It even feels like my eyes are stinging now.

He takes a moment to refresh the rag and then comes in close, putting the warmth against my neck. A bit of water trails under the collar of Liberty's shirt. "You're not giving yourself enough credit."

It's damn near impossible not to watch his face as he brushes the washcloth over my cheeks and the bridge of my nose. "Guys don't give me the time of day."

He lowers the rag and uses a wet finger to swipe away a strand of hair clinging to my jaw. "That's not true."

Adler and I have been this close before—we became reigning co-champs of Twister when we agreed to tie at Liberty's twelfth birthday party, and he's literally sat on me to steal the remote at least once each summer since he moved into the neighborhood—but it's never felt like this. I can't breathe. Damn Catthew.

"Well, I have no evidence to the contrary," I say in a small voice. "So, forgive me for not believing that. You just want me to end up alone, like you."

He shrugs with one shoulder. "Well, if we're both alone, then we could be alone together."

My eyes drop to his lips only for a fraction of a second, not long enough for him to see the movement, hopefully. There was no trace of a joking smirk on his mouth. "That . . . wouldn't be alone, then."

"Oh yeah. Well, then we could just be together."

He moves even closer, eyes dancing between mine and my mouth, until his nose is almost touching mine. *Someone call 911 now.* Am I about to get my first kiss from *Adler* of all people?

The realization hits me like a punch to the stomach. It's a *pity* kiss. I can't let him go through with it. I'm going to suffocate. My throat is closing up. It's not a reaction to the cat at all; it's Adler. How am I expected to process this? What is *happening*? I DON'T KNOW!

His serious look cracks into one of doubt and, in a second, he's pulling away. He steps away and throws the rag into the sink with a disappointing and wet thud. With the faucet on and his back to me, he says, "Wow, your face. Wish you could have seen it."

If that was some kind of game of chicken, he absolutely had me fooled. I take a quiet, steadying breath. "I only wish that if there are fewer hives on it."

I catch a glance at myself in the mirror over his shoulder. Thankfully, it doesn't shatter, and the swelling and redness on my skin don't seem too bad anymore—or at least it's all blending in with my blush now. Maybe I can still make this date with Jackson. Maybe it will help me forget that I'm a joke to everyone, even people who are supposed to be nice to me because of their best friendship with my sister.

"Since you *are* terribly alone and have no dates to attend, would you mind taking Lily home?" I have to put some distance between us. I must pretend like he didn't almost give me a pity kiss and then turn it into a joke. I am *not* a laughing matter. I will *not* be alone forever.

His shoulders stiffen, but he keeps his eyes down on the sink. "You're just going to leave—"

"Thanks." I pull out my phone to order a Lyft—my parents

put twenty dollars on my account at the beginning of the summer for emergencies, and this counts as one to me. "I've got a date to get to." Hopefully it ends happily ever after so I can never think about this moment again. I can't believe I got so caught up. I'm suing whoever makes Adler's soap for all they're worth.

He leans his back against the sink, arms crossed. The humor has disappeared from his face, and now it's left blank like a Twister mat with no dots. "And what do I tell Harry?"

Harry. Oh, Harry. I wish things went differently for us. He's so beautiful and had so much potential, but he's seen me at my hive-iest and we can't come back from that.

"Tell him I died." I leave Adler in the bathroom, where hopefully he gets trapped for the rest of the day to think about what he's done. A wall of heat greets me when I swing open the café's back door. "He can count me as his mysterious first wife."

Ten

The Junkyard is not as word-of-mouth and mysterious as Jackson made it seem—it not only has a website, but also various social media accounts that post on an impressive and consistent daily schedule to keep patrons updated with what's happening. And what's happening, I discover during my Lyft ride when I googled the address, are tournaments for card and video games, arcade private parties, and a weekly Trade-In Tuesday where people can attempt to sell their gamer-ish goods for store credit.

By the time my feet hit the sidewalk outside the Junkyard, I've shaken off the weird feeling Adler left me with and, miraculously, most of my hives—at least, the ones I can see. A quick glance in my front-facing camera revealed only the slightest pinkness on my cheeks and chin. I already texted Lily that when she gets home, she needs to start deep cleaning—it would be hard to hide the fact that she brought a cat inside without Mom and Dad's permission if I'm suddenly and mysteriously breaking into hives.

The Junkyard stands before me a moody brick building painted black and oozing loud music from the cracks around the single entrance door. I really try not to judge books by their covers, but this book does not seem like the book for me. At least, not the real me. The new and improved just-for-Jackson version of Lahey? Yeah, possibly. I try to inhabit that mind space and trudge forward with confidence (read: naivete). I think about the last video game I played—*Fantastic Lorenzo's Planet*, with Adler and Lily, when Liberty ditched us to meet up with Sophia for the hangout before their first official date. I did not win (Lily did), but I also didn't lose (Adler did).

Inside, a young boy smashes the buttons of an old arcade game that's lined along the wall with a bunch of other games. In the center of the room sits a worn pool table with two beaten and broken cues laid across it. Beside that sad mess, a couch and several armchairs surround a TV stand with consoles and their controllers tangled underneath—no TV, though. A worker behind the register watches something on his phone that emits an inappropriate amount of expletives. There are only two people in this room aside from me.

"Need help?" the employee calls without looking up from his phone.

"I'm supposed to meet someone, but it looks like he's not here."

I texted Jackson, but he hasn't responded yet, which makes me think I'm being stood up. *Or,* I panic, *that I accidentally texted Kabir Khan instead.* He texted me on the way here, just striking up a casual and kind of pointless conversation—which is honestly a great sign that he was thinking of me, but very inconvenient when I'm working on another guy!

"I'll just—" I pivot to leave, unlocking my phone in a hurry to check my messages, but then the arcade cabinet closest to me starts moving on its own.

I'm halfway to a heart attack when I realize it's not falling, but sliding to the side—to reveal Jackson and an increase in music and crowd volume by at least five hundred percent.

"Lahey!" Jackson's breathless, with pink cheeks that match his lips. He wears the color well. "You're late. I'm up next."

He motions for me to follow him into the hidden room behind the cabinet, and I do, with a lot more ease and peace of mind than when I walked into the Junkyard originally. I almost don't even care that he said I'm late when I'm not. I'm a very punctual person, who respects start and stop times for activities. Maybe he meant for me to meet him earlier but mistyped the time. It doesn't exactly matter at this point, because I'm here now and he's happy to see me.

The slightly narrow hallway behind the arcade game opens into a larger room—but not very large in the grand scheme of things—packed from black wall to black wall with people of all ages. Bits of scrap metal hang from the ceiling on fishing line, giving the appearance they're floating. It's kind of like rocket ship debris. It's very avant-garde, and Poppy would love it.

In the center of the dim room is a fenced circle flooded with light. It's not until Jackson has maneuvered us near it that I worry I'm about to see some kind of animal fight. My fingers clench into a fist, and I'm ready to break every single one of them on Jackson's face when his friends from the mall join us and they hold up—

"A robot?"

Jackson rubs at his neck a moment before accepting the robot and nodding at me. It's about the size of several Roombas glued on top of each other and has googly eyes stuck on two rods protruding from its head thing.

"Uh, I guess if you want to run, now's your chance," he says sheepishly over the noise.

"I don't know what's happening." I probably should, though. I glance around the room and see a few others holding similar-sized machines. Someone hops into the fenced area to sweep up a mess of plastic and metal—robot parts. "Oh my god. Is this a robot-fighting arena?"

His face flushes even pinker. "Yeah. I—I don't know. It's a hobby I got into from Tech Club at school. It's just fun. I'm not that good."

Something about how he's playing this off like it's no big deal is endearing. Maybe because guys are usually so confident in things that it's nice to see some insecurity, some humility. I'll gladly validate him.

"No, this is really cool. I could never make a robot."

He examines my face, his eyes flicking from side to side. "I thought maybe you'd think this kind of stuff was dumb."

"What? Why?" What an assumption to make about some-one he barely knows.

He shrugs. "You hang out with the art kids, and your sister

is a jock. I could never picture you here before our conversation today at the mall. I didn't know you let your geek flag fly sometimes."

I try not to bristle. "I don't think you're a geek. You're just smart and happen to enjoy a mainstream fantasy series."

"Sci-fi series," he says.

I offer a tight smile. If we were to ever date for real one day, this movie series would need to be off the table. It's exhausting just talking about it. "Star Wars is fantasy. It's about people with magical powers. Wizards."

"It's sci-fi. It's futuristic."

"No, it takes place in the past."

He wears his own fake smile on his face. "*No—*"

"It says at the beginning of the first one that it's 'a long time ago'—"

"She's got you there," one of the friends says. I still don't know their names, and suddenly it's bothering me that Jackson hasn't introduced us—does he not think I'm worth introducing? "But it's the fourth movie, actually. It just came out first."

Is it hot in here, or am I just in hell?

"Nah, Jackson has this." The other reads from his phone, the screen turning his pale skin blue. "'Science fiction deals with advanced technology, space exploration, time travel, extraterrestrials, and parallel universes.'"

Jackson grins. "See? Sci-fi."

I wish I was in a parallel universe right about now. One where this didn't matter.

"Ha ha, you're right." I nod at his robot stiffly. "So, what's its name?"

"Rex," he says. "Spelled like *R* hyphen three *X*."

"Cute." I clasp my hands together, struggling for more questions. To be honest, our argument—whether I was wrong or right—has left me with a nasty aftertaste.

All three boys raise their eyebrows at me.

"Oh. Not cute," I correct myself. "It's very manly and . . . technologically sophisticated or whatever word you're looking for."

Jackson exhales out his nose in one of those silent laughs, and I take that as water under the bridge.

I smile at Rex—sorry, *R-3X*—and bend to his—its?—eye level, even though I'm pretty sure it can't see me. "When do you fight, buddy?"

"In a minute." Jackson faces the arena with a somewhat blank expression, his robot clenched in white-knuckled terror.

"Against who?"

"Flametron," all three of them say in unison.

Jackson points across the arena at a robot twice Rex's size being held by a guy twice Jackson's size and age. "He's a reigning champ. I almost beat him last year, but then he destroyed me in a last-minute move. It took me months of after-school hours and club time to rebuild."

"It only took two days to reach a thousand views, though," his one friend adds unhelpfully over Jackson's shoulder. He goes back to the other, showing him something on his phone.

Jackson rolls his eyes. "It was pretty cool, I'll admit."

I give up waiting for Jackson to do the polite thing. "Who are your friends?" I ask quietly, into his ear. "They don't go to school with us, right?"

He glances over his shoulder. "No, I met them through the Junkyard. They helped me improve my build and technique." He taps the one closest to him on the shoulder. "This is Quaid." Then he moves the same hand below the other's phone and pops it out of his grip. It clatters to the floor, and Quaid and Jackson laugh while the other boy scrambles to pick it up before people step on it. Jackson calls him Smith.

Smith stands straight and tucks the phone into his pocket. He doesn't even look angry at Jackson. "Those are our last names, by the way. I'm Matt, and this is Tyler."

The music stops suddenly, cutting me off from introducing myself, since Jackson didn't seem intent on doing it. Suddenly, neon lights cascade to the center of the arena. The effect gives me goose bumps.

"Oh, shit, guys. It's time." Jackson grips Rex a little tighter.

My heart starts working faster in anticipation. Maybe if Jackson gets into his element, we'll see some sparks fly—between us, not the robots . . . unless that's a good thing.

He and his competitor enter the arena through a makeshift gate and place their robots on opposite ends of the enclosure. Assuming everyone here knows the drill, the Junkyard employee overseeing this event doesn't bother to explain what happens next, so my ignorant self is left on my own to figure out everything. It seems pretty simple, though. Two go in, and one comes out.

Once everyone clears the arena, a deep prerecorded voice counts down from three over the loudspeaker and then the music starts up again. People holler and taunt the robots like they're thirsty for some bloodshed. Someone calls Rex a "poor excuse for a pencil sharpener" and a chant of "wreck it" starts up. Jackson uses a controller to advance Rex toward Flametron.

"It's so cool that you know how to make something like this," I shout over the music. I think I said this already, but it's true—plus it seems like he likes hearing that he knows something I don't.

"I barely know what to do when Siri doesn't work," I add, apparently embracing my "dumb blonde who can be fixed to have all the same opinions as me" persona.

He barely registers that I'm speaking, his mouth hanging open as he keeps his eyes locked on Rex. "Uh, thanks."

"How did you get into this?"

"I'm trying to focus!" His eyes dart to mine for one second. "Sorry."

Appropriately chastised, I take a step back and just watch the show. It's obvious he's busy. I don't know why I tried. We'll have time to chat after. I should just cheer him on for now; that's what he wants from me, and I am a people pleaser!

Rex and Flametron do a scared little dance around each other until Flametron's arm, a long machete-type thing, swings out to Rex. But Rex is faster and dodges it. I scream along with Quaid and Smith, already having forgotten which one is Max and which one is Taylor. Rex stretches out his own arm and knocks the machete from Flametron's body.

"PVC pipe!" Jackson screams gleefully as Quaid pats him on the back excitedly. "Suck it!"

A tiny thing that looks like a pizza cutter—*oh, it might actually be a pizza cutter*—pops out of Rex's chest cavity and, when Jackson makes him advance, this time at a much faster speed, Flametron isn't quick enough to unleash his own weapon. Rex rams into the other robot and all the life drains from it.

Jackson throws his hands up in the air, a shout of victory falling from his lips as the boys tackle him in an embrace. He remembers I'm here and goes to hug me before realizing how weird that would be. I offer a high five, and he takes it with a warm smile.

"Great job!" I say over the noise. "What happens now?"

"I get to go against the next competitor." He points to a small tissue-box-shaped thing. "And it looks like I'll clean the floor with it."

"Oh yeah," I agree. "Rex will kick its ass."

This false confidence earns me another smile from Jackson, and for just a second, the lights and the noise fade away so he and I can exist in our own perfect little bubble of contentment. He's smart and good-looking, and I bet I could clean him up nicely for Summer's party—undoubtedly after telling him the T-shirt tuxedo he owns is funny, but not up to dress code. But then our bubble pops when Flametron is swept to the side and Rex's competitor is placed into the arena.

The dismembered robot scraps hanging from the ceiling grab my eye again. I wonder what you have to do to be immortalized like that. Clearly, not win.

Windmill, Rex's opponent, raises a tiny little windmill with sharp objects attached about three seconds into the game. Jackson doesn't seem surprised or worried.

"I could beat this guy in my sleep." He even takes a moment to look at me, relaxed. "*You* could probably beat him."

"I'd love to try." I lean in but give him space to still control Rex. "Maybe I can do the killing blow."

He hesitates for a moment, no doubt debating if he should let me, or if he wants to give up that satisfying moment.

"Please?" I bat my eyelashes.

His eyes dart to my mouth. "Yeah, I guess."

I grin. "Thank you!"

He attacks Windmill with a renewed sense of self, pulling out all the fancy moves on Rex and showing off in such an extreme way that I should find it annoying or ridiculous, but instead I'm a little smitten, like, *That's* my *robot operator guy.*

He gets Windmill into position, beaten down and slow-moving, and then reluctantly gives me control.

"Just press this," Jackson says, pointing at a red button on his controller. "It's over from there."

"Put him out of his misery!" someone in the room chants. The crowd picks up a chant of "Misery! Misery! Misery!"

I press the button with glee, but I'm not fast enough. Windmill was only *pretending* to be hurt, if robots can pretend. It springs up on legs that it hadn't shown off before and lets Rex ride right under it. It lowers when I stop in shock and lands right on Rex. I don't know what to do, and Jackson seems to be in similar shock.

Then it self-destructs.

God, I wish I could.

Jackson and his friends scream in agony as I stand there try-ing to understand what just happened. Neither of the robots is in one piece, but Windmill is announced as the clear winner since it ended it all in one fatal and literal blow.

Jackson rips the controller from my hand. "*Thanks.*"

"I—I'm sorry. I pressed the button. I didn't know that was going to happen." My shoulders practically meet my ears. "I just did what you told me to."

"I shouldn't have let you do it." Jackson rolls out his neck. "It was too important."

"I'm sorry." I blew it. Any chance of another date with him is ruined because a robot got the better of me. We can never allow them to take over.

"Months of work ruined. . . ." He turns to talk to Quaid and Smith, whose agonized faces are practically mirror images of one another.

I wait a moment before realizing he just dismissed me. I no longer warrant being part of any conversation, apparently.

I regret saying sorry and letting him steamroll over my opin-ions. I wore this too-tight unisex T-shirt to be here for him and he's just cut me off! I tap him on the shoulder. He *ignores* me. What a child. I know you have to kiss a lot of frogs and all that, but this is like trying to kiss a *worm*.

"I said sorry," I say loudly, dropping my forced niceties. "You can be upset, but I didn't do it intentionally."

He glances over his shoulder and *down his nose at me*. "Yeah. I'll text you."

Seriously? I have other options. Better ones. Guys who text me just because and who wouldn't get mad at me for something like this because they have boring, low-stakes hobbies that I can't ruin.

"No." I look him up and down. "Don't."

JK

JACKSON KELLER, 17, through the eyes of Lahey Johnson, who has spent a regrettable forty-five minutes in his presence

How I know him: ~~he's in my grade at school~~ wasted good flirting on him, should have known nothing good comes from a shopping mall

He likes: ~~Star Wars, tech stuff, wearing black T-shirts with black-washed jeans, probably a band called To Die For~~ cutting girls down, asserting his dominance, breaking his friends' phones

He dislikes: ~~English class, waiting for teachers to sign hall passes, cheese fries~~ moisturizer, others' opinions, the chance to lose his virginity one day considering how he treats prospective partners after basically just meeting them

Dating history: forever alone

Bio: who cares

Wednesday

Eleven

Liberty slams on the brakes in the Twin Ponds East parking lot, throwing me into the painful clutches of my seat belt, and basically kicks me to the curb. Because she's doing me a favor, I choose not to tell her that if I could, I would give her driving zero stars.

Noah reached out at an ungodly hour this morning, claiming that despite his flirty texts with Justin, he was not ready for a one-on-one hang and needed me to chaperone his first date. Because I was already texting with Kabir, warming him up to a hangout of our own today, I decided to consolidate my missions. Justin and Noah agreed to go ice-skating and, in a twist of fate, Kabir *loves* ice-skating. I would have thought he'd want to do something more musically inclined for our first outing because he's the second-chair violin in the school orchestra, but apparently he's extremely into ice-skating as a break from the demands of a string instrument he plays second-best in our high school. Naturally, I tell him that I'm very good at skating, despite it being the thing I might be the worst at, aside from having a successful dating life. We texted all last night about our summers, school, hobbies, and more. It feels like we have a connection, and his blinding-white teeth make the butterflies in my stomach do a tango. It's time to test that connection when it's not relying on minute-long breaks in the conversation while I type-delete-type responses catered specifically to him.

Poppy still insists that I just accept defeat and go solo to Summer's party or, at the very least, stop lying to my dates, but Poppy's single, too; her advice can't be trusted.

Against my entire personality, I arrive late to this afternoon double date because Liberty didn't know that Twin Ponds West had closed so she originally drove me to the wrong place. In her defense, I didn't know it had closed, either. The last time we were at the skating rink was Summer's tenth birthday party. Though he hadn't shown up, her father had rented the entire building for Summer and her guests and had supposedly paid the employees double their hourly rate to keep it open late.

Noah, Justin, and Kabir are in a semicircle outside the building, waiting for me. Once my body is ninety percent out of Liberty's car, she takes off with her music blasting. She seemingly doesn't think even once about leaving me to fend for myself against three guys. Movies really made me think my relationship with my older sister would be much different than it is.

"Hey, Lahey." Kabir leaves the little bit of shade the guys found to greet me. He wears a gray long-sleeved shirt and dark blue jeans. Meanwhile, a dribble of sweat slides down my back as we stand under the beating sun.

"Hi," Noah calls from behind. Justin offers a wave. After everything I did for them, the cowards won't brave the heat for me for even a second.

Kabir takes my hand without asking and then leads me toward the door. "Want to head in?"

"Yeah, I'm sweating." Maybe not the most appealing start to a date, but it's the truth and totally visible to the naked eye. It's almost ninety degrees today, and I'm wearing a cardigan and leggings with my dress. Ice-skating rinks are cold, and goose bumps aren't cute.

Justin and Noah, *who seem perfectly fine without me*, clasp hands (!!) and walk ahead of us as if we're not the other half of their double date. I'll be giving my friend a lecture later about wasting my time. The only thing keeping him safe from a *stern* lecture is the fact that he isn't wearing some kind of hideous video game T-shirt today. I'm proud that he styled such a cute outfit without me: medium-wash jeans with a short-sleeved button-up shirt covered in dainty black roses.

Kabir ignores my comment to inspect me head to toe. He even uses our joined hands to spin me around slowly, which is easy for him because he hovers over me by quite a lot. "Oh no, did you forget your skates in your sister's car?"

Ah. Yes. Because I love and am so great at skating. My skates.

"Actually," I draw out, "I just donated them. To a charity. That teaches kids to skate." He holds the door open, and I use this as an opportunity to break free of his grip and roll my eyes at myself. Between this and the skateboarding lessons, I'll be single-handedly responsible for turning the next generation on to alternative means of transportation. "I'll just rent today."

"What's the charity?" he asks. "I've worked with a few."

If given the time, I could come up with a great skate pun of a charity name, but— "Oh, it's . . . a secret."

He laughs. "No, really. Was it Thin Ice, that group that mentors kids who've gotten in trouble?"

Damn, that's a good one.

"No, you've probably never heard of it, actually."

"The Great Eskate?"

"No."

"Am I getting warmer?"

I force out a laugh. "Yep, and you should be careful not to melt the ice." I nod along to my words, convincing myself and him—or maybe just myself. He frowns, but I play it off like I'm being flirty and follow Noah and Justin into the lobby.

I'm eager for someone else to say anything to get me out of this awkward conversation. Noah obliges.

"We were thinking we'd skate first and get some food after?" He looks from me to Kabir for confirmation, and I want to scream *Yes, thank you!* but I smile and nod instead.

"Sounds like a great plan. Skating always makes me work up an appetite." Kabir pats his nearly nonexistent gut. Between AP classes, violin, and skating, I wonder when he even finds time to eat. Or date. When Noah and Justin head to the rental desk, I linger behind for a moment.

I know why I asked Kabir out, but I have to admit that I'm curious. "Why'd you agree to go out with me?"

His easygoing smile drops. "What do you mean?"

"You're probably super busy, but you still said yes to this date. Why?"

His brown cheeks bloom into a faint pink tinge. He re-adjusts the bag of skates on his shoulder. "This feels like a trick question."

I huff out a laugh. "I promise it's not. I'm just suddenly worrying that I'm not worth your time. You could be doing so many other things."

"Don't say that." He scratches the back of his head and wets his lips. "I'm . . . trying to say yes to more things. Things that aren't obligations."

I guess I can't fault him for making me part of an experiment when I'm making him part of a lie. "I like that."

"Why did you ask me out?" He looks like he's leaning out over an edge to ask me this.

I could continue my lies, but there's something about the sweet way he waits for an honest answer that makes me want to give him one.

"Poppy dragged me to the school musical last year. I saw you in the orchestra pit and you—" Okay, maybe lying here is for the best, because I can't very well say that I picked him as a potential suitor based off how lovingly he stroked his violin. "You seemed so passionate and sincere. I just liked that."

"Oh," he says, releasing a grin. "*Cool.*"

Noah and Justin leave the rental desk with skates, so I step forward to get some of my own, but there's only a wall of cubbies housing the used ice skates. While everyone else would assume I *am* the ring-the-bell type, I'm *not*, so it doesn't bring me joy to have to do it now.

And who but Adler Altman pops his head up from below the counter?

"Are you kidding me?" A knowing smirk cracks his face, but I don't let him speak. The only thing he has going for himself is that he's good-looking, and I wouldn't want to let him ruin that. "Do you work everywhere?"

He leans his elbows on the counter and settles in like he has a a a a l l l l l l day. He might. There aren't many people here. "No, just places I like."

"Because you suddenly like ice-skating?"

"I like hockey."

"You like *watching* hockey. I saw you wipe out on Roller-blades before our parents stopped letting us go to Fountainblu because there were more sketchy drug deals than skating happening, and a Wayne Gretzky you are not."

He tucks his hair behind his ear. "Is that the only hockey reference you could think of?"

"I'd like to see *you* make one, Mr. I-Like-Hockey." I cross my arms and wait.

"Gritty."

"Gritty doesn't count; he's transcended hockey. He's a Pennsylvania god."

Kabir steps up next to me and clears his throat. "Uh, we'd like to rent her some skates."

My cheeks heat when Adler ignores him, turning around to the wall of cubbies. God, why can't he function like a normal human being? It's not just me he's being a pain in the ass to right now. "*Adler.*"

He spins and deposits a pair of skates on the counter. "Size seven." He raises an eyebrow at me in question.

"I'm a seven and a half." But that was impressively close.

"You need a half size down—" Adler and Kabir say at the same time.

Kabir frowns at me. "What size were your skates?"

"She doesn't—" Adler starts, but I slam my fist on the counter to silence him. He reels back a foot, and I tamp down the immediate flashback of him pulling away in the Purrfect Match bathroom.

I unstick my hand from the handwritten sign for $5 skating lessons I accidentally demolished and snag the skates off the counter. "Let's go, Kabir."

"We didn't pay," he says, reaching toward his pocket. "How much do I owe?"

"Nothing, man," Adler says, raising his hands. "I owe you for getting her away from me."

I take the nearest bench, which unfortunately sits directly across from the rental counter, and start locking my feet into these skates.

Logically, I know you can't breathe from your feet, but the skates are so tight that I feel like my feet can't breathe. There must be a word for it— Kabir bends down in front of me, making me realize just how badly I was fumbling the laces. He takes care to lace them up, and all the while I'm glaring at Adler over his head.

Noah and Justin have already tied themselves into their

skates and are giddily holding on to each other near the rink entrance. I'm not even sure why they're waiting for us at this point. We are very clearly on two separate dates.

"You don't skate, do you?" Kabir asks lightly, his eyes on the task before him.

I swallow. I can't lie about this, not when he's about to see firsthand that I am not the avid skater I claimed to be. "No. I just wanted to go out with you."

He shows me his bleached teeth in a smile. "That's fine. I'll teach you."

Something inside me warms, despite the chill in the air, and I watch as he expertly ties his skates. He stands up with ease and then pulls me to my feet. I'm unsteady on the blades, but he keeps a hand on my elbow as we meet Noah and Justin and head to the ice as a foursome. Two little kids leaning over orange traffic cones get lapped by the handful of other skaters on the ice, carefree and skilled. Everyone is in their own little world, so I don't feel too embarrassed about being taught to skate— Noah and Justin take off with hands held and I wish I had better balance so I could take a photo for them.

It's not until we reach the break in the rink wall that I realize exactly what I signed up for today. Not only is it cold, but that ice looks *hard*. I know I have more cushion on my body than some people, but not nearly enough of it is on my butt.

Kabir steps onto the ice ahead of me, and he makes it seem so easy, so fun. He reaches out a hand, and I take it but resist his pull.

"I'm just—I need a second." I stare at the ice, release one

anxious cloud of breath, and then step out.

The problem is that I can't seem to make my other foot move. I hope it endears me to him instead of annoying him. Patience is key in everything, and if he doesn't have it, we won't even make it to Saturday night.

He swaps my hand for my waist, pulling me over the edge. My legs split like a newborn deer, and I land on my tailbone. Off to a *wonderful* start.

"I'm sorry," Kabir says, swooping down. He wraps his arm around my waist and takes my hand with his free one, helping me up, but my skates just slide against the cold surface. "I—"

"I've got it." I pull away from him and flip to my hands and knees, crawling into a standing position by sheer willpower and the stability of the rink wall. I pause there to catch my breath and inspect the damage done. I don't think anything is broken, but people also go an entire pregnancy without knowing they're pregnant sometimes, so the human body is *wild* and *mysterious*, and I won't be counting anything out. I dare to remove one hand from the wall to swipe away the bits of ice stuck to my dress. Imagine my surprise when I feel Kabir's hand already there and doing the work. I yelp and slam into the wall to get away from his touch.

"I'm sorry," he says with a cringe, coming to stand next to me along the wall. "Sorry."

"It's okay," I say, out of habit.

"Here." He skates behind me with grace and puts both his hands on my waist.

He doesn't mean any harm. He doesn't mean any harm—

He presses his fingers into the fat on my hips and pushes me forward without letting go. "Don't even move your feet," he says into my ear. "I'll push you until you get more comfortable. You'll be doing this by yourself in no time."

This isn't the most romantic, or even secure, skating position, but it's something. He's trying, and I'm not letting my fear of him letting go, causing me to smack nose-first into the ice, stop me from doing this. We make it maybe halfway around the rink, my hands out in front of me to brace any falls, when his hands slide lower.

I stutter forward to avoid him full-on grabbing my ass again, which just makes me lose my balance. I actually manage to right myself, but that doesn't stop Kabir from planting his hands on my ribs just under my boobs, fingers grazing up like he thinks he's got a fucking chance.

I know from our conversations and everything his social media could tell me that he likes to go go go. He barely stops for a breath. He aces his classes, is an accomplished musician, volunteers at charities, hikes mountains, and has started planning his life beginning the day after graduation. But I am not about to be on his schedule when it comes to him getting his hands all over me.

So, I spin around to let him hear all my thoughts on using someone's vulnerability to cop a feel, even if it might ruin what could have ended up being an easy option for Saturday night—but then Adler stops next to us, pushing shaved ice onto my skates. His green Henley sleeves are pushed up to his elbows, and his jeans fit perfectly around a black pair of skates—he looks like he belongs here.

"Hey, pals," he says with a forced smile. His cheeks are bright red under the fluorescent lights. "Someone in need of a lesson?"

"We're okay, thanks," Kabir says, wrapping his arm around my shoulder.

I break away, gripping on to the wall. "Actually, I think I need one."

Kabir frowns. "I can teach you, though."

I bite my lip, searching for a response, but it's Adler who replies.

"Nothing beats a professional, right?"

"How much is it?" Kabir says, exasperated, but really trying to hide it. "I'm basically a professional."

"It's free."

"Okay, fine. I'll see you after a few laps." He adopts what I think is a flirty tone. "I expect to see some progress when I'm done." He skates off, leaving Adler glaring at his back.

"What a tool." He gestures to my arms wrapped around my torso in a hug I didn't know I was giving myself. "Can I?"

"Oh, no—you don't actually have to give me a lesson." I search through the skaters and find Noah and Justin laughing with each other. "I'll just take a seat and wait this out."

"Do you need help getting off the ice?" Both our eyes dart to the exit, which is now very far away.

"Yes."

He gently unfolds my arms and places his hands in mine. Without a second thought, he starts moving backward, pulling me along slowly. "We have to stay going with the flow of traffic."

I clench tighter on his hands when my skate hits an entirely too slippery spot, but he keeps me steady. "Thanks."

"No problem. I was going to punch a hole in the plexiglass if I saw him make another move on you when you needed help."

My heart does a perfect triple axel at the thought of him looking out for me. The concept typically annoys me, but I really did need some good old-fashioned alpha male vibes to ruin the mood this time. "I meant thanks for helping me not fall right now, but, yeah, that, too. Why were you watching exactly?"

"Because you don't know how to skate."

I roll my eyes. "Just couldn't wait for a face-plant, could you?"

"Not what I meant." He looks down at my skates and then at my face. "You're not doing too bad now. Move your feet wider and then let them slide in. That's it. Nice."

I start to get the hang of it but panic when his grip loosens. Not only is he keeping me upright, but he's keeping my hands warm. "No, don't leave me."

"I won't. I've got you."

People skate around us in warp speed, but it feels like we're moving in a separate, safe reality. I spend half the time staring down at the ice, at his hastily tied skates.

"Lessons aren't free," I say, glancing up. "I saw the sign."

"Yeah, well, I'm not trained to give lessons anyway." He smiles, all teeth and squinty eyes. "We both knew if there was a fee he wouldn't have left."

"He didn't pay for my skates, so it's not like I've been an expensive date so far."

Adler tsks. "He didn't even know your size."

"Okay." I laugh, feeling confident enough to skate a little closer to him now. "That's not something a random guy would know. I don't even know how *you* knew it."

He shoots me a wounded look, half joking and half serious. "Those Converse you've barely ever worn?"

"What about them? I wore them yesterday!" They're at the back of my closet again, where they belong. I might have to donate them after the traumatic experience I had in them with Jackson.

"*I* bought them for you."

"No you didn't."

He stops with the tiniest flick of his heel, but I continue sliding toward him until my chest bumps into his. Despite that, we both stay steady, his hands bracing me near my ribs until I'm able to shift away from him.

"Yes I did. There was a buy one, get one free deal online. I got them for your fifteenth birthday." He adopts a snooty expression. "Didn't even thank me. I guess I shouldn't be too surprised you didn't remember; I didn't get to give them to you myself."

"*Liberty* bought me those." Adler did seem confused during every interaction we had after my birthday for at least two weeks, though. He was waiting for a thank-you or, at the very least, to see me wearing the shoes. (I had thought I wanted them and then when I got them, I realized I was delusional. They do *not* work for me.)

"No, she *brought* you those." He examines my bemused face

for half a second before his own explodes into tamed outrage. "Oh, that *sneaky little—*"

"Even if that *is* true, you didn't buy them. They were free; you said so yourself."

"You know what?" He skates backward again, thumbs in his pants pockets. "Get to the exit yourself."

I reach my hands out toward him. "Don't leave me to fend for myself against him," I joke in a whisper.

He rolls his eyes and skates toward me, accepting my outstretched hands. Kabir stops next to us.

"How is it going?" He looks eager to take over teaching duties, so I cling to Adler tighter.

"Awful," Adler says at the same time I say, "I suck."

"She's gonna need another year or two of training before I feel comfortable leaving her, even in your very capable care," Adler adds.

Kabir glances from Adler to me and wets his bottom lip. "Okay . . . Maybe after we eat, we can hang out just the two of us? If we go to my house, I can play something for you."

I don't know what the patriarchy puts in the water to make so many women docile while we're screaming inside, but it's a real bitch right about now. "Maybe, yeah."

He grins slyly and leaves us once more. Kabir may be saying yes more, but I think he needs to hear no more.

"What's he going to play for you?" Adler asks with a furrowed brow.

"Absolutely nothing because I don't plan on going to a second location with him."

We've actually passed the exit by now. Another lap won't hurt. I'm almost getting the hang of it.

"What about with me?"

I use the back of my skate to come to a stop, like he showed me. "What about you?"

"The barbecue. I was about to leave, but then you came in." He points to my skates. "That was good, by the way."

Oh, right. I'd been fine with skipping the annual family and friends barbecue when this date had seemed promising—now I can't imagine what I was thinking. At the end of every summer, Adler's family and mine get together to pig out and cram a whole summer's experience—and food—into one night. We've been doing it since they first moved in.

"Why would you want to be here with that douchebag eating boiled chicken wings instead of your dad's famous hot dogs?" he asks.

"You mean his famous *store-bought* hot dogs that he does nothing to except grill?" I free my hands from his to push some hair behind my ear. Adler, subconsciously or consciously, mimics the action. "But yeah. I could use a ride."

His hands dangle awkwardly at his sides now that they aren't latched on to mine. "So we're ditching Kabir?"

I spot Kabir on the other side of the rink. "I think he'll be fine."

This is the second time this week that my date has found a replacement, this time a slender girl who looks like she was born with skates on her feet the way she glides around. That was fast.

I search the rink for Noah and Justin but don't find them . . . because apparently, they left the rink completely and exchanged hand-holding for lip-locking on the bleachers at some point. Noah should have given himself more credit. He could have done this on his own. I wish I could say the same.

Twelve

"So, we're probably going to head out now. . . ." Liberty's preferred "goodbye" is punctuated with the crunch of a potato chip and then silence as the rest of us at the picnic table stare at her. It's an unspoken rule of the cookout that you don't leave unless you're going to sleep, no matter how badly you're being bitten by mosquitoes.

If leaving early was an option, I'd have begged off to cry in my room by now. Every last one of my remaining date options is busy tomorrow, except Tyson, who has left me on read for hours, completely shooting my confidence in the figurative foot. And yet I'm still here, because it's tradition.

"But Dad made his famous hot dogs." The words slip out of my mouth before I process if they're even a joke or not. My eyes cut to Adler hiding a smirk in his palm and then to my dad, who looks like Liberty told him he wasn't invited to her wedding.

"We've got a movie to catch," she adds, glancing at our parents. Sophia winces and then swallows the last of her virgin sangria Adler's mom made. "Is it cool if we go?"

My dad wipes a bit of macaroni salad from the corner of his mouth, stiff, but amiable like always when his heart is broken. "Yeah, of course. Have fun."

This stupid barbecue is so important to him. It's the whole reason for the picnic table we're sitting at in the first place. It's not like Liberty can't hang out with Sophia *here*. It's only one night.

Lily perks up. "Can I hang out with Cecily, then?"

She either doesn't notice or care that all five of the adults at the table—our parents, Adler's parents, and Aunt Madison—exchange frowns.

I speak up because I know they will tell her it's fine and it's not. "What about s'mores and sparklers later?"

She shrugs, pulling out her phone. "We'll stop back here maybe."

I'm suddenly met with the crushing realization that Lily's too old to be kept around solely by traditions now. She's off to see a friend, Liberty's leaving with her girlfriend. It's just Summer, Adler, and me—how tragic. I guess I could see if Poppy's home from work and adjust my plans for the night, or I could risk totally turning Tyson off with a double text asking if he got my first text.

My mom smiles at Lily. "Yeah, that's fine, as long as you're home by nine."

Lily's too busy texting Cecily to even say thank you. I shift in my seat, poking at the watermelon Aunt Madison brought. I didn't know when I scooped it onto my plate that it's horrible, rotten and soggy, so now I'm here with several handfuls of bad watermelon and no respectful way to get it as far from me as possible.

Conversation starts back up as Liberty and Sophia stand to leave. I overhear my sister reluctantly ask Adler if he wants to go with them. He shakes his head, but it's so clear to everyone, except perhaps Liberty, that he doesn't want to be left behind. They leave, and he watches their retreating backs like he might call out for them to please wait.

Things seem fine between Adler and me now, but with everyone around, it doesn't feel like I can be as open with him as I was at the rink. I want to tell him that Liberty's kind of a jerk for always ditching him for Sophia, but I doubt he'd appreciate my pity when there's an audience. I wouldn't. Instead, I elbow Lily.

"What?" she huffs.

"Ask Adler to play cornhole," I whisper.

"Why don't you? I'm about to meet Cecily."

"I saw her text," I say, nodding to her phone screen, which she keeps on full brightness at all times. "She's still eating dinner. Just go play while you wait."

"Do it yourself. You clearly need something to do or else you start inserting yourself into everyone's business."

"I'll play the winner." I'm exceptional at cornhole; it seems only fair.

Lily narrows her eyes and then smirks, turning to where Summer sits quietly picking at her own terrible watermelon. Then she ruins my night. "Summer, will you play cornhole with us?"

Summer glances up from her paper plate with wide eyes. Apparently, she's as surprised as I am that she's been asked. "Uh, sure."

"Great. You can be on Lahey's team," she says, scooting away from the table and sticking her tongue out at me. "Adler, you'll be my partner?"

He stands and brushes dirt off his jeans even though he knows my dad would never allow such a thing as dirt to sully his precious picnic table. I meet this sorry group of cornballs by the boards and claim the one facing away from the setting sun, leaving Summer on the other side to squint into the glare. When she tries to say something about giving a guest the better spot, I point to my glasses. My mishap at the public pool led to scratches on my prescription sunglasses, so these are all I have right now, and for a long while, according to my mom.

"I can't see anything with the sun in my eyes. That would give the other team an advantage."

"Yeah, and you couldn't have that," Lily says sarcastically to herself. She collects the beanbags in the crook of her arm. "It's not like you could win this game blindfolded or anything."

Adler offers Lily the free spot on my side, but she just slams her head forward abruptly, her sunglasses sliding down over her eyes. "I came prepared to win," she says.

He removes the sunglasses at his shirt collar and tosses them to Summer. I try not to roll my eyes at the way she slides them on and poses for him. The Summer Show is beginning, and the worst thing is that we turned it on and sat down on the couch for it. *Thanks, Lily.*

The game starts normally enough, in that I'm doing great, Summer is frustratingly bad, Adler can't sink a beanbag to save his life, and Lily takes after me when it comes to this specific athletic prowess. At least the teams are fair this way, but I obviously would have preferred playing with Lily on my team. This would be over sooner.

Summer engages Lily in some conversation we're too far away to hear—probably claiming I take steroids to be this skilled. Adler leans in.

"Did I hear you say at the table that you wanted to play the winner?"

I blink. I was *whispering*; how did he hear that? "I was trying to keep it an even playing field."

"Maybe you should offer to play the loser in the future. Seems like you've gotten a little rusty."

I turn to him, my mouth hanging open, and smack him on the shoulder with my remaining beanbag. "*Rusty?* Says the guy who hasn't even gotten on the board! You know, it's an absolute wonder you're single with how complimentary you can be."

"Speaking of being single, should we tell everyone here how poorly your hunt for a date is going?" He bites his lip to hold back a smile—it doesn't work.

"Sure, and we can tell them how spectacularly your eighteen-year hunt for a personality is failing, or . . . did you give up and you're just embracing this *meh* vibe you give off?"

"Do you guys need a minute or can we finish this game?" Lily calls, hands on her hips.

It's hard to see with their eyes behind sunglasses, but I imagine the looks my sister and cousin are giving Adler and me are quite judgmental.

"Sorry," I can't help but say sarcastically, "were we stopping you?"

I notice the beanbag in Summer's grip. It was her turn before

Adler started antagonizing me. What has she been waiting for?

"Yes," Summer says indignantly. "It's hard to focus with your bickering."

"Use us as a target." I wave to the area in front of Adler and me. "Maybe you'll make it in."

"I'm not a bat, okay? I don't need echolocation; I need the two of you to be silent."

"That won't ever happen," Lily says.

"I'll be quiet." Adler even backs a step away from the cornhole board, giving Summer silence and space.

Appropriately peer-pressured, I shut up while Summer throws. The beanbag arcs through the air and lands with a thud and hiss as it slides right into the hole. Summer freezes when I cheer, like maybe she did something wrong, but relaxes when she sees I'm yelling in excitement instead of anger.

"Oh, come on," Lily complains, her head tilted to the side and the rest of her body nearly limp in annoyance. "This was only fair when Summer and Adler both sucked—no offense," she adds to Adler.

"I'm sad about this turn of events, too," he says. "Good job, Summer."

She smiles shyly, and it's the fact that she says nothing—her humility showing for one brief moment—that propels me to say something nice.

"Yeah, that was good. More of that." I even give her a thumbs-up.

She turns her smile to me, and I see it so rarely in its full glory that I had forgotten how perfectly straight and white her teeth are—another present from her dad.

We start getting into a rhythm. Adler *almost* hits the board—I'm starting to think he is purposely missing, because it's entirely too difficult *not* to hit it, even accidentally. Lily and I both sink beanbags right into the holes every single time. Then, in a miraculous feat, Summer's toss manages to push Lily's off the board. She and I scream in surprise and meet in the middle of the yard to hug, as if we've won.

We quickly split apart, but not before Aunt Madison makes a point of loudly cooing over the moment.

"If Lahey gets this point, we win and then the game is over, right?" Summer asks. Despite our family religiously playing this game every summer, she still hasn't caught on—actually, this may be the first time I've ever seen her playing.

I raise an eyebrow at Adler and mutter, "*Watch who you call rusty,*" and then turn to the cornhole board opposite us, ready to win this thing.

"Yeah, Lahey! Show those girls who's boss!" Aunt Madison cheers, raising her red Solo cup in my direction.

"We're on the same team," Summer says.

Apparently, her mother doesn't know how the game works, either.

"Oh. Well. Go, Lahey!"

With my arm winding up to toss, Adler's hand sneaks to my side and brushes *just the right amount* to make me flinch, and the beanbag goes soaring toward the picnic table. Aunt Madison bursts into laughter, falling into Adler's dad's side, face red.

I spin in his direction and I'm unable to keep the laughter

from my voice when I say, "That one doesn't count!"

"She should be able to go again," Summer says, agony in her voice. "That was, like, an illegal move."

I point at her. "Exactly. It's in the official rule book."

"Is it?" she asks quietly, leaning forward as if she and I are able to have even half of a private conversation in these positions.

"No, of course not—you think there's a rule that says no tickling?"

She stands straight and shrugs, arms folding across her chest to watch me go again.

Adler offers me his beanbag, and I guide him farther back so he can't ruin my shot again. I take a deep breath, zero in on the hole in the board, and then—glare at Adler over my shoulder because he's creeping up behind me with his tickler hands out in plain sight! I throw the beanbag down on the ground and wrap my hands around Adler's wrists to push him so far back that his butt drops into the lone swing we still have hanging from the tree in our yard. I stomp back and take my final shot at victory.

And I would have made it if Adler hadn't tackled me.

I don't hit the ground—he had the decency to maneuver us into a position where his back hit the grass and I hit *him*—but the wind is still knocked out of me.

Somehow, it's not knocked out of him. Probably because of how much he gasses himself up all the time. He has an extra store of oxygen or something in his body. "Does this count? Did we win?" he shouts at Lily through a tangle of my hair in his mouth.

"Obviously not," she says with distaste. "But if nobody cares about the game anymore, I'm out."

She grabs her skateboard and helmet from the back porch and then waves to the adults, effectively ending our game. In her absence, Summer organizes the beanbags by color and I try to collect myself, all too aware of Adler's solid thighs pressed against mine. I roll away and adjust my dress, hoping I didn't flash anyone, and stand. I don't offer him any help up, though he asks for it with an outstretched dirty rotten cheating hand.

I debate going back to the table but remember the rancid watermelon waiting for me.

"Well," I say, wiping my sweaty hands on my skirt. "It's been a time."

Summer stands awkwardly next to the cornhole board, beanbags in her hands. "Are we playing another game?"

I don't really want to play another game. I didn't want to play the first game. "We don't have enough players now."

"Don't you just need two?"

"It's not as fun."

"I'll play," Aunt Madison calls, trying to untangle herself from the bench. She's a little too tipsy to do so, though. "I want to be on Lahey's team."

"You could be on mine," Summer says, watching her mom fail to get up.

"I want to be on the winning team, though," Aunt Madison says with a laugh.

Summer's face goes so blank that it's obvious even with sunglasses on.

Adler's still on the ground, but he's in a seated position, his arms laid atop his bent knees. "I'll play again."

"I'm actually going to clean up the kitchen," I say, wiping my hands on my dress. I can't focus on cornhole now that Adler's been all over me. "Maybe do some dishes."

"That's a good girl." Aunt Madison plops herself back down and picks up her drink.

"Adler, help her with that, will you?" his mom asks.

"I don't need help; it's okay." I step toward the sliding door that leads to the kitchen, but she won't accept that.

"No, he practically spends half his time at your house. He should help out."

"I don't mind," Adler says quietly to me, standing up.

"Fine." I rush inside and use the second alone to catch my breath, which has mysteriously caught in my chest for I'm not even sure how long. I don't know why I'm so flustered. But the last few times I've seen Adler—like, now that he's acknowledging my existence again—it's felt like there's something off. He used to hold back on the teasing in public, at least a moderate amount; he definitely was never tackling me or tickling me in front of people, especially our parents. I don't know what to make of it, but suddenly Adler is right next to me in this kitchen that is much messier than I believed it to be when I volunteered my services and I don't have any more time to think about it.

At least with the two of us, we'll finish sooner and then I can leave. I'll go to Poppy's and get some fresh air, and my parents can't even be mad that I ditched the cookout because my sisters did it before me *and* I helped clean up.

The sink is by far the biggest disaster. It's an oversized farm sink capable of holding every dish in the world, plus my crushed hopes and dreams of ever escaping this chore, with room for water and soap bubbles. It's full to the top.

I push my hands into some blue rubber gloves and turn the faucet as hot as it can go.

"Do you have any gloves for me?" Adler stands next to me in this space that is really meant for one person. Heat rolls off him and clings to me. It was nice earlier at the rink, but now it's smothering. "I have to keep my hands nice and soft."

"You work at a garage. There's no way your hands are soft." Plus, he could pack food up in Tupperware instead. We don't both need to do the dishes.

He accepts the challenge, seemingly already forgetting that I had my hands in his earlier today and know they're soft, like rudely soft. All the moisturizer in the world couldn't do that for my hands. He holds his right hand out, palm up, and I let him watch me glance from my one wet, gloved hand to the other. I lean my cheek down into his palm and he bursts into laughter.

Aiming my hot face toward the sink, I clear my throat and say, "There are more gloves here." I give a gentle tap to the lower cabinet with my foot. Who am I to be ungrateful for his help?

He pulls out a hot-pink pair of gloves and puts them on. We clean in silence for about a minute before he says, "Hey, Siri? Play some music," and she starts playing whatever he was listening to last. The sound comes from his back pocket, so it's muffled on top of being hard to hear over the sloshing water and clinking ceramics, but it's the thought that counts.

"Are you okay, from earlier?" he asks. "I didn't think you'd actually fall."

I brush away a strand of hair and feel the water from my gloves trickle down my face. "Don't worry; your massive ego cushioned my fall."

He grins and then steps back to better look down at his pants. "*Massive*, you say?"

I roll my eyes until they fall on the sink sprayer in my hand. If I can just keep the grin off my face, maybe Adler won't see it coming.

"Don't even think about it," he says in a low warning.

Is that a murderous rage in his eyes or a dare?

I aim the sprayer at his face—just so the temperature of his matches mine—at the same moment he lunges at me. We wrestle over the sprayer, water flying into the air, on the counter and floor, and all over us. My hands threaten to slide right out of my slippery gloves and lose this battle, but I tighten my grip like my life depends on it. I must put up more of a fight than either of us thought I could, because Adler gives up and crushes me to his chest, effectively lodging the sprayer, now shooting icy-cold water, between us. For a second, the only sounds in the kitchen are Adler's tinny music, our ragged breathing, and the constant *drip drip drip* of the water.

"If you were hot, all you had to do was say so; I could have turned the air conditioner on." I try to wiggle the sprayer free from its place smashed between us, but it's no use. The entire front of my dress is drenched.

His smile is tight as he locks his fingers together behind my back and squeezes us even closer. The drip lessens, more of the water getting caught in the fabric of our clothes. "Oh, me? You thought *I* was hot?"

"You know what I meant—"

"You were the one with the red face. I think *you* needed to cool down."

I break eye contact first and stare at where our chests connect. Adler has hugged me a total of four times in my life: after I took a nasty fall from the monkey bars, when he left the spring dance early in eighth grade, the time I was bedridden in the nurse's office with period cramps, and at the start of his graduation party . . . before I messed everything up.

It's not many times considering the years we've spent in orbit of each other, but they were significant enough that I remember how our bodies felt in relation to each other, how his made mine feel. It's different this time, and I'm not sure it has to do with the water.

My eyes meet his while I process this moment slowly—most of his green irises are blown out black by his pupils. His breath, a sweet combination of virgin sangria and chocolate, fans against my cheeks.

"Do you want to call a truce?" I wish I could glue my eyes upward, anything so they would stop falling to his mouth and the slight smirk he wears there. "We're wasting water and making a huge mess that I'm going to have to clean up."

"You started it."

"Doesn't mean I can't stop it."

Without a word, he unlatches his hands and turns the water off at the faucet. The sprayer goes limp in my grip, useless for protection now, so I toss it back into the sink, where it lands in a puff of soap bubbles. We barely made a dent in the dishes.

I gather my dress at the seams and bunch it up in my fists so I can squeeze some water out, on top of Adler's shoes. "Those didn't look nearly wet enough."

"Thanks." He slides the heel of his right foot against the floor and it squeaks loudly. "Yes, perfect." He does the same with his left. "Just what I wanted."

"Really?"

"Yep."

"Hold out your hands, then; I have another surprise."

He does, closing his eyes like a little kid about to be presented with a puppy. I lift my dress high enough to scrunch the excess water right into his waiting palms. He flings it back into my face without even opening his eyes.

"I thought we called a truce!" I push him back, knowing his balance is precarious at best, and he latches on to my shoulders to keep upright. The movement pulls us close, our chests hitting each other with each breath. He tucks a wet strand of my hair behind my ear, but it doesn't stay.

It feels like whatever happens next will be big. Maybe that's why neither of us speaks.

"So, does Liberty know about the two of you?" My heart leaps to my throat with the appearance of Summer at the sliding door. She dumps her plate of watermelon straight into the trash and gazes pointedly at the immense space now between Adler and me. I don't even know when we scrambled apart.

"What do you mean?" I push the stubborn strand of hair Adler tried to tame behind my ear; it stays with ease.

She smiles. "Oh. She doesn't."

"There's no—us—two—*no*."

If Adler hadn't already moved an entire planet away, I'd be fighting to shove him into a dark little box far from here so she could never suggest such a thing in front of him again. I have to end this terrible conversation before Adler does something heroic and embarrassing, like lie to her that we're together because he feels bad that I'm failing so hard to get a date for Saturday.

"So Adler isn't the one you're bringing to the party, then?" She crosses her arms over her chest. "Who's the mystery date who doesn't mind you flirting with other guys?"

"A literal physical fight is not flirting," I blurt out, ripping my rubber gloves off and throwing them into the sink, where they disappear beneath the dwindling bubbles. With my hands free now, I pull myself into a hug. *A hug!* I *am* pitiable. "You'll meet him Saturday, like I said before."

"Will I? Because I heard that you went out with a guy this week who now has a girlfriend. Your roster's getting smaller, huh?"

My stomach drops to the floor and shatters. "Excuse me?"

"My friend Wilson works at the stable where I take my riding lessons; he told me all about this girl he went on a date with who hooked him up with their waitress." She moves through the kitchen with intention and stops at the refrigerator. "He said she seemed desperate, so he went out with her, but it turned out to be the best thing he could have done. He got with his girlfriend that day. So, I guess that takes him off your long list of guys you could bring, right?"

Does a date to her party even matter if she knows how badly I've struggled to get one? Wilson, the supposed gentleman, told her I was desperate.

"It was just a scheme to get him with his crush. I do that all the time. *You* of all people should know. How's Tommy?"

"He's real and actually interested in me, as you know."

Adler leans his back against the counter and witnesses my humiliation all over again. Summer seems to revel in it, her eyes dancing in the fading light streaming in through the door. How twisted does one need to be to get amusement out of someone else's pain?

"What's his name, Lahey." It's not a question coming from my cousin's lips. "Show me a picture. Prove that there is one guy willing to go on a date with you."

"I said I will Saturday." I grind my teeth. "You'll feel stupid. In fact, that's the only reason I'm not sinking to your level right now. Seeing your face when I walk in will be the icing on your birthday cake."

She opens the refrigerator like this is her house, like she's welcome anywhere but the depths of hell, and grabs a green juice that only my dad drinks. I guess when you're used to getting whatever you want, you can feel comfortable anywhere. "If you had just been honest and told me I was right not giving you a plus one, *you* wouldn't feel so stupid now. I was giving you an out. I tried to help you."

She cracks the seal and takes a sip. I don't even know what to say. It would be embarrassing enough as it is, but to have Adler here witnessing it in silence . . . this is torture.

"Sure, you help a lot of people find love, but it doesn't change the fact that you will never find it yourself."

She turns and hands Adler his sunglasses with a smile. "Anyway. Thanks for letting me borrow these."

He stares at them in his hand but doesn't say anything. I leave the room before either of them can leave first.

Thirteen

"She just spelled out my total lack of datability in front of Adler like it was the ABCs. I'm so annoyed and so—" I don't even let the phone line fully connect before I bombard Poppy with my emotions, my body loose and lifeless spread across my bed. "Humiliated," I whisper, hating the sound of the word. Even the rhythm of it is terrible. Like a roller coaster. "I thought we were kind of getting along tonight."

The door is locked and everyone who's still here is outside, but I don't want to breathe too much life into the words by having them heard by anyone else—which means I'm definitely not mentioning that Summer accused Adler and me of flirting right now. I hope the floral peel-and-stick wallpaper I put up last winter on my side of the room acts as a sound barrier in addition to being very cute (and slightly crooked).

"Who are we talking about? Summer?"

"Who else?" I take a calming breath and close my eyes. "Like, it's Adler, okay, whatever. But it's still so rude and wrong, and

I regret ever helping her with anything, even saving her from choking on chicken nuggets."

"Did that actually happen?" Poppy's voice was somewhat monotone earlier, but now I hear some emotion coming through.

"No, but before now, if it *had* happened, I would have saved her! I hope she orders a ten-piece and goes to town tonight."

"Okay, evil genius, calm down."

"I can't! Can we hang out?" Outside, I spy Aunt Madison offering a sip of her drink to Adler. He refuses, and passes the test she pretends she was giving him. "I need to get out of here. Both my sisters abandoned me, and Adler hasn't left, so I just—I can't face anyone else right now."

There's some rustling on her end, but no words.

"Poppy? I need you!"

"Sorry," she says, not sounding sorry at all. Then, "It's just that—I have a problem of my own."

"What? What's wrong?"

"They're all fucking gone." I tense at the distress in her voice, but let her continue. "Every bottle I collected—every beautiful bottle—has been recycled. I even told them not to. I told them exactly where I was putting the empties and—gone."

Apparently, someone, whether it be her parents or a well-meaning employee, has recycled all the bottles Poppy had stored away for her fundraiser centerpieces. They were the main structural piece of her art, and the world is ending now, apparently. Mine, too. We should galivant across this postapocalyptic world together and just burn it all down.

"My family is finishing off their second bottle right now, if you want me to donate to the cause."

"Please. I'm going to ask Francesco and Peter to see if they have any empties I can take tonight. If they do, will you come with me to pick them up? I'll need to make another trip tomorrow night, but at least I can start working on the centerpieces in the morning this way. Between your bottles and theirs, I should have like ten."

Francesco and Peter, her parents' couple friends, must go through plenty of wine during the dinner rush at their Italian restaurant, Pane Caldo. I'll agree to go so I can get out of the house and, if I'm lucky, get some bread scraps. They have the *best* bread. One night when I was there with the Nguyens, I made sure to tell Francesco and Peter this. They and Poppy's parents laughed and laughed, because I, a seventeen-year-old with two years of high school Spanish under her loosened belt, did not know that the restaurant name translated into English is "warm bread."

I haven't held it against them. Because of the bread.

"I'm already texting them and heading to your house, so just say yes." I hear her ignition turn over in the background.

"Yes. A million times yes. Please save me."

Leaving the house after nine o'clock at night, even though it's the summer and I'm almost an adult, can be a tricky thing. It's made way less complicated when Poppy's idling in the driveway and the two other children in the household are already out. Plus, they should focus on Lily, who is still out despite agreeing to a curfew. They tell me goodbye, even though the disapproval is on their wine-stained lips when I creep to the backyard to tell them I'm leaving. Adler tries, and fails, to meet my eyes before I disappear. I almost feel bad for abandoning him with all the parents and Summer, but what was I supposed to do? Invite him as an afterthought like Liberty did? Plus, it would be so uncomfortable after the eviscerating verbal lashes Summer gave me earlier. And . . . the weirdness before.

In the tense silence of the car ride, my gut works itself into a knot as I piece together the sentence I want to use to break the news. It feels safer in this bubble, just Poppy, me, and no chance of being overheard or judged.

"Um, I think maybe Adler and I had a moment."

"What do you mean?" I catch sight of her wide eyes as a car's headlights pass over her face. "What does that mean? And how can you say it so casually?"

"I think it was like an I-feel-sorry-for-you thing. He did it the other day, too, kind of." I roll my eyes. "Or he could be messing with me still, because of the matchmaking incident, but I felt like we were past that. Regardless, the important part of this story is not that, but the fact that Summer walked in and said I was basically cheating on my imaginary date for Saturday, and then—*and then*—she tells me she knows I've been hounding guys for dates and essentially called me pathetic and undatable, as I said before."

Not to mention the dig at my self-esteem, which, as I just said, I will not mention. I like myself very much, though—too much, according to some people—so I don't even know what she was trying to get at with that comment, aside from on my nerves.

"She's good." Poppy's grip tightens when she merges onto the highway even though there isn't another car in sight. She just barely passed her driver's test in January. It started snowing the morning of, and she hyperventilated on the way to the DMV. But she did it, technically. "How does she even know?"

"She has henchmen in unexpected places." The more I sit with the fact that Wilson called me desperate, the more I doubt he actually did. Summer was probably exaggerating, or just straight-up lying to further her agenda. Would a grateful guy with a new girlfriend—and me to thank—insult me like that to anyone, let alone my cousin?

"As most evil people do."

"I don't even know where she gets it from. My aunt is super nice."

"Maybe her dad."

I bite my thumbnail from nerves. "You think evil is genetic?"

"Well, you just made a case against it being nurture in the nature-nurture debate."

"I never expected Mr. Crocker's class to come up in a real-life conversation. I thought it was like algebra. I don't want to talk about Summer anymore."

"We were actually talking about Adler, but you steered the conversation to safer waters."

I groan, throwing my head back so hard it hits the seat and bounces. "I don't know. Things feel different between us. I thought it was just because he was mad at me for so long and now we're getting back to how things were, but I'm not sure anymore. He could be pulling a long con and trying to get back at me for setting him up with Brighton—like letting me lower my defenses before attacking—or, *or*, he feels bad for me, which might be even worse than retaliation in the form of psychological warfare."

She shoots me a strange look, eyebrows squished together and a tilt to her mouth.

"What?" I ask.

"Or maybe he likes you."

My stomach drops, but I pick it up immediately. "You're too optimistic. It's gonna get you murdered one day."

"I just mean not everything has to be suspicious—sometimes it's exactly what it seems. He's known you for years and you think he's over the matchmaking incident, so . . . there could be feelings there. You're awesome; it's not that much of a stretch. You should ask him to Summer's party!"

"Why, so he can reject me? Or worse, so he can say yes and then stand me up—or *worse*, show up at the party and embarrass me somehow? He and Summer could team up to bring me down once and for all." I hook my thumb on my bottom row of teeth and gnaw. Poppy swats my hand away. "Or, because he knows I'm desperate, he'd say yes and then it's a whole awkward thing, and we'd have to explain to Liberty and everyone that we're just friends—but are we even friends?"

She blinks. "I think you're being paranoid. You can't let yourself see what's right there in front of you because you feel like you don't deserve it."

"No, it's coming from a place of self-preservation, and pride." I pull the side of my phone case away from my phone and then release, letting it snap. I can't stop fidgeting. "I know I deserve someone nice and cute who actually likes me."

"Maybe that's Adler!"

"Maybe you're delusional and—you're about to miss the exit!" I point out the windshield, but it's not necessary.

She slides into the exit lane. "I'm sorry," she says, and it sounds like she means it. "I'm stressed and don't want to think about my own problems. Your problems seem more fun."

"They're not fun for me." I wake my phone to check for a response from Tyson, but my text from hours ago sits unanswered and alone. It looks so tragic there by itself. I might just text him about something else to give him an out so we can continue the conversation and move that text message up, up, up, until it can't be seen on either of our screens any longer. "It's no fun to have to think about Adler's motives all day. And it's no fun at all to be ignored by a guy I thought I was making real progress with. Tyson Garcia left me on read."

She just bites her lip. I can see how stressed she is.

"Hey. It's okay, you know," I say, rubbing her shoulder. "We'll get the centerpieces made in time, and they'll be excellent. Everything you make is amazing."

"What if they did this intentionally?"

"Who?"

"My parents. What if my parents recycled the bottles—or had someone recycle them—so that I can't make the centerpieces?"

"Why would they do that?"

"Because they don't believe I'll make something good."

I scoff, which turns into a light laugh until I notice she's not laughing with me. "Poppy, no. Your work is amazing."

"Maybe they don't know how to tell me that I suck and they're worried I'm about to throw my life away."

She pulls into the parking lot of Pane Caldo in Hershey with a white-knuckled grip. I lay my hand on top of hers, the air-conditioning gliding over our skin.

"That's not it," I say softly. "I think it was an accident."

"I don't want to blow this for them," she says, equally as quiet. I don't remember who started the whole "if it can't be heard, it's not true" thing, but we both do it so regularly that it's obviously just ingrained in us. "It's a big deal."

"That's why they're trusting you to nail this. They believe in you."

She exhales and turns the car off, pocketing her keys. "Or I was their only free option."

"Or that." I wait for her to laugh before doing it myself.

We leave the temperature-controlled space of the car and head inside Pane Caldo, the usually dim dining room welcoming us with lights bright enough to stun. Employees clean tables and booths, vacuum, and refill the sugar packets. A girl tells us they're closed, but Peter comes from the back and waves her away.

"Family friends," he says with a smile. "Hey, Poppy." I think he forgets my name, but why should he remember it? "Hey there."

"Hi." I try to stuff my hands into my dress pockets but remember that I had to change my outfit after the water fight. I cross my arms instead.

"The bottles are in the back by the walk-in. If you pull around, you can have Tom put them in your car."

When she blinks in confusion, he clarifies. "He's a new hire. About your age. Red hair. Has a name tag on."

And then Peter gets back to work, counting money from the register with what looks to be another new hire. I guess business is booming. Warm bread never gets old—stale, maybe, but not old.

"I'll pull the car around," Poppy says to me. "Will you go meet the guy?"

I nod and head into the kitchen, which feels scandalous because it's not the kitchen at Feather, yet I have full authority to enter. A few guys elbows-deep in the sink and loading the dishwasher turn to look at me with raised brows but don't bother trying to stop me. They don't get paid to care.

"Where's the walk-in?" I try to inject some confidence in my voice, but I think uncertainty is what comes out.

One jerks his head over his shoulder, confused, but too interested in what I'm going to do—maybe steal the frozen cheesecakes?—to stop me. I head in the direction I was . . . jerked . . . in to find the back of a skinny guy about a foot taller than me, red hair sticking out from underneath a black delivery hat.

I hesitate for one moment, because it couldn't be— "Tommy?"

He turns around and it *is* Tommy. Tommy Porter, Summer's boyfriend. The one *I* helped her get. I really should apologize for setting him up with such a demon.

"Oh, hey, Lahey." He scratches at the back of his neck, which is littered with freckles like the rest of him, and takes his cap off to reveal messy, sweaty hair. "What are you doing here?"

I nod at the box of bottles by his feet. "I'm here for those."

"Small world." He bends down to pick up the box. "What are you going to do with them?"

"They're for my friend. She's using them as centerpieces for some—" He's totally tuned me out, staring at the bottles. "How have you been?"

He blinks back to attention. "Oh, great, thanks. Worked a long day. You?"

"Fine." I point to the back exit. "Should we . . . ?"

"Yes, totally."

I open the door for him, retracting my hand when it meets something sticky. Outside, Poppy makes room in her trunk for him to deposit the box with care, but the glass bottles still jangle against each other.

"Thanks," she says timidly, closing the trunk. Her being the driver isn't the only reason she went to bring the car around instead of finding Tom, someone she's never met before. I find her so endearing, it makes me sick sometimes.

"Poppy, this is Tommy, Summer's boyfriend."

She finishes a double take. "Lucky you."

He laughs but takes it as the compliment it's not. "Yeah, seriously. I don't know any other girl like her."

And you still don't, because you and Summer were probably the fakest matchmaking I ever did.

"You said it," Poppy says with a sneaky smile at me.

It hits me like a truck then. I don't need to panic and stress over finding a date—I mean, I'm still *going to*, but I don't need to. There's a plan B staring me right in the face.

Poppy gets into the car, and I motion for her to wait a minute. She nods and closes her door, the engine turning over a moment later.

Even if I can't find a date of my own, I *can* try to prevent Summer's date from going to the party at all.

"Hey," I say, catching Tommy before he can go into the restaurant. "I—I just feel so guilty . . ."

He frowns. "About what?"

"Well, you mentioned Summer . . . I . . ." I don't have to blow up Summer's relationship like this, but she didn't have to embarrass me like she did tonight, either. We were having a completely fine time and, out of nowhere, she pointed out all the things I'm totally *not* insecure about, and in front of Adler, too.

Tommy watches me with a frown. "What about Summer?"

She acts like she's so much better than me because she has a boyfriend. But if I had everything she had—if I had someone to match me with a great guy—we'd be even. It's ridiculous that I'm letting her get away with making me feel inadequate. I take a deep breath and let it out, all of it.

"It only feels fair to tell you that a lot of what she said to you before you were together was a lie. Like, the stuff about tiny homes." *God, this guy and tiny homes.* His parents started a company that builds them, and he's obsessed. He even tries to live a minimalist lifestyle so he's ready to live in one someday in the future. "She doesn't like them. She hates them, in fact.

She thinks they're stupidly small and inconvenient. I think she even said she thought your parents' business would go under in a year or two. But she thought you were cute and knew you guys had nothing in common, so . . . she said she liked tiny homes. And hiking. And Solo and the Wookiee—she would rather bang her head in a microwave door than listen to that band's first EP. Sorry, those are her words, not mine." I suck in a breath, letting my shoulders rise, and then release. "I suppose it's quite the compliment, though! She made herself into the perfect girl for you even though she hates everything you love."

He stands there in silence.

"I'm sorry that I helped her lie to you. It's been eating away at me. I'm honestly surprised she hasn't told you the truth yet."

"I—don't understand?"

He's really going to make me spell it out for him, huh? Well, I will.

"She's fake. I'm sure you guys are great together now," I rush to say, like I'm trying to correct things for Summer's sake, but really to emphasize that their so-called solid relationship started on lies, lies, lies. "It's just that your whole relationship is built on falsities stemming from cyberstalking. I'm sorry she did that to you. I just felt like you deserved to know."

He exhales suddenly out of his nose, body rigid, and says "Excuse me" before going inside. I watch the door swing shut and allow my adrenaline to settle before I slip into the passenger seat.

"What were you talking about?" Poppy asks, scrolling

through her phone for the perfect song.

"Just making a contingency plan."

If I do, unfortunately, show up by myself on Saturday, at least I might not be the only one.

TOMMY PORTER, 16, through the eyes of Lahey Johnson, who is seeing smirking devil emojis everywhere she looks

How I know him: my darling cousin Summer

He likes: doesn't really matter, does it?

He dislikes: doesnnnnn't matterrrrrrrr

Dating history: Summer, and maybe now NO ONE

Bio: I know quite a bit about him from my time researching him for Summer but, again, it doesn't matterrrrrrrrrrr because Summer's going to eat a kangarooooooooo!!!!

Thursday

Fourteen

As a general rule, I sweat for no one.

But when Tyson Garcia sent me an extremely charming and apologetic text this morning explaining why he couldn't answer me yesterday along with an invitation to play tennis today, there was no way I was saying no. No way. Not only do I still need a date, but he's currently my number one choice. Even with the heat and unwanted physical activity? Game set match or whatever. I'm *yours*, Tyson.

"What if we played, like, baby tennis?" I huff out after running to the ball I missed for the seven hundredth time. "Like, we play really close to the net? And don't hit the ball very hard? And then we don't have to run as far to get the ball when one of us misses?"

Actually, maybe getting closer to each other is a mistake. I'm soaking through my T-shirt and can feel the sun's effects on my face—I'm splotchy. Tyson hasn't even broken a sweat, which is honestly a shame because he'd probably look good with the sheen on his golden-brown skin.

He laughs at my suggestion, but jogs to the net. I meet him there after trying to subtly wipe the sweat from under my eyes. With my glasses on, the airflow to that region all but stops and insecurity puddles there.

"How about we just take a break?" He leans on the net with ease, his tennis racket under his palms.

A break? As in, we'll play *more* later?

"Yeah, great. I love tennis." I follow him to the shaded area by the courts where we stowed our bags and keys. "Can't wait to get back to it."

He releases a bark of a laugh. It's my favorite thing about him. He can't help but put his entire body into laughter. He throws his head back, crams his eyes shut, and holds on to himself like he may combust. One of my favorite pastimes in World Lit was watching Tyson trying not to laugh when Mrs. Phillips would, mid-lecture, misplace her notes, give up, and then move on to the next piece of work that the class hadn't even read yet.

"We can be done," he says when his laughing fit is over. He sits next to me on the grass before he cracks open his water bottle. "If you don't like tennis, why did you agree to play?"

"I wanted to hang out with you." I stuff my hand to the bottom of my bag to find a semi-melted protein bar. I offer him half of it with zero hesitation. I don't typically like eating in front of guys. I accept my body, I love myself, et cetera, et cetera—but I'm only human. It's hard to live in a fat body and not sometimes fear being judged for eating, even when I'm eating something healthy like fruit or vegetables. It's like some people think that because I'm not skinny, I must be on a journey to being skinny, which obviously means I shouldn't be eating. I don't deserve to eat until I have what they think is the ideal body. It's really a whole thing I could go on about for days, but I don't need to, because I don't feel uncomfortable eating around Tyson, and it's probably because he's big himself. Not fat in the same way I'd refer to myself as fat, but solid and sturdy. I have areas of fat, holding my weight in my stomach, arms, chin, and thighs; he's just thick all over.

He bites into his half of the bar and leaves a smudge of melted chocolate at the corner of his mouth. "Well, I appreciate it. I've been working a lot, and it's been hard to see friends and not just become one with my couch when I have time off."

I point to the corner of my mouth to indicate he's got some leftovers to take care of. He gets the message loud and clear, using his thumb to wipe the area clean. "Happy to be your other bird," I say.

His tongue darts out to lick his thumb. "Bird?"

"Two birds, one stone."

"Wow, I know you don't like tennis, but am I really *killing you* right now?"

"Not *right* now; right now we're on a break, so . . ."

"The chances of you dying while playing tennis are low, but—"

"Never zero." I down the majority of my water bottle in one go. I can't recall the last time I felt this thirsty. "You've still been working at your grandma's grocery store?"

"Yeah. I'm trying to save up as much as I can before school

starts, because then I won't be working much, and with college next year . . . expensive."

Tyson's been raised by his grandmother his whole life, but I've never asked why. During the few classes we've shared, he's mentioned his father in passing, but not in a way that made it seem like he's around, so I've kept my curiosity to myself. When we were freshmen, Tyson started working at his grandmother's grocery store, Abuela's. I met Abuela herself once when my dad randomly decided our typical white people taco night would not do. My dad and I were only slightly overwhelmed by the selections until Mrs. Garcia came over to help us, a smile on her face the whole time. I think she loved my dad for his self-deprecating jokes about the level of spice he could tolerate—and probably also for his earnest desire to have authentic food and learn something new. He even invited her and Tyson over, but she claimed they had plans to eat some white people food that night. My dad loved the joke.

"What about you?" He pats me gently on my sweaty knee. "Weren't you working at the daycare center in the summers?"

I nearly shudder at the memory of the kids' perpetually wet hands and temper tantrums.

"That was appropriately short-lived." It was too long, actually. "I learned that I don't like children," I say carefully. Often enough, this is quite the controversial phrase coming from a young woman, even though I'm basically still a child myself. "They don't seem to like me, either. It's a mutual dislike and distrust."

Tyson leans back, eyes narrowed at me. "I could see that."

"See what? Do I have child-hater written on my face?" I grasp at my face, but he stops me with a gentle pull. I let him lead my arm down and stay perfectly still as he wipes my chin.

"No, just chocolate," he says simply.

My heart hammers much too fast in my chest as I wait for him to fulfill my sexy rom-com dreams and lick the chocolate away or just swoop in for a much-desired first kiss. I'm not picky, or expecting too much.

But this *isn't* a sexy rom-com dream; it's midsummer in humid Pennsylvania, and that would be the saltiest chocolate he's ever tasted. I'm so glad he wipes his finger on the grass as opposed to doing anything else. I free my trusty hand sanitizer from my bag and offer him a dollop.

"Oh my god." I freeze in realization. "I don't like kids because they're messy, but do they not like *me* because *I'm* messy? Are we . . . hypocrites? We should get along, right?"

He breaks into his full-body laughter once more, clutching his chest and falling backward onto the grass. I watch him for a moment, a goofy smile on my mouth, and then lie down next to him. This is the most comfortable I've ever been with a prospective date. It doesn't even feel like a date because . . . I've just been me. I really feel like Tyson likes me for *me*. Butterflies beat their wings against my rib cage, and I steal a glance at him from the corner of my eye. He's looking at me, a grin on his face.

"I've never once considered you messy," he says.

"Maybe not in appearance—except for today—but surely in personality?"

That boisterous, addictive laugh again. "No, not even in

personality." He stares intently at my face. "And you look great."

Now's my chance . . .

"Will you be my date to my cousin's birthday party this weekend?" I blurt the words out so fast that I'm unsure what order they actually come out in. "It's a big party with a lot of people from school, so you don't need to feel awkward—it's not like it's family-only or something."

"Um." He sits up, elbows casually over his knees even though his demeanor is stiff, and clears his throat. "I don't think so, no. But thank you. I appreciate the offer."

I gather myself into a seated position, too, frozen. Firstly, from shock, and secondly, because he must be about to give me a reason why, right? He's probably working, or already has plans. Summer knew what she was doing, dropping this plus one thing on me with such little time.

A long pause follows his words, so long that I realize it's not a pause. It's a period.

"Oh."

I want so desperately to ask why not, find out what he has going on, sift through any excuse to find out if it's me—*it has to be me*—but I say nothing. A no is a no. I'm not perfect, but I do have enough of my wits about me to not question or guilt him.

I choke out a laugh and smile, avoiding any chance of looking at him by searching for Liberty's car keys in my bag. She and Sophia carpooled with a friend today, and she graciously left me her vehicle—and tennis racket—for this disaster. "Well, okay, then. Thanks for the tennis. We should definitely not do it again."

Tyson nods, a forced smile on his face. "Maybe baby tennis next time."

"I would kick your ass in baby tennis." I stand up, bag and keys clenched in one hand. "I have to meet my sister, though. It was good to see you."

I want to add that I'll text him, or he should text me, something to turn this from a period to an ellipsis, but I don't. I'm too close to crying. I'm in such shock that things were going great, I was feeling great, and I still got rejected so fully. He didn't say no to a character I created or a lie I weaved; he said no to *me*.

I didn't have to meet my sister—at least not until Tyson politely broke my heart. But once the words were out, it felt like fate. My plans for tennis had brought me to Adams-Ricci Community Park, and Liberty's plans for tubing down the Conodoguinet Creek with Sophia and friends have her floating right past this place in the next few minutes. I know this because Liberty has to share her phone's location with the family when she goes tubing because duh.

I try not to shift unnecessarily on the weathered bench beneath my legs, but I've already been waiting here for an hour since picking up some food for the girls, and the fidgeting has become unconscious. According to my phone, they're just around the nearest bend in the creek. I don't exactly know what I want her to say. Mostly, I just want her to fix things in my favor. She's in a loving relationship, so she should have advice. At the very least she should be able to tell me, with her searing older-sister honesty, what is wrong with me.

Ah, shit. Speaking of people ready to tell me everything that's wrong with me. Summer won't stop texting me.

So much time has passed since last night, when I threw a grenade at her relationship, that I was starting to think Tommy didn't say anything to her about it. But there's no denying that these angry and strongly worded texts means *something* happened with them. I wish Tyson hadn't just rejected me, so I could thoroughly enjoy this moment.

Instead, I'm just feeling nauseous. I'm not ready for this confrontation right now, so I clear her What the fucking hell did you DO text. For good measure, she's sent a follow-up text: You have no relationship of your own to wreck, so you thought you'd ruin mine? ANSWER ME!

I head to the water's edge with the two lukewarm-at-best chef salads I picked up—mostly to counteract all the soda and junk food Liberty and Sophia probably inhaled on their morning leg of the hours-long tubing trip. The first of the tubers comes around the corner, and I recognize the bright orange bikini top as my sister's. When she gets close enough to recognize my face, she waves ecstatically.

"I brought food!" I hold up the bag with the salads.

Liberty rolls off her tube and into the water with a splash. It laps above her knees when she straightens, just in time to catch her tube before it disappears down the creek. She wades over to Sophia and holds her tube still so she can slide off more gracefully. They push toward the bank, water sloshing around their legs as they navigate the rocks under the surface.

"Did you bring enough for everyone?" Liberty asks, throwing her tube off to the side and grabbing the bag from me.

"No, I'm not everyone's sister."

"She means thank you," Sophia adds, putting her tube on top of Liberty's. Being a redhead, Sophia is very careful in the sun, but a bit of pink has crept up on the tip of her nose.

"Yes, thank you. What do I owe you?" She practically puts her whole head into the bag and sniffs. "How did you know I was starving?"

"You owe me nothing but some wisdom."

"You can't afford my wisdom." She hands Sophia a salad, then frees her own. "What knowledge do you come seeking? Maybe Sophia can help you. She was valedictorian."

"I also tried to be the dungeon master for my mom's D and D game once, but it went terribly," Sophia adds, cracking open her Styrofoam container and plopping down on the grass. "Will one of you remind me to reapply some sunscreen before we go back out there?"

"Of course," Liberty says, kissing her temple.

We join Sophia on the ground as others in the group swarm the bank. The area is a designated entrance and exit for the creek; a porta potty sits up the hill for those who are too classy to pee in the creek and a few picnic tables make for good spots to unload more substantial food from the coolers they brought.

"I just don't think I'm going to get a date for Saturday night." Something rolls in my stomach when I admit this aloud. I blink away tears, feeling the sting of rejection all over again. I was so confident, so sure, before. "I can't win."

"Why does it matter so much to you?" Liberty asks, chomping into a big piece of lettuce. My stomach growls. "There's nothing to win."

"Easy for you to say when you have a date."

"I just mean that it's not the end of the world to go alone—or, hell, to not go at all."

I brush some dirt off my knee. "If I hadn't made such a thing of it, sure. But she knows I'm struggling to find a date, and now I can't just *not* show."

"Why not?" Sophia asks around her fork. "You two clearly have issues. It would probably benefit you both to stay away from each other."

"You're seventeen now," Liberty says, Catalina dressing dripping off her fork as it stalls before her face. "You and Summer don't have to like each other just because you're family; that's clearly never worked."

"Okay, whatever." I wave away the direction this conversation is going in because it very obviously isn't in my favor. "I'm not here for therapy. I want dating advice."

"Uh . . ." Liberty's eyes flick between Sophia and me. "You set us up, so I'm not sure I can help with that."

"But that's it, isn't it?" Sophia says excitedly. "You're so good at this. Look at what you did!" She pulls Liberty in for a kiss on the cheek. "You can do it for yourself, too."

My sister and Sophia were the only couple I've set up with honesty instead of carefully crafted half-truths. They're a fluke. A one-off. Never to be replicated, especially not for myself. Tyson is evidence of that.

"I'm running out of options. The dating pool is drying up." I shake a fist at the sky, but I'm mentally shaking it at every single guy I've texted this week. "Thanks, global warming!"

Behind us, Liberty's friends splash around in the water, yelling and tackling each other in the sunlight. How can they be so carefree when my world is falling apart around me? It's so inconsiderate. Did they not hear my somber tones over their laughter?

"I know you and Poppy pretty much stuck together in school, but you did have other friends, right?" Liberty's eyes widen. "Did I not notice that you had no other friends?"

I roll my eyes. "I had other friends."

"Any guys?" Sophia asks.

"Yeah."

"Ones interested in girls? Like, romantically or sexually?"

"Yes, okay? And I'm not good enough for any of them, apparently!"

"You're a catch, Lahey," Sophia says, dropping a light hand on my shoulder. She looks like she might cry. "You're good enough for anyone you think is deserving of your time."

Liberty nods. "Eloquent. You see why she was valedictorian?"

"It's important to me that you know that's not how I became valedictorian," Sophia says seriously.

"Yeah, your good looks helped, too."

Sophia plants another kiss on Liberty's cheek and then turns back to me. "Maybe you're putting too much pressure on yourself, and on the guys you're trying to date."

"But there *is* pressure. The party is in two days." I try to imagine a world in which I'm not stressing about this. Who is that naively calm girl? Couldn't be me. "You're suggesting I just wait and let a date fall into my lap?"

"No, but you could maybe approach a guy without the intention of making him your date from the start. Your nerves are probably making you fumble without realizing it."

"You'd hate if a guy started talking to you just because he's desperate," Liberty adds unhelpfully. "Maybe they can smell it on you, like animals with fear."

Sophia motions for Liberty to zip her lips before grasping on to both my shoulders, her pruning fingers digging into my shirt. "Stop dipping your toes in and telling me it's cold. Just dive!"

"I think I understand . . . like I'm . . . overthinking it? Putting too much pressure on the moment and thus ruining it?" I glance at the few guys roughhousing in the water. The thought of just walking up to them and chatting is terrifying—there's always the chance they're dickheads and would be cruel to me. I'm in a too emotionally precarious state for that! This is why I need a screening process in which they can't hurt my feelings to my face first!

I can say I'm not putting pressure on the situation, but it's there, lurking in the water like an alligator—are there alligators in the creek? Is that a thing I need to be worried about on top of literally everything else?

"Yes, exactly," Liberty replies.

"Okay. Well. That's not actually that helpful. Maybe you

should leave the romantic advice to me in the future."

"Hey, you asked for it." Liberty chucks a tomato from her salad at me as I stand. "Where are you going?"

"I'm going to go be casual," I say slowly, like I'm convincing myself that it's true.

Don't jump the gun. Be natural. Don't try too hard. Be yourself, but not too much of yourself, because that doesn't work.

I tell myself that striking up a conversation with cute boys in swim trunks is a good idea and head toward the water. Relief washes over me at the same time the sun does, illuminating the previously difficult-to-make-out faces of the four guys in front of me—I know(ish) them. Casey Collins; a guy with medium-length blond hair in two very short French braids; Sam something-or-other; and Ben Whitaker. I can use this as practice. They won't be rejecting me for anything because I won't be asking for anything.

Who to approach? I instantly cross French Braids off my list because I don't actually know him. Then I cross Sam off because he's not interested in girls. I quickly look between Casey and Ben, but it's an obvious and easy decision to make. It can't be Casey because when I was a freshman, he snapped my bra strap against my shoulder so hard it left a welt. He didn't get how that was full-on sexual harassment.

The plus side of these slim pickings is that Ben is really cute, he adores my sister (and me, by default), and I've always gotten a good vibe from him. He's perfect for this little pick-me-up.

I start to untie my shoes, but then Liberty stops me.

"Lahey, you can't go in barefoot."

"Are the rocks really that sharp?"

"She means because of glass," Sophia interjects, wiggling her water-shoe-clad feet at me. "People are assholes."

"Well said," Liberty says, "once again."

I sigh, tying my shoe back up, and wade into the water with it on like a dumbass. It's warm, and I can tell from just a few steps that keeping shoes on was the right call, but the water seeps in slowly so that each movement becomes more sluggish. Liberty won't let me use her car anymore if I keep making a habit of soaking the interior.

I make it to the middle of the creek, where Ben and Sam have anchored their tubes down somehow and are trying to kick a soccer ball into the holes.

"Hey." I grimace at how nervous I sound. "Hi, Ben."

He spins around, his brown skin gleaming with water droplets, and his face lights up. "Lahey Johnson!"

He pulls me into a hug, and I'm not even mad when he gets my shirt wet. He's happy to see me, and it's such a relief after feeling so unexpectedly unwanted earlier.

"I asked Liberty where you were, and she said you had better things to do." He tucks the soccer ball between his hip and his forearm.

"What a liar. She didn't even invite me." Now would not be a good time to mention that I had plans, or that they ended in humiliation. I have to sell myself here—but not too much.

"Did you invite yourself, then?"

I push him gently. "I brought that brat some lunch!"

We laugh about inconsiderate older sisters for a moment and

it feels so meant to be. But I cannot rush this. I cannot be thinking several days in the future. I am here; I am now.

He tosses the ball to Sam and then dips his hands into the water, letting it puddle in his palms before splashing it across his lean shoulders. My face heats up, and I'm so grateful that the sun gives me the perfect excuse.

"We could swap, if you want." I flick my gaze to where Liberty sits now, talking animatedly to Sophia. "Sisters. I'd take yours if you'll take that one."

"Nah, Madeline's a pain, but she's *my* pain, you know?"

I give him an exaggerated frown. "I don't. If I could get rid of Liberty, I would."

He raises an eyebrow conspiratorially. "That's because she's Liberty."

If any other guy talked like this about her, except for maybe Adler, I'd introduce his groin to my foot. But Ben's done soccer with her since elementary school, and there's only platonic love between them. If we got married, Liberty would be so happy to have him as a brother-in-law. She's always trying to start soccer games after Thanksgiving dinner, and no one wants to play with her because that's obviously ludicrous. Ben would be down.

I'm getting way too deliriously ahead of myself. Again.

"You make a great point, but no, it's because she's not away at college yet. I'm sure I'll miss her and think of her fondly when she's gone. Naively, but fondly." His sister is a few years older than him, and away at school, so I can't fault him for misremembering the years they had together. I'll be dopey like that, too, when I forget all the times when Liberty dragged me out of the bathroom so she could use it or when she would put literal tape on the floor of our bedroom to keep our sides divided because she was pissed off about something or other.

That bedroom will be all mine until I go away to college, though.

"You know," I start dangerously, "I'm glad I saw you today."

No, Lahey. Abort. Stop. Stop sabotaging yourself.

"Oh yeah? Why's that?" He grins, aiming his pearly whites at the sun, and then gestures to himself. "Aside from the obvious."

He's expecting a joke, and I can't say what I was going to say because I can't rush this, so I just say, "I wanted to tell you a joke."

"Okay, hit me."

Sam kicks the ball our way, and Ben catches it without flinching. "I wasn't talking to *you*," he says, sending a mischievous glance at his friend.

"I forgot it, actually."

This makes Ben laugh, at least. He doesn't put his whole body into it, but there's a way it sounds that makes me feel like it's genuine. A kind of full-bodied *essence*. "Well, when you remember it, text me."

"I can do that."

Honestly, why hadn't I put Ben on my list in the first place? He seems so obvious now.

Some of the other tubers start jumping onto their rafts. As the only person standing here without a bathing suit or tube,

I'm starting to feel like I've overstayed my welcome. The theme for the day.

I aim my thumb over my shoulder, taking the hint. "I have to go."

"Nooooo," he says dramatically. He tosses the ball to Sam and then wraps me in another wet hug. "Don't go yet. Do the last part with us."

"Oh, you mean, the last *four hours* of the tubing trip? Without a tube, bathing suit, or any preparation?"

"Spontaneity." Light bounces off the water and the reflections dance in his eyes. "And it's only like three hours. The water is pretty fast today."

"Maybe we can catch up some other time."

"Yeah, what about tomorrow? Movies?"

He says it so casually. He *asks* it so casually. Me, on a date. With him.

My foot slides on a rock and just as I'm about to slam into the glass wall of water, Ben catches me and rights me. *So* romantic. I even have an excuse for why my legs suddenly gave out on me. He doesn't need to know that I'm beyond shocked and excited.

"Definitely." We laugh off our awkward detangling of limbs, and then I head to the bank, where Liberty and Sophia are taking photos together. "I'll see you tomorrow, then," I call over my shoulder.

"Can't wait," he says with a smile. "I'll text you."

"Don't forget sunscreen," I tell Sophia as I climb out of the creek, my face aimed at the ground so I don't trip in my dumb-founded state.

"Thanks!" she says as I pass. "Looks like you could have used some. Your face is already all red."

I cannot believe that haphazard advice Sophia and (barely) Liberty hacked together for me actually worked. Is it this easy for everyone else? Do dates just throw themselves at you if you aren't actively searching for them? Not even Summer's continued stream of pissed-off texts can kill my high. Things are finally turning around.

Fifteen

My dad yells for me later when I'm lying on my bed, watching my phone as new texts and missed calls from Summer pour in. He rarely raises his voice, so I figure I must have *really* messed up the load of laundry I put in this morning, or something.

Instead of finding him waiting at the bottom of the stairs, he and Mom stand in front of the couch with Lily caught beneath their glares. Any sudden movement might set them off, the tension in the room feeling like its own physical being. I'm two steps in reverse before my mom calls me over.

"Not so fast, Lahey." Mom's arms cross over her chest to match Dad's. "Lily, would you like to tell your sister what you told us?"

"Not really," she mumbles.

As I come around the back of the overstuffed couch, I spot a lively plant on the coffee table between my parents and sister. My parents have never been the type to decorate with plants— my mom prefers homemade crafts and photos over things that perish from neglect—so that means plants stay outside or are doomed to a short life in Lily's room.

"How about you do anyway?" my dad asks, his tone firm but soft. He's used to getting his way with toddlers at work. He's had years of practice.

Lily sighs, crossing her own arms.

"I got a plant," she says to the rug. Her lip looks recently gnawed on, a sign that she did something she wasn't supposed to. But since when is she not allowed to blow her allowance on plants? Something about this scene isn't adding up.

"A special plant." My mom tries and fails to meet her eyes. "And what's special about it?"

Its leaves are waxy green and maroon, and it stands only a few inches tall in a muddy brown pot.

"It will live forever."

"She means that it's fake." My mom picks up the plant. "And she said it was your idea."

"Whoa, whoa, whoa." I put my hands up in surrender. "You're just going to believe her?"

"You *did*," Lily says with wide eyes. "When I—"

If she's going to rat me out, then I'm certainly going to bring up that she— "Brought a stray cat into the house? A *dirty* stray cat?"

She shoots me a burning look. "I cleaned the house," she hisses.

"And then threw me under the bus," I hiss back.

"What are you talking about, a dirty cat?" My mom can say a lot with just her eyes. Her eyes are telling me to plant my butt on the couch right this minute or suffer the consequences.

I flop down and glare at Lily. "She brought a stray cat into the house earlier this week!"

"And Lahey *n e v e r* mentioned it to you two," Lily adds.

My mouth drops open. "Neither did you! Instead, I took the cat to a shelter to be adopted."

"Adler did that."

"It was my idea for Adler to do that."

"Girls," my dad says calmly.

"And it was *your* idea for me to buy a fake plant. I don't understand when I'm supposed to listen to you and when I'm not. This isn't my fault—"

"*Girls*," my mom adds with more intensity.

"It's literally your own fault," I say. "Did you lie when they asked you about those scratches?"

"I get beat up from skateboarding all the time; who's to say if these were cat scratches or signs that I intimately met the ground—"

"Lahey! Lily!" My dad's face is red, and he takes his glasses off to wipe beneath his eyes. We're both under-eye sweaters. "Shut up."

My mom raises a brow at him. "What your father means is be quiet."

"Yes, that one." He slips his glasses back over his nose. "You both seem to have been part of this, so it feels fitting that Lily, who thought she could pull a fast one on us, should be grounded, and Lahey, who gave her the idea, should have to babysit her."

"I don't need a babysitter."

"You're right. You need a warden. No electronics or skate-board tomorrow," my mom says, nodding. "Lahey will make sure you stay bored and at home."

My heart starts ramming in my chest. But I'm supposed to go to a movie with Ben tomorrow. I can't be stuck here on a Friday, *the* Friday before Summer's party.

"But I have to help Poppy with her centerpieces." It's not even a lie. I did plan to help, but it definitely wasn't going to take all day.

"Some other time—"

"No," I interject, clasping my hands together tightly. My finger pads slide into the grooves my knuckles make. "The centerpieces are for Saturday. She has load-in time Saturday morning at the hotel so that they can prep food after. She's already behind because someone tossed her materials."

My mom sighs. It's one thing to punish me, but to punish Poppy? Unacceptable. "Take Lily with you, then."

"Kate," my dad says in a low voice. "I think that's punishing Lahey a little more than Lily."

"We can't leave Lily by herself; she'll find a way to talk to friends through carrier pigeon. Or she'll just watch TV all day."

"What about Liberty?" I wipe my sweating palms on my knees. "She can stay home and watch Lily, and then that frees her car so I can use it to go to Poppy's." A genius idea, if I do say so myself.

And apparently, I need to, because no one else is saying it.

They share a silent glance before sighing in unison, like the literal parental unit they are.

"We can approve of that," my mom says, like she and Dad just had a telepathic discussion about it. They are the literal definition of soul mates. "But your own punishment is still coming."

"Why am I being punished for something Lily did?" I refuse to look at her. I just know she's smirking.

"Because you gave her a rotten idea. You knew she'd be lying and manipulating us." My dad frowns, like this is the first time he's ever considered that his daughters might have a few small dishonest bones in their bodies.

"And there's the whole thing about not telling us Lily brought a cat home."

"It kind of feels like Lahey did just as much damage as I did," Lily says lightly.

"Nice try," my dad says.

"Worth a shot."

I return to my bedroom, diving onto my bed, and go back to wishing for Tyson to text that he changed his mind about Saturday, for Ben to call me and say he can't wait until tomorrow to see me, for one of the Tamburello brothers to make a damn move already. None of those things happen, but it doesn't mean they won't. I have another day—almost *two* days, if I look at this optimistically—and anything could happen.

Later, I hear a car door slam outside, announcing Liberty's return home after tubing. She'll be sunburned and exhausted, and I don't want to be around when she receives the bad news about how she's going to spend tomorrow. I sneak to the back-yard and pass the time on my phone, until her loud arguments have died down and the house falls asleep. I creep into our shared bedroom, but there's no need for the stealth—Liberty is unconscious, with her noise-canceling headphones on her ears and a tight frown on her face.

Friday

Sixteen

I wake up at an ungodly hour to get dressed and leave before Liberty can even dream of stirring. By ten thirty, I haven't yet heard from Ben about what time the movie is, or which one we're even seeing, but I keep my hopes up that he'll whisk me away from this agonizing manual labor Poppy has me doing now. I stare at my phone screen for ten seconds, then fifteen, but it stays dark. It taunts me with its nothingness. No Prince Charming push notification means I'm stuck here in Poppy's studio, where I will definitely die alone and unloved because no one will find my hot-glue burns attractive.

About a year ago, Poppy's parents turned this partially finished basement into a space for her art. Her parents were just about to put carpet in when Poppy proposed an alternative use for the room—it was originally going to be a movie room (read: girls-get-out-of-our-living-room room), but with Poppy leaving for college, there wasn't much need for one. Once she's gone, they can throw some carpet down if they still really want to. For now, the concrete floor remains cold and paint-splattered. The worktable in the center of the room is one big slab of wood, and the stools we sit on now were Poppy's first and only attempt at making her own furniture. They creak when we breathe, so it's safe to say she's far from a career in carpentry.

"You've got your sad face on and we're not even halfway done." She doesn't look up when she speaks, her eyes focused on the tinted bottle in front of her. She pulls a dry brush from her overall pocket to Bob Ross some paint on the glass. "What is it? The party still?"

"Of course." I try to stop my bottom lip from jutting out, but I can't *not* pout right now. "I'm starting to think Summer was right. I can't do, so I teach."

"Summer said that because she has some sick obsession with putting you down. It's probably because of her mother."

I set down the X-ACTO knife I've been holding, not using. "What do you mean?"

"Uh, 'cause your aunt is kind of mean?"

"What? No she isn't." She has her quirks, sure. I mean, she's very loud, for example.

"Mean to *Summer*," Poppy says. "It doesn't give her an excuse to be a bitch to you about being single, though."

She takes a ripped patch of burlap and wraps it around the bottle. "It's okay to be single," she adds quietly. "People without partners aren't always tragically single; it's a choice."

I shift in my seat. "No, of course not. There are people out there who don't want relationships, but I *do*, and that's the problem. This is about me, not anyone else."

"Lahey," she sighs. She's preparing her Lecture Voice. It requires one massive inhale before she annihilates me with words. "You can't force a relationship for yourself. That might work for getting other people together, but that's because you can see the bigger picture, because you've got distance from them. You can't be a bystander *and* someone playing the game. You just need to believe in yourself and *be* yourself."

"If I had the confidence you think I should have, I'd have a boyfriend—maybe I would have had several by now—and I'd also rule the world."

"Oh please." She sets down the burlap. It didn't look right anyway. "Have you forgotten who you *are*? Have these idiot boys really broken you so much this week?"

"Go on."

"You're the girl who just decided one day that she was going to make red lipstick work for her. You're the girl who wears what she wants, says what she wants, and doesn't let people belittle her. I'm so proud of you—*you*, not the girl you pretend to be for a bunch of people who don't deserve any version of you."

"But there's nothing to be proud of. I've accomplished nothing. I'm *wrong* to have been so confident."

She examines my face for only a second, but finds something I couldn't stuff behind a mask. "I'm sorry you feel that way. You really shouldn't."

I pick up the glue gun. "People keep telling me how awesome I am, and I want to believe them, but I don't feel awesome. And I definitely don't get treated like I'm awesome."

I scrub a hand down my cheek. "I'm sorry, I'll stop talking about this. I'm not trying to be a downer. It's just getting pretty frustrating to have so many people talk me up when guys are still turning me down. It's truly pathetic."

"It's not," she says. "It's brave to put yourself out there like this."

"You think it would be braver to go to the party solo, though."

She tilts her head, debating between a twig and a leaf for the wine bottle she's working on. "Yeah, I think honesty is brave. But I also think it's scary, so I get where you're coming from."

"It's scary over here on the dishonest side, too."

She smiles, a sad, defeated thing. "I'll keep my fingers crossed for you."

"Thank you. I need it."

"No you don't."

We work silently for a while. Despite my dilemma, I'm productive and helpful. It's fulfilling work, helping an artist with their creative vision. Our two-person factory churns out seven beautiful and noncontroversial centerpieces—wine bottles of varying heights and colors decorated as different trees native to Pennsylvania (the compromise she and her parents came to)—before my phone finally, blissfully goes off.

My heart lurches into my throat, and I get my hopes as high as the Eiffel Tower that it will be The One, the guy I've been waiting for to show me a perfect Saturday night and, ideally, many perfect Saturday nights in the future. Ben or Tyson or *anyone* at this point. I am no longer even a smidge picky.

But it's Liberty.

I send her to voice mail. Liberty does not like this and starts texting my name over and over and sometimes in capital letters. She asks when I'll be home, and when I ignore her, she starts calling again. Honestly, if I were her, I'd just make a deal with Lily that I "stayed home all day to watch her" and she "didn't do whatever she wanted." It's a win-win where we'd both get what we want. Mutual destruction if the other gives up the lie. Though . . . that didn't go well the first time. But I guess that plan wouldn't even work out for Liberty because I have her car.

I'm flicking away notification after notification, until I get into a groove and accidentally flick away a message from Ben. *Ben!* I open it to find he's invited me to an 11:35 matinee at the Camp Hill AMC. I've always thought movies were a terrible first date. It's loud and dark, and you can't talk. There's also a chance of popcorn getting stuck in your teeth or your cute shoes sticking to something spilled on the floor.

I respond with more exclamation points than necessary and stand up from the worktable.

"Are you going to get snacks?" Poppy asks without looking up. "Even if you're not, please bring me some Twizzlers. I need fuel."

I slide my phone into my back pocket and pick up my bag slowly, my aching knuckles popping in pain. "Actually . . ."

"Where are you going?" The panic in her eyes guts me for a lingering moment.

"I told you I had a movie date."

"*Now?* Who goes to the movies this early? I thought I had

you for at least a few more hours."

The thought of that makes me grimace. She droops.

"I need help. I haven't even gotten to the wall art." She looks at the scattered bits of materials on the table. "You promised . . ."

I do want to help her, but I have to help myself, too. On Saturday night, I'm not going to be at the fundraiser and Poppy won't be at the party. We can only help each other so much until we have to fully take over our own duties.

"I'll be back as soon as the movie's over."

"I need help—"

"I know! I'll be back." I head to the stairs and glance over my shoulder.

She doesn't look like she believes me at all.

In fact, she doesn't even look surprised.

Seventeen

Despite an entire trope created from romantic moments happening in the rain, I nurse anxiety in the pit of my stomach as I flee Poppy's house into an unexpected and inconvenient downpour. We'll be inside for the majority of this date, so it doesn't really matter what's happening outside, and I refuse to let anything crush my optimism. *Ben Whitaker asked me out* and I will jump through whatever rain-slicked hoops I need to for us to hang out today.

Admittedly, as I come to a four-way stop outside of Poppy's neighborhood, the car tires sliding j u s t a bit, I'm already daydreaming about tomorrow even though Liberty and Sophia said I need to stop getting ahead of myself. Ben's the total package. He's kind, cute, and funny. According to Summer's incessant texts that I reap joy from ignoring, Tommy has completely iced her out since telling her he learned some "new information" about their relationship. She wouldn't be able to stand the beautiful sight of Ben on my arm even if her relationship wasn't on sharp, pointy rocks. Now that it is, she'll combust and blow away with the wind. They'll rename this season after me. Winter, Spring, Lahey, and Autumn.

The person in the car behind me lays on the horn. As the wipers whip across my windshield, I press on the gas, startled. The car stutters for a moment and then lurches into the intersection, just in time for another car, whose turn it was to go, to collide with the nose of Liberty's car.

I think the realization that I'm not making my date hits me harder than the impact.

Though that does hit pretty hard.

I don't immediately know what to do besides tense up. I've never been in a car accident before. My nerves are buzzing, and my breath comes out short, but other than that, I feel fine. It's the shock that hurts most, the consequences of my stupidity weighing on my lungs. I'm going to be late for my date!

The car that hit me—or maybe it was me who hit them, since it wasn't my turn—eases backward until it's out of the intersection. I follow, hoping nothing important falls from Liberty's car. Oh god, Liberty is never going to let me hear the end of this.

I park on the side of the road just in front of the other car and step out to inspect the damage. I'm about to have a good old-fashioned spiral when I remember to have some human decency about me and check on the other driver. Cars can be fixed, lives cannot.

She exits her shiny black Acura with some paperwork already in her hand.

"Are you okay?" I ask. Of course the rain is easing up now that it's already ruined my day.

She sighs, sliding the hood of her raincoat down from her dark curls. "Yeah. You?"

"Yeah." I know I'm not supposed to admit fault and, because of who I am as a person, I don't want to anyway, but I say, "I'm so sorry."

"You need new tires," she says unhelpfully, looking around Liberty's car. "I'm not surprised you couldn't brake."

Yes. Because I tried to brake, but the tires slipped on the wet road.

Yes. Not my fault.

She gestures to the papers in her hand and it shakes me to my senses. I dive into the passenger side to wrestle free my parents' insurance information from under about sixteen packs of tissues in the glove compartment, and then I pull my license from my wallet. We swap to take photos and then assess the damage of each other's cars, taking more photos. I can feel a migraine starting by the time we're finished. She wasn't the kindest, but I can't blame her. I think it also frustrated her that I needed to be walked through everything, but it was my first accident!

At the very least, she didn't yell at me.

My sister will take care of that.

The front right of Liberty's car is smashed in, the headlight broken. When I turn the ignition, something jangles under the carriage. If I speed, I can make it to the movies. But I know that in reality I need to get to Adler's mom's garage. In a brief moment of clarity, I make the right decision, accepting that this whole mishap was actually a sign, and that maybe Ben and I can rain check, literally—I text him about what happened and try not to ooze with panic when I ask him to meet me after the movie for lunch somewhere.

I pull into the parking lot of Auto-Correct, the body shop Adler's mom, Hannah, opened when the Altmans moved here, and shakily pull the keys from the ignition. This is the only place Liberty takes her car for inspections and repairs, so I feel like the one smart thing I can do in this situation is to leave this in Hannah's hands. She's a whiz with tools, and it doesn't hurt that she also never seems to charge Liberty for the work. I hope that generosity extends to me; it's the same car, after all.

The front office is empty when I walk inside, but it doesn't deter me like it might others. I walk around the counter and through the door that connects the space to the actual garage. Loud rock music plays, and a warm breeze winds its way through the open garage doors. A drop of sweat slides down my neck as I approach the lone car being worked on with its hood up. I expect Hannah to be behind it, but it's Adler.

A streak of grease runs across his nose like misplaced war paint, and it might as well be the way he tenses at the sight of me. "What are you doing here?"

I haven't seen him since Wednesday, not since that awkward tension between us turned into Summer accusing me of flirting with him, *my sister's best friend.*

I put my fists on my hips and decide to ignore my nerves. If I play this cool, then everything is cool. "Do you speak to all your customers like that?"

"What makes you a customer?"

"Promise not to yell?"

He straightens slowly, eyes serious. "I guess . . ."

I motion for him to follow me through the open door and around the side. As soon as his eyes land on Liberty's busted car, he whips around to me. "Is Liberty okay?"

"She's fine. It was just me in the car. I got T-boned, kind of." I slide away when he reaches for me. His hands are filthy. "I'm *fine*."

His eyes slide over my body like he can't take my word for it, and then he wipes his hands on his work pants. "Mom went to pick up some lunch." He licks his bottom lip. "I'll take you home when she gets back, and then we'll give you an estimate once we're done with this Toyota."

Home. To face Liberty and the consequences of all my actions.

No thank you.

"Thanks, but I'm going to order a car probably."

I pull out my phone and freeze. A car to where? Ben hasn't messaged me back. He probably went into the theater, expecting me to show up as planned, and put his phone away. He's such a good guy, and I blew my shot.

I throw myself into a chair in the waiting room, Adler on my heels. I ruin everything; Summer's right.

"Why would you do that?" Adler asks. "I'll just take you home."

"I'm not going home." My frantic tone almost cracks me up. Am I going *anywhere*? My day is currently wide open like a gaping abyss. I need to make backup plans. Screw taking things slow. Screw no pressure.

"Where are you going, then? I'll take you." He pushes his hair behind his ears. He'll have to cut it or really grow it out soon. This length is unruly and has to be hot in the summer—and a static nightmare in the winter. He uses X-ray vision to bore through the wall behind me and see the damage to Liberty's car again. "You better be going on the run. Liberty's going to kill you."

"It's not totaled, is it?" This is my first incident—I've decided to call it that instead of accident, because it sounds less dramatic and less my fault—and I don't know what a totaled car even looks like.

"Doubtful." He scratches the back of his neck. A new smear of grease appears there. "I don't know. I don't want to get your hopes up. Berty only paid like a grand for it. It might not be worth it to repair."

I sink farther into the seat; the cushion is flat as a pancake. "Awesome. *Only* a grand."

"If you got hit, though, the other driver's insurance should cover it—"

"I got hit, but it was my fault. And then I couldn't make my date, so Ben doesn't want anything to do with me, and my love life, or my attempt at one, is over forever. Summer will mock me and post my failure on the internet. I probably won't even get into college because of it."

He blinks. Fine, I will break it down for him.

"I was meeting a date at the movies before I was a dumbass

and totaled Liberty's car." I suck my bottom lip between my teeth to stop my pout. "Now I have pick to which of the Tamburello brothers I want to pursue—but who am I kidding, neither of them will like me."

"Lahey."

The conversation I had with Tyson comes to mind. "Maybe I could kill more birds with fewer stones. . . ." I squint, staring into the middle distance. "That would certainly help with the no-car situation. I could have both of them meet me at the same place, but at different times. Maybe I pad some time between them to make sure they don't run into each other, but who—"

"Lahey?"

"*Yes*, Adler? You're interrupting some brilliant brainstorming here."

He shoots me an amused smile. "Brilliant. Yeah. I'm gonna go finish up the Toyota."

"Okay," I say with little care. "I wasn't stopping you."

He bristles and then disappears into the garage. If possible, the music gets louder, or maybe that's just because he leaves the door open. From my seat, I have a good view of him bending over the hood. His black pants stretch with the movement and— *Focus*.

By the time Hannah arrives with two massive burritos and a to-go bag of chips and salsa from Neato Burrito, I have fully spiraled, but in a *genius* way.

I plan for Cameron and Brad Tamburello to meet me at

Woodworks in Harrisburg, a restaurant with an ax-throwing area and wreck room. I've given them two different times, to avoid them running into each other. It's the perfect spot for first dates and employee outings, according to the website. It also has separate spaces, so if Ben decides he *does* want to go to lunch with me, I can keep him in the restaurant area away from Cameron in the ax-throwing space and Brad in the wreck room. I'm a date-planning savant; no wonder people trust me with their meet-cutes.

My plan is to have a great time with Brad; I'm not as familiar with him as I am with Cameron, so I'll give him my full commitment until it's time to part ways. We'll do so amicably and with positive vibes. Then, in case Cameron says no when I actually ask him out for tomorrow, I can fall back on Brad and insist we get to know each other more . . . at my cousin's sweet sixteen, naturally. He's exceptionally extroverted, so I think a social setting would be ideal for him, and he wouldn't bat an eye at the idea.

As Hannah takes hurried bites of her vegetarian burrito, I explain to her what happened to Liberty's car. She offers me some of the chips, but I'm saving my appetite for my dates. I've had a hankering for a chocolate milkshake since my botched date with Wilson, and I plan on getting one today even if I have to buy it for myself!

"I'm sorry about your movie date, but hopefully he wants to do lunch." She wipes her hands on a napkin. "It would be his loss if not."

"I'm trying to stay optimistic about the other dates just in case. If this week has taught me anything, it's to be prepared for disappointment."

"It's everyone's loss if they don't want to be your date." She winks at me and then gestures over her shoulder at Adler. She lowers her voice. "He'd be happy to take you, you know."

Suddenly I'm back in the cage of Adler's arms in my kitchen. He's about to kiss me. He's about to kiss me. He's about to—

I force out a loud laugh. "I'm desperate, but not that desperate." Hannah raises her eyebrow, unimpressed. "I just mean, a pity date is just *not* what I'm looking for."

She accepts my answer since it's not technically insulting Adler. Not that anyone could even insult Adler! He's good-looking, he's hilarious, he's kind and loyal. I still don't get why he doesn't have a girlfriend, why he wouldn't even consider going out with Brighton under my supervision. But I need to worry about my love life right now, not his.

We watch him for a moment in content silence. He slams the hood of the Toyota, and Hannah says quietly, "He hates it here."

"What, the shop?"

She keeps her voice low as Adler turns the car on and drives it to the parking lot. "He hasn't said it, *in actual words*, but I know. He doesn't want to work with cars. He *can*, but he doesn't want to. It's why he's desperately trying to find other ways to save for school. This isn't fun for him."

"Is it *fun* for you?" I could understand my parents finding some enjoyable aspects of their jobs, like finger painting with sugar-high children and working on publicity for nonprofits in need, but working on cars seems like it would be stressful. You have someone's life in your hands!

"Totally." She leans on her elbows to get closer and more comfortable. "I love solving problems and changing out parts so an old car can run like a new one."

"But the *filth* . . ."

She bursts into laughter. "Yeah, well, the nice part of that is when you get to clean yourself off."

"What are we laughing about?" Adler asks, coming in through the shop door and hanging the keys on the wall. "Lahey's love life?"

I smirk. "No, the grease mark on your nose."

Hannah throws a clean rag at Adler's face, but he swipes it before it can fall. "Clean up and have some lunch." She heads into the garage and shoots me a look over her shoulder. "Lahey, just be yourself with these boys."

I groan, unattractive and loud. "That hasn't worked."

"You have two dates set up?" she asks.

I nod.

"You've got two more chances to perfect it, then."

My phone chirps with a new text message.

"Three!" I call after her, excitedly waving my phone in her direction. Not that she can see Ben's response this far away. "Three dates now!"

Ben's not ignoring me or mad; I was right that he went into the theater and put his phone away like the model citizen he is. I, very casually, ask him to meet me at Woodworks in the specific bubble of free time I planned between the Tamburello dates, and he responds with a yes immediately.

What a relief. He's going to meet me at Woodworks.

Oh *shit*. He's going to meet me at Woodworks.

Adler steps into the small bathroom and washes his hands with the door open, like he's inviting conversation, but I can't form any words just yet.

He grabs his burrito and drops into the seat next to me, his elbow brushing against mine. "Shaken up from the accident?"

"I have three dates at one location at almost the same time." I can't muster up the energy to put emotion into my voice. I have to conserve it all for later. It will take all of my being to pull this off. I can't half-ass any of these dates, because any of these dates could be The One. "Why didn't you tell me how bad of a plan that was?"

He freezes, burrito nearly in his open mouth. "What happened to you being brilliant?"

"I've never been good at multitasking! You should have talked me down. They'll put a cross in the Woodworks parking lot to mark the place of my sudden and untimely death from embarrassment. This is your fault!"

"What do I have to do with this? You're just going to do what you're going to do, no matter what I say. You're asking for disaster." He takes a massive bite.

"No, I'm simply asking for my time and effort to be rewarded with just one guy to bring on Saturday. Just one."

"You might be asking too much. This isn't a Build-A-Boy Workshop."

"These three are my last hopes." My stomach growls. I've

been around other people eating for too long. My inner monster pops out, and I pull Adler's hand holding the burrito to my mouth so I can take a bite. It only makes me hungrier. "Will you give me a ride?" I ask, mouth full. "And another bite?"

He pulls the burrito out of my reach. "Yes, I'll give you a ride."

"Thank you." My eyes flick to his still-outstretched burrito. "And the bur—"

"Don't push it."

I roll my eyes. "I think it's more than fair."

"For me to give you a ride *and* my burrito?" He takes a large bite, probably to rub it in my face. "Doesn't seem fair. What's in it for me?"

"You'll be getting to watch me humiliate myself, most likely. And you could see if they're hiring."

"Do you think I can be in a hundred places at once or something? I'm already struggling with the four jobs I have."

"This really calls for a lengthy bitchfest about how minimum wage is still way too low, but I'm on borrowed time and limited mental resources. How about you just go to make sure I don't get murdered or kidnapped?"

"You keep adding responsibilities to my plate but nothing to yours."

"Use a different phrase; I'm *hungry*."

He takes another bite, but his mouth is already exploding with food. He grins around it. It's disgusting and *adorable*. My stomach flutters from more than just hunger pangs. I need to land a date before I get hypnotized by whatever Adler's got going on and actually beg him for that pity date.

"Fine, I'll remove a responsibility. You can be there to make sure I *do* get murdered or kidnapped, whichever you're feeling in the moment."

"Now *that* I'll agree to. You've been a pain in my ass this week."

"Not intentionally!" Despite the insult, it feels nice to be his *something. His* something.

He folds the tinfoil over what's left of his burrito and stands. "Let me just throw this out and then—"

"Adler!"

He tosses me the last few bites of the burrito, and while he tells his mom what's going on, I enjoy a final moment of peace before the chaos of my afternoon.

Eighteen

I can't stop my leg from jiggling. It might puncture the floor and start jackhammering into the concrete below if Brad doesn't show up in the next minute. It's ten minutes past when we agreed to meet, and the clock keeps ticking toward the time Cameron will show up for ax-throwing, which means the clock keeps ticking toward the time Ben estimated he would be here. In hindsight, I should have allotted more than forty-five minutes each for the first two dates. I didn't consider that not everyone is as punctual as me. Some people will be late and some people will be early.

All of a sudden I'm *very* afraid of the possibility of Ben and Cameron being early.

Adler catches my eye from across the room and gives me a cheeky thumbs-up. He's been sitting at the very edge of the busy restaurant section, nursing a soda and mozzarella sticks while being blissfully unaware of his teenaged waitress's attempts at flirting with him. At this point, I'm just as frustrated as her that he hasn't noticed, but I learned my lesson about matchmaking him last time, so I remain on my stool, legs fidgeting and internal organs shutting down in panic.

The door to the recreational side of the business swings open, and Brad—frantic, well-meaning Brad—stumbles in from the afternoon light. I jump from my seat to meet him, air vacating my lungs in relief.

"Hey," I say breathlessly.

"Hey, sorry. There was traffic."

"Sorry there was traffic."

He frowns. "What?"

"*I'm* sorry that there was traffic."

"Ha. No worries. Have you ever been here?" He walks into the space like he definitely has, and I follow.

It's hard *not* to follow Brad. He's hulking in size, but not in a scary way—more like a friendly giant way. He has kind eyes and a contagious smile that says he'd lead you out of the dark forest the evil witch chased you into. He'd make sure to tuck you in at night with the warmest, softest blanket. Brad is a rescue pit bull in a bow tie.

He blinks. "Lahey?"

"Sorry, no." I shrug sheepishly. "I just thought it sounded fun."

"Have a lot of pent-up aggression you need to get out?" He heads to the touch screen beside the see-through door on the wreck room. The whole thing is see-through, actually. People partaking in the ax-throwing and dining can see in. I didn't realize that when the website said the areas were separate, it didn't mean by traditional walls that would help a girl out when she's trying to have three dates at once, like an overachieving dumbass.

"I already have us booked for the room." I check my phone for the time. "For about thirty more minutes."

"Sweet." He puts away his wallet and then thinks twice. "How much do I owe you?"

"Oh, nothing. My treat." It was *forty* dollars, but I like to think it was an investment in my future, or at least tomorrow. I think Ben will be chivalrous and pay for lunch, but if he doesn't, I'm content with water and an appetizer. The half of Adler's burrito I had weighs heavy in my stomach as it is. And Cameron will definitely pay for the ax-throwing. He was always doting on his girlfriends and bragging about it.

I type my reservation pass code onto the touch screen and the door pops open. Inside, old computers, phones, desks, couches—really anything you can think of that would be satisfying to break—cover the floor, sometimes in a few pieces and sometimes still, miraculously, whole. The music that is subtle in the restaurant area blares into this room from a few speakers in the corners. Brad helps me into the face mask we're required to wear after I pour some sanitizer on it. I can only imagine the face grease and sweat that's embedded into the soft cushion of the headband. He looks ridiculous in his, so I have to believe I do, too. He requests to take a photo together despite our appearances—or maybe because of—and I allow it. A little butterfly dares to take off in my stomach. This could be the first photo my boyfriend and I take together.

He grabs the metal baseball bat hanging on one of the

plexiglass walls and hands it to me. "This will probably work best for you." He grabs a crowbar for himself. "And now you just, you know, break."

It feels kind of illegal and dangerous, but I step forward and whack the small TV perched atop the shredded couch. It falls over the back and onto a pile of vinyl records.

"How was it?" Brad asks, glee written into every smile crinkle on his face. He's frozen in time, waiting for my reaction before starting.

As an answer, I drive the bat into the TV screen, cracking the glass and sending some records flying into the air. He whips his crowbar into the couch and pulls down, tearing the fabric with a satisfying *riiiiip*.

"Switch with me!" I extend the baseball bat and accept the crowbar.

I swing at a china cabinet that's in perfect shape except for the one door hanging off the hinges. I knock it free and then shove the crowbar through the glass panel. The glass shattering is the most relaxing sound I've ever heard. It's like all the tension from this week fell with the shards. Brad and I take turns trying to snap the records over our knees when my phone vibrates in my pocket.

As Brad stays distracted with pulling keys off an old gray typewriter, I check my notifications, the screen filled completely by messages from Adler instead of Ben or Cameron like I expected.

Adler

When you said Ben, did you mean Benny Whitaker?

Adler

Ben Whitaker?? LAHEY

Adler

He's here

Adler

Oh this is too good

Adler

I'm sorry in advance for how much I'm going
to make fun of you for this

Adler

I will keep him distracted for now, but you really
don't need me to . . .

I nearly shriek. I manage to keep my scream somewhat con-
tained, but it's enough to freak Brad out. He swings around, his
crowbar sliding from his grip, and it hits my phone out of my
hands. We watch in slow motion as it clatters to the floor and
lands screen down.

We stare at it for a moment, both too afraid to turn it over.

"I'm so sorry."

For a moment, I forget about Ben and Adler and the
triple-date drama. I can't afford a new one, and I definitely can't
ask my parents for one after what's sure to come from Liberty's
car repairs. I squat down, my dress pooling over my knees, and

brace myself with a steadying breath. I grasp my phone around the edges and turn it over.

Cracked.

Still functioning, but cracked right down the middle.

"I'm so sorry," Brad says again.

"No, it's okay. You didn't mean it."

"Do you have insurance on it?"

"I can't remember . . ." The screen lights up, but I can't tell what's happening through the spiderweb of broken glass. It's all a jumbled mess, and not knowing what these texts say will give me an asthma attack, and I don't even have asthma. "I have to step out for a minute—"

"I'm sorry." He completely drops the crowbar and lifts the face mask. "What can I do?"

"No, it's honestly fine. I just have to call my parents so they know."

"Here, you can use my phone." Naturally, he has his in a durable case that covers it front and back. "My pass code is 0504. I can't leave the room with you or we forfeit the rest of our time. It only lets you in with the reservation number once—"

"I get it." I hold his phone up. "Thanks. I'll be back in a few minutes."

"0504," he calls. I'm only a few steps from the room, the music faint again, when he turns around, puts down his face mask, and starts breaking things with more vigor.

I don't need his phone, so I put it in the opposite pocket of mine. I yank off my face shield and swing into the dining area, the sight before me stopping me in my tracks. Ben sits at Adler's table . . . with his friend Sam. This is not good.

"Hey," I say in a shaky voice. "You're early."

Adler pulls out the chair next to him. "There's our girl," he says with a knowing smile.

I sit, sending Ben a charming smile that I let dull by the time it gets to Sam. I did not realize this was a group hang. No wonder he still went to the theater.

"How was the movie?" I ask stiffly. I don't even know what they saw. I hadn't planned on paying much attention anyway.

"Shit," Sam says with a pointed look at Ben. "Like I said it would be."

"How was I supposed to know that it was going to be shit?" He looks across the table at Adler. "Don't see the new *Scream* movie. After the last one, I thought it would be kind of progressive, but this one was cringe as fuck."

"Noted." Adler bites back a smile. He takes a mozzarella stick and pops the entire thing into his mouth like an ambitious five-year-old. Chewing, he says, "So, what do you three have planned today?"

"Oh," Ben frowns, glancing between us. "Do you have to leave, Adler?"

"No, I'm just curious what we're in for."

"Lahey, what, did you just drag him here?" Ben asks with a good-natured laugh.

"She used me for a ride." He fixes a piece of my hair so it lies flat.

"That's—I mean, it's not entirely true." I realize quickly that

I cannot defend myself in this situation. I don't want Ben to think that *I* thought this was a group hang . . . or do I? Can this almost-date be salvaged? Or should I wrap things up with Brad and just move on to Cameron?

Shit. Brad and Cameron.

I try to subtly glance over my shoulder toward the wreck room. Brad might as well have come here alone with how quickly he forgot about me. It's for the best that he stays consumed with pulling apart a grandfather clock.

"Used you for a ride?" Ben looks over the menu. "Is that what we're calling it these days? I bet my aunt would like that better than me calling Sam my annual summer fling."

"*I* don't like you calling me that," Sam replies, tone hard.

"Wait, what?" I feel like they're speaking a language I don't.

The table falls silent around me and *looks* are exchanged.

"Sorry," Ben says with confusion. "It was just a joke . . . I don't mean it when I say that. Just, like . . . using Adler for a ride?"

I blink and then turn to Adler. "I'm not understanding."

Sam laughs. "Adler's your—well, I mean he might not be your boyfriend, but you're together, right? This is clearly a double date, or . . ."

Sam and Ben lock eyes again, but it's brief. They both turn to me with such sympathetic expressions that I may combust from the warmth. I can't seem to close my mouth.

"Lahey," Ben says sweetly, wrapping his hand over mine, "Sam is my boyfriend."

Adler shifts in his seat, his mouth a straight line as he watches

Sam burst into laughter. My insides freeze. So do my outsides.

"Sam," Ben hisses.

"I'm sorry." Sam tries to contain himself, wiping away a tear. "I'm sorry. He's just *so gay*. How did you not know?"

"It's not like I formally announced it or anything—"

This is why Adler was surprised it was Ben Whitaker. My nose is numb and my feet are cold and my fingers are tingling— am I having a heart attack? I'd google symptoms, but my phone is broken.

"I'm so sorry," I blurt out, cutting off whatever conversation was happening. I push my chair out from under the table and stand. "I totally misread . . . everything. I'm sorry. I shouldn't have assumed."

"It's okay, Lahey. Please don't go." Ben grabs for my hand again, trying to gently pull me back down to the table, where Adler has to be exploding to make fun of me with Sam. "It's totally reasonable you didn't know. I never told you outright."

"No, but you didn't need to. Please don't try to make me feel better. This was my mistake," I say, resisting his tug. "I'm sorry. I have to go."

"Go where?" he asks. "What about Adler?"

"He must *actually* be her ride, then," Sam adds as an aside.

"Shit, man," Ben says, turning to Adler. "I'm sorry—"

"This is the funniest fucking thing," Sam says to himself, smiling at the table. Sam's actions yesterday and his tone now suddenly click into place. I'd be kind of prickly if someone was hitting on my partner also.

This is all too much. Ben's out, Brad's still in the wreck

room, and Cameron will be here soon for ax-throwing. I have to make one of the brothers work. Brad might feel so bad about breaking my phone that he goes with me tomorrow, but maybe I could get Cameron to go without a guilt trip. I don't want to pick the wrong brother. . . .

"Uh," Adler says, clearing his throat. "Yeah, you do have to go." He nods behind me, and I swing around.

Brad is leaving the wreck room, because our time is up, and Cameron is strolling through the door, a whole thirty minutes early.

Jesus, I should have just put all my eggs in Cameron's basket at the beginning.

"What's happening?" Ben asks, watching as the brothers meet in confusion.

"It's a great story," Adler says as I scamper off to defuse this bomb, my heart beating seven thousand and thirty-eight miles per hour.

"Brad, Cameron." I say their names so quickly that it sounds like a joint name. Brameron. "What a weird coincidence that you're both here."

I have to pick, right now: do I girlboss or gaslight? Turn this into a *Bachelorette*-esque competition for my heart, or tell Cameron that I have them both saved in my phone as "Tamburello" and thought I was talking to him when I was talking to Brad? Because Brad is kind, and he does owe me for the phone, but I'd rather spend a night of misery with Cameron. We actually know each other, have inside jokes, and he's the cuter of the brothers—dimples and piercing blue eyes, small muscles and big hands. Plus, I know what I'm getting into romance-wise since he has such a public relationship past.

Cameron has his hat on backward, which I've always found really cute, and a frown on his full lips. "Am I missing something?"

I exhale through my nose. These two are my last hopes. There are basically twenty-eight hours standing between me and Summer's judgment, and I'm panicking here, hoping that one of the Tamburello brothers will feel sorry enough for me to make my cousin regret crossing me.

I look at Brad, then Cameron. I see no way out of this. I'd be surprised to end this day with even one of them as my friend still, which I should have foreseen. I should not have assumed that just because they're guys, they wouldn't talk about their lives to each other. "So—"

"Sweet." Adler claps a hand on my shoulder and squeezes me into his side. He's warm and sturdy, and I shouldn't sink into him in this moment, but I do. "Everyone here now? We're throwing axes next, right?"

My panicked eyes meet his steady, calm green ones. Inside them, I find my own calm.

"Ben and Sam are just waiting on some appetizers for the group, but they'll be over in a minute." Adler smiles at Brad and Cameron, whose expressions are clearing one second at a time. "Thanks for putting this hang together, Lahey."

"Yeah," Ben says, arriving in the recreational area with Sam in tow, plates of potato skins and kabobs in hand. "Thanks, Lahey. This'll be fun."

Brad's gaze roams over everyone and then stops on me. "Oh, cool. I didn't realize—"

"Sorry. I'm terrible at planning." *If any of these guys took one second to think that statement through, they'd realize that was not true until this day.* "I'm not sure who got what memo."

"I was confused, too." Cameron laughs and then lowers his voice conspiratorially, so only our group can hear him. "I actually thought maybe this was a date."

I force a hysterical laugh—because it's funny to him, dating me. "No, I'm so sorry. And here I was thinking, why didn't the Tamburellos drive together? Don't they want to save the environment?"

I pull Brad's phone from my pocket and hand it back. "Thanks."

The group falters in awkwardness for a moment and then rights itself, like this was the plan all along. The brothers join in a conversation with Ben and Sam, who Adler must have roped into this lie, and walk over to the ax-throwing area, which is understandably the least connected part of the business. Can't have axes flying past your head when you're trying to fit your burger into your mouth. Adler attempts to follow them, but I pull him back, both of my hands wrapped around his. He faces me with a subtle hint of surprise in his eyes.

"*Thanks*," I say, deflating in relief.

"You're welcome." He smiles down at me. "It was fun for a little, though. To watch you squirm."

"Well, there's plenty more where that came from. I have to face Liberty later to tell her about her car, and then I have to ask my parents for a new phone." I free my phone from my pocket, where it's been vibrating almost nonstop for the last few minutes of turmoil, and hold it up.

His smile turns into a Cheshire grin, glee in his eyes. "Oh, you are in *so* much trouble."

Nineteen

I didn't walk away from that disastrous triple non-date with even one escort for tomorrow, but at least it was fun and I was able to momentarily forget this catastrophe of my own making. Thanks to Adler. And the axes. When we pull into his driveway, I tell him again how screwed I was without him and how badly I owe him.

"This is the eighth time you've thanked me since I put the car in park." He glances to the left, where my house, a white two-story colonial, sits innocently like a photo on the front of an expensive residential community brochure. No one passing by on their evening walk would be able to tell there's about to be a storm inside. "Stop procrastinating and get this over with."

"But . . ." I look around his car for a distraction. "You have an exceptionally clean car. Let me guess—you've been dabbling in car detailing for money and used yours for practice?"

"Lahey." He stares down his nose at me, but there's humor hiding in the corners of his mouth.

"Nooooo," I whine, throwing my head back and closing my eyes. "I'm scared. She scares me when she's mad, and I'm about to make her so mad. I'll be lucky if she forgives me by the time she graduates."

"I'll go in with you." He even unbuckles his seat belt to show me how serious he is, and I would never admit how much better it makes me feel.

"Yeah, you will. In front of me. As my shield."

"I'll let her know the damage didn't look too bad."

"Before that, though, maybe you can tell her a really funny joke or possibly something that you did that will make her so mad she doesn't hear me tell her about her car because there's too much cartoon steam coming out of her ears?"

He sits there, a silly little smile on his face, and then suddenly turns toward his door. "Nope, let's go."

"I know this isn't your first time as moral support for a Johnson girl, so I feel comfortable telling you that you're not very good at it." I meet him on the other side of his car.

"I think Lily would disagree."

"Lily's a menace, and so are you."

He practically has to drag me up the walkway to my house. I can feel the heat from Liberty's rage pouring out the front door when I open it. I pause before entering. I can still flee. I can still pretend this didn't happen for a little longer—nope, Adler is pushing me inside, using me as *his* shield.

"Liberty," he calls, his hands locked over my shoulders to keep me in place.

Liberty comes stomping down the stairs, sounding like a

herd of cattle about to run me over. "Hey—*Lahey*." She jumps the last three stairs and lands in front of me like the most boring superhero. "Why haven't you been answering my calls?"

I pull my phone from my pocket. "My phone broke."

She stares at it, which gives me one last moment of normalcy before she murders me, but as I'm examining her reaction, I notice her eyes. They're puffy and red, and faint mascara lines curve over her cheekbones and under her jaw. She was crying.

"Oh my god, what happened?" I can't stop my brain from filling in the missing pieces. Liberty: distraught and trying to get ahold of me. "Is Lily okay? Mom and Dad?"

She blinks at me and then seems to understand. She wipes away the already-dry remnants of her makeup and tears, and huffs. "They're fine, but my relationship is *dead* thanks to you."

Adler's hands drop from my shoulders and I'm suddenly freezing cold, left here alone under her icy gaze.

"What? How is it my fault? You two already agreed to break up."

"You took my fucking car," she croaks out, tears welling in her eyes. "I had to stay here to watch Lily because of something *you* apparently told her to do, and then I couldn't follow through with my plans to see Sophia and ask her to stay my girlfriend. I had a big idea worked out, and I couldn't do it over the phone. I had a picnic of just pies! And a list of ways we can make our relationship work long-distance! All my stuff was in my trunk and you had the car! She thinks I chickened out on saying bye to her in person, and now she doesn't want to see me because she's upset and has to finish packing. She leaves *Sunday*."

I've tried to keep my mouth shut about her stupid breakup pact, because it's her life and her relationship, but when she's blaming me for its scheduled demise, I simply cannot stay quiet.

"I didn't even know you had something planned! How is it my fault? I needed to find a date for tomorrow—"

"Everyone's tired of hearing about the date, Lahey! It's not that important. This is my *real* relationship we're talking about."

I shrink a little into myself. It's one thing to be demeaned like this, but an entirely other thing for it to be done in front of other people—Lily's crept into the living room, a literal bowl of popcorn smashed against her chest, and Adler's still looming behind me.

"Why isn't my problem as important as yours?" I ask.

"Because *you* are the root of your problem!" She crosses her arms. "And you're the root of *my* problems, going all the way back to the beginning. If you had just let me have my idiotic crush without sticking your nose in my business, I would never have asked her out and—"

"Liberty." Adler's voice cuts through her next words. "That's enough."

Her eyes flick to him. "*What?* You of all people are going to defend her meddling?"

"You knew you were getting into a long-distance relationship." He steps a little in front of me, and that simple action has the ability to make me cry. Or maybe I was already crying. "I'm sorry. I know that you're sad—"

"Do you?" Liberty asks, a gleam in her eyes teetering toward deranged. "How? You've barely been around all summer to know how I feel about her."

Something in Adler's demeanor changes, tightens. "I've been working, and you've been with Sophia *every day* this summer, leaving me waiting for you to want to hang out with me. You're going to be hours away in a few weeks and I don't think it's even crossed your mind that you're not going to see me for months. And I've tolerated it." He shakes his head. "It's not Lahey's fault you two broke up. Why would you rather pick a fight with her than ask her for help fixing your mistake?"

"What are you even doing here?" Liberty sags, defeated.

Adler puts his hands in his pockets and rocks back on his heels. I can tell by his position that he might deliver the news bluntly, which would not help me one bit. I step forward before he can say it so indelicately. He's trying to help me and that would do the opposite.

"He gave me a ride home because I got into an accident in your car."

A piece of popcorn falls out of Lily's open mouth.

"Where's my car?" Liberty asks tightly.

"It's at the garage," Adler says. "My mom said that pending a full inspection, the damage is minimal and you can consider the repairs a graduation present."

"For *Lahey*," she bites out.

I think post-sobbing fatigue is the only thing stopping Liberty from mopping the floor with my back as she pulls me around the house.

"No, I'll pay for it," I plead.

"With what money? Mom and Dad's! But it's not their fault, and they shouldn't have to pay for it on top of everything else they pay for. And you'll just walk away from this somehow; Dad will be like—" She adopts a low voice in an imitation of our dad and says, "'Her car looks *better* with scratches anyway. Adds character!'"

"You can't blame Dad's ridiculous optimism on me, too, and you know I'll be punished for this. I'll get a job."

"She can borrow some of my money," Lily says. "I'll give her half of my allowance until—"

"No, she can't borrow your money, because you still owe *me* money from the last five hundred plants I helped you buy." Liberty aims her laser focus on me again. "I can't believe you. It's just . . . cosmically unreal, the way you get yourself into messes. I hope you have a great time, *alone*, tomorrow night."

The rage fills me the same way satisfaction filled me the day Liberty and Sophia became official. "Well, same to you."

Twenty

Adler has to take the knife away from me like I'm some hysteric slasher victim being laid with the blame of ten grisly murders.

"You're not mad at the potatoes," he says, setting it next to the chopping board. "You're mad at Liberty. Why don't you wash some green beans instead? Seems safer."

After the blowup, Adler directed me to his house, and then his kitchen, where we began making some beef stew for his family's Shabbat dinner as a means of calming my boiling rage. I started in on the potatoes like I had a personal vendetta against them while he went to his dad's garden to collect some vegetables. He came back to me basically making mashed potatoes with a butcher knife, and I can't say I blame him for getting me away from the danger.

I grab the colander he offers now and dump the green beans into it one fistful at a time. I pass behind him to run them under a stream of lukewarm water while he unwraps a huge hunk of beef and begins dicing it up.

"Why was your first instinct to cook dinner?"

He pauses slicing the meat. "It wasn't."

"What was it, then?"

He shrugs. "To get you away from her."

I snort, turning the faucet off and grabbing a paper towel to lay the beans on. "It's not like she was going to punch me."

He pulls a face. "Eh, I don't know. She might have."

"You really think so?"

"Couldn't chance it, could we? You can't go to Summer's party with a black eye."

My laugh rips from my throat, harsh and sharp. "Yeah. Summer's party. I'm not going."

"Of course you are."

"No." I pat the green beans dry and rinse out the colander. "I'm not. My own ambition ruined my last two date options, and I can't show up alone."

"You won't be alone." He uncaps some seasoning and liberally shakes it atop the mini mountain of beef he's made, eyes on the prize. "I'll go with you."

I tilt my face down, like I'm really invested in my work putting these green beans back in the colander for more washing, but, really, I'm just trying to hide my blushing cheeks.

"I don't want a pity date. I already told your mom."

He freezes. "You talked to my mom? About what?"

"She said you'd go with me, and I told her I'm not *that* desperate."

"Wow, thanks." He scoops up some beef and drops it into an oiled pan for browning. "Aren't you?"

I whip my eyes to him, first in offense and then in panic. The party's tomorrow and I've run out of guys. Seven billion people in the world and no one to go to the party with.

"Do you think you could give me Harry's phone number?"

"I told him you passed away, remember? It was your dying wish."

"Damn." I put the washed green beans to the side of the sink and lean a hip against the counter. "I guess I am, then. Desperate."

He frowns at the pan. "You know, I'm sure a lot of girls would be excited to go to a party with me. I'm not a pity date."

"*You're* not the pity date; I am. I know girls who want to date you. I've met some of them firsthand. There was your girlfriend of, what, ten days? Her name was Melanie, I think?" I start washing a carrot he pulled earlier. "And there was Quinn, and Anita." I hand it to him for chopping. "And Brighton . . ."

We've skirted around this topic for weeks. It's time. I must unleash the long-awaited apology.

The skin between his brows pinches. "Yeah. Brighton."

He takes the carrot from me and cuts it into uneven chunks.

"I'm really sorry about all of that, by the way. Truly. I just felt bad that Liberty kept ditching you." I bite my lip. "I mean, I was kind of right, wasn't I? You do feel like a third wheel with Berty and Sophia. You said it yourself earlier, she keeps you on deck."

He throws the carrot pieces into the Crock-Pot and turns to me. He takes a deep breath, and I prepare to be put in my place. Instead, he says, "Yeah." He nods to himself. "Yeah. I knew we'd go our separate ways soon, but I didn't see us parting like this, having barely seen each other all summer. She had Sophia, and I had my hundred and one jobs."

I nod. "I guess considering how everything turned out, I'm sorry I got the two of them together." It would have saved Adler some anguish and me a lot of verbal abuse.

"No. It's fine. They love each other." He wipes his hands on the little towel hanging off the stove. His mom bought it at the apple festival last year and snagged a matching one for our house. "And for the record, Brighton's great. I'm sure she'd be a good girlfriend. I just wasn't interested in her."

"Why not? I'm *really* good at setting people up normally." I'd be lying if I said a part of me wasn't interested in what went wrong. I thought I read all the signals right. I thought I found a perfect match. If I can find the flaw, I can avoid it next time.

As an answer, he just stares very seriously at me, and I don't know what to make of it. I laugh nervously and drum my fingers against the counter before pushing off and wandering around the kitchen. "O-kay, then. What should I do next?"

"Look at me." His voice is low.

Nope. I don't want to do that. I cannot—*cannot*—get pulled in by those green eyes and the dimple and the thought of him kissing me . . . and then breaking my heart by feeling bad for me. Plus Liberty's already mad enough at me; I can't kiss her best friend.

I trail my finger across the back of the nearest dining chair. "Do you forgive me?"

"Lahey, look at me."

His voice comes from right behind me this time. Goose bumps travel down my neck as his breath hits my skin. I close my eyes to absorb his words into every pore of my skin, hear his voice tunnel into my ears and find a comfortable place to rest in my brain.

"I wasn't mad at you for trying to set me up with Brighton." He takes a steadying breath. "I was mad at myself, for believing you were interested in me when you kept asking me all those questions. I just thought you wanted . . . to know me."

I turn, letting my eyes drink in the soft curves of his nose and cheekbones, the cut of his jaw. "I did want to know you when I asked those questions." I needed to know if he was a good fit with Brighton—he was, in my opinion—so I grilled him about everything. I already knew most of it, but I needed to view it in the context of a relationship with her.

"I thought you were asking for *you*. Not for her." His eyes bore into mine, begging me to understand.

His words hit the protective wall I've built up over the past week like a wrecking ball. There's no time for me to build it back up and stop the realization from flooding in: *Adler Altman likes me. Adler*, of all people, likes me. Somehow, despite my swings and misses this week, I have hit a freaking home run. I cannot believe it.

No, I really can't believe it.

I'm terrified he's joking.

"Shut up," I say with a small laugh, pushing him gently.

"I'm serious, Lahey. Do the math."

"You know I'm not good at math."

"Okay, well, do the English." He raises an eyebrow. "Read me loud and clear."

I try to push him away again, my tongue going numb and stopping me from speaking, as if I even had the words. His hand captures mine, freezing my fidgeting.

"I think you're saying that you like me, you little creep," I say in a lighthearted voice, just in case he's not being serious.

He doesn't deny it. He just grins . . . *smitten*. "Why am I a creep?"

"I'm your best friend's little sister!" I step closer to him, despite it. "She'd be so mad."

His cheeks pink. "You're only a grade below me; don't be dramatic."

"So, that's it?" All this time I thought he was the only one with the power in our dynamic, but he's had a *crush* on me. "You like me? Seriously?"

His lips part, and I can't look away from their softness or the dimple they create when he says my name. "Lahey, I more than like you."

My head spins with this revelation, so I plant a palm on both his shoulders to keep myself on my feet. "Okay."

"Okay?"

"So, you forgive me?"

He barks out a laugh. "You're ridiculous."

But suddenly I'm not laughing. "I just have to know. I have to know that things are . . . that it's just you and me, nothing standing between us. You really mean this."

He shuffles forward, only a whisper of air able to glide between our bodies. "I forgive you," he spells out. "There's no pity in my offer—in my *request*—for a date tomorrow. In fact, the only thing unforgivable about you is that you haven't told me how you feel about me yet."

I grip onto his shoulders tighter. "Sorry. I—this is a lot."

He nods. "If you need to—"

"No!" I completely squeeze the last bit of space between us from existence. His chest is warm, his heart beating so hard that I can feel it through our skin. "It feels right. I mean, it makes sense. *You.*"

He smiles, understanding my nonsense like he always has. "Will you go to Summer's party with me?"

"Yes." I return the dopey grin.

"She's going to feel like an idiot tomorrow when she finds out that you didn't even have to ask me; I *begged* to be your date."

"No, she'll definitely still think you just feel bad for me, but I appreciate the help." My hands slide over his shoulders now, stretching out behind his neck and intertwining.

"Will she believe us if we spend the whole party kissing?" The rumble of his low tone makes my stomach clench. "Would that be enough to convince her?"

I have never been this close to a boy—except, I guess, Adler, in various other situations—so I don't know how to handle this sudden influx of underarm sweat that my body has started to rudely produce. Don't know how to handle the increase in my heart rate, the sensation that my throat is swelling up, the urge to fling myself at him and silently tell him to literally put his mouth where his money is.

"Maybe if we practice," I say, clearing my throat unat-tractively. "Then we can really sell it."

"Great. I have all night."

I glance around his shoulder, unable to look over it, and raise an eyebrow at the half-made beef stew.

"My parents can order takeout," he says dismissively, "and I can take you out."

All this time and the date I wanted—the *romance* I never dared to admit I wanted—was right here. Right next door. In my bathroom, at the cat café, guiding me around an ice-skating rink. I suddenly can't think of a more perfect place or time to have my first kiss. Despite the history between us, *this* is our meet-cute. It's like we're seeing each other for the first time.

I push up to my tiptoes and rest my lips against his, our noses brushing in a delicate, tickling way that I couldn't have ever predicted when I was lying in bed at night visualizing and planning this moment with faceless strangers.

His hands slide against my lower back to rein me into him, but I lean away. "Um." I clear my head of the lust that's built up. "That was . . . that was my first kiss."

"I know. How was it?"

I can't even think of words to properly describe all the wonderful emotions I'm feeling, so I just nod, and he understands. He always understands. He places another slow, sweet kiss on my lips.

"That was your second," he says quietly, lovingly.

"Somehow as good as the first."

His grin brushes against my mouth in response. I'll gladly spend all night here, sucked into his orbit, our lips pulled to each other, but the front door opens. I leap away from him and fan my face. He twirls back to the counter and turns the Crock-Pot on just as Hannah strolls in.

"Oh," she says, smiling at the sight of me. "Hey. How'd it go today?"

"Fantastic," I answer, still breathless.

She gives me a thumbs-up and then kisses Adler on the cheek. "Thanks for making dinner. You're welcome to stay, Lahey."

"Thanks; I'd love to. Liberty isn't too happy about her car and stuff." I tuck some hair behind my ear, unsure what the hell to do with my hands now that they aren't on her son. "I better lie low for a bit."

Hannah winces, turning on the faucet and washing her hands of the leftover grime she couldn't get off at the garage. "It'll be okay. The damage didn't look too bad."

"I'll make sure to tell her that when she's beating me senseless in my sleep tonight."

Adler clears his throat, finally speaking up. "You could always stay here."

She smacks him lightly upside the head with her wet hand and then towels dry. "No sleepovers" is all she says.

"I didn't mean in my *bed*," he says loudly. "You . . . pervert."

Hannah leaves the room, shaking her head. Adler watches her go and then whispers to me, "Yes, I did."

My face, which had almost calmed down, begins to burn again. I need to run far away from him while simultaneously needing to be as close as possible. My hormones are raging. "Don't get me kicked out; I haven't even had dinner yet."

He walks up to me with an annoying pep in his step. Absolutely ridiculous. Absolutely adorable. "Can I tell you something?"

"Yes."

He bites his lip, holding in his classic cheeky smile. "I hated seeing you with other guys this week, until I realized how badly the dates were going."

I cross my arms. "You loved my failure."

"No. I was just amused at how you avoided seeing what was right in front of you."

"Maybe I need my prescription checked."

"You don't have to change for me, you know?" He plants his hands on my hips, and meets my eyes. "You were working so hard to be who those guys wanted you to be. But my favorite version of you is just . . . you. Pajamas, messy hair, glasses on crooked."

"A low-maintenance guy. Nice."

"Yeah, I try." He leans in, stopping a few inches from my lips. "I've missed Liberty this summer, but honestly . . . I missed having excuses to be around you more."

"I won't tell her that you've been using her to get to me as long as you kiss me again. Or, like, a hundred times."

"A *minimum* of a hundred."

Saturday

Twenty-One

Last night was the most perfect night of my life. I don't even care that my happiness has peaked at the age of seventeen.

Despite the disastrous day that came before, I went to sleep last night feeling giddy, thinking about that one last stolen kiss with Adler before I reentered my house to face the consequences of my actions. Even that ending couldn't ruin it.

But waking up, reaching for my phone, and finding a shattered useless device in its place did the job quite well. I want to text Poppy a play-by-play of this major life plot twist, but the memory that I abandoned her yesterday hits me like ice water in the Sahara.

And now I've forgotten to meet her for transporting the centerpieces.

I shoot out of bed and dash around my room, putting myself together piece by piece—and I see a small flash of the girl Adler says he likes most. Me, with my long hair tied up, no makeup, mismatched pajamas—despite owning several matching sets—and oversized glasses. He likes a mess. A total mess who let her friend down and who will do it again if she doesn't kick herself into overdrive and convince a parental unit that she deserves to borrow one of their cars. Liberty's side of the room, which is usually a disaster, is in perfect order, and she's nowhere to be found. I hesitate at our door for only a moment, to wonder if she murdered me in my sleep and this is some kind of purgatory where I'll have to live out a life where *I'm* the disorganized child.

In the kitchen, I'm happy to find signs of life. My mom and dad dance around each other while making brunch, one of their phones playing soft music. They've always been way too big of fans of combining meals, but it does make for fewer dishes that my sisters and I will have to do later, so I keep my mouth shut. Plus, breakfast has always been my favorite meal of the day.

"The problem child has awoken," my dad says, whisking some eggs in a glass bowl.

I glance at the microwave and see that it's only 10:34. While my day isn't completely shot, any chance of helping Poppy like I promised is fading away with each minute closer to eleven. I must resist the call of French toast.

"Can I please borrow one of your cars?" I swear the phone even goes quiet.

After sharing a pointed look with my mom, my dad stops whisking and says in a stern but apologetic tone, "Your mother and I politely decline that request."

"I'm sorry about what happened, but maybe everyone should be thanking me for discovering the flaw with Liberty's tires in a way that did no damage to a living being? It could have been way worse, and Mrs. Altman is probably covering it anyway."

My mom peeks in the oven at some muffins, which smell incredible, and shoots me a raised eyebrow over her shoulder. "You don't actually think we'd ever allow that, right?"

I twist my fingers together in front of me. "She's done it before."

"Like hell she has," my dad mutters, dropping a piece of thick bread into his eggs. He dunks it and then plops it onto a frying pan that sizzles at the contact. "We always pay."

"It's a frustrating three-step process," my mom says. "First, she refuses to take our money. Second, we threaten to shove it down her throat. Third, she accepts."

"Liberty always brags that it's free."

"Yeah, for *her*." My dad sighs and leans against the counter. "No cars for you for the rest of the summer."

"That's not fair!"

"It's not?" my mom asks, gasping. "I forgot that everything has to be fair."

I bite my tongue and wait out the lecture.

She continues. "If that's the case, it doesn't seem very fair that Liberty stayed here so you could go out and wreck her car when we thought you were at Poppy's."

"Well, you let me do it," I mumble.

"Lahey," they chide.

"Fine, no car. Should I hitchhike to Poppy's right now, or will one of you drive me?"

"After brunch," my dad says diplomatically. "And then one of us will take you later to get your hair done."

My breath catches in my chest. "No, I can't wait. I have to help Poppy with her centerpieces *now*. And I don't even want to get my hair done."

"The centerpieces lie again?" My mom pours herself some orange juice. "You used that one yesterday."

"It wasn't a lie! I just had to leave for a little—I'm still looking for a date—"

Or I was. I can't tell them I'm going with Adler, though. We have to tiptoe around this until we figure out what's going on between us, and then tell Liberty first. She might be a brat, but she deserves that much.

"I'm—"

"Your sister is very upset," my mom interjects, pulling the muffin tin from the oven. "And we are, too."

"So am I! I was in a car accident yesterday and then I was blamed for Liberty's scheduled breakup happening on time, and now you two aren't willing to help my best friend—she's going to be so mad at me. And it's *your* fault." I cross my arms. "I hope you're happy with that. You claim to love Poppy."

"Your bicycle is in the garage." My mom frees a muffin and hands it to me. I accept mostly because I am dumbfounded at this abrupt and rude dismissal. And because I love a good muffin, even when it's so hot it's burning its way through my skin.

"Wear a helmet," my dad adds, his back to me.

I wait a second, hand still outstretched in shock, and nonverbally beg him to turn around. I think if he had to see the utter outrage and offense he's caused on my face, he'd break down and drive me. My mom joins him at the stove and keeps a hand on his lower back, anchoring him there and silently instructing him to be strong. I hate when they're a united front.

With a sigh, I search Lily's box of miscellaneous things by the door until I find an old helmet. Inside the garage, I pluck the pale blue cruiser from against the wall and check the tire pressure. The last thing I need is to get halfway down the street and realize I have to reverse and pump some air into them.

I stuff the entire muffin into my mouth for sustenance, but spit it out instantly when it burns me.

By car, Poppy lives about five minutes away. By bicycle, and with my slow pedaling, it's about fifteen minutes. I'm lucky to catch her still at home. Her car sits innocently in the driveway, the rear passenger door open, and I drop my bike on her front lawn. One box of centerpieces has already been loaded inside, but I made it. I made it!

Sweaty and out of breath, I knock on the front door. My fist leaves a wet mark on the paint that I attempt to wipe off with an equally as sweaty palm just as the door swings open. I come face-to-box with Poppy.

"I'm so sorry I'm late. You would not believe what happened—here, let me help." I try to take the one end from her, but she holds firm.

"I've got it," she grunts.

"No, that's—let me—Poppy." I pull at the side closest to me, but her fingernails dig into the cardboard and she glares over the top of the box.

"I needed your help yesterday. And earlier. But now I don't."

259

She huffs out a breath, having carried this enormous box of delicate centerpieces all the way up from her basement by herself. "Get out of the way, Lahey."

I slide from her path and watch as she precariously carries the box to her car, one step at a time. Her right foot catches the edge between the paved driveway and her lawn, and her ankle rolls. She falls in slow motion, but I'm there to catch her in an instant. The box nearly clatters out of her hands, but I push my arms underneath to give it some additional support.

Again, Poppy doesn't appreciate this. We stand across from each other, the box between us, and I say, "What's your problem?"

"Are you joking?" She tries to pull the box from me, but I sink my own claws in. "Let go."

"I'm sorry I'm late. I have a wild story to tell you about yesterday—"

"I literally could not care any less."

I blink. "That's a little harsh."

"You bailed on me. You bailed on me *all week*. I gave so many fucks for you, but you couldn't even give me one. You couldn't even answer your phone to tell me that you weren't coming back yesterday."

The box starts to weigh in my arms. I don't know how she was carrying this by herself.

"That's *not* true." I try to take the full weight from her, to show her that I'm here and helpful and sorry, but she won't budge. "I can care about more than one thing at a time. And my phone broke yesterday! I was in a car accident!"

All my excuses start pouring from my mouth, but she doesn't want to hear even one.

"Anytime the conversation turned to me, you'd bring it back to your stupid date. No one cares if you have a date to Summer's party except you and Summer, and you don't even like her, so why do you care what she thinks?"

She yanks again, but I double down on pulling the box away from her. It feels like whoever gets control of the box will have control of this conversation.

"Obviously there's a lot to unpack there, but I'd like to start off with the fact that I've never had a real date of my own, it's always about whoever I'm setting up—"

"Whose fault is that?"

"I know you're not implying that it's *mine*."

"You're literally doing the thing that I said you did that you're arguing that you don't."

I stop tugging to think through her sentence—it's like turning down the music to see better when driving—but

then I'm falling,

and so is the box.

All the centerpieces—*half* of her supply—break when I hit the ground. In the silence that follows, I'm not sure that's the only thing that broke.

Her voice is shaky. "Lahey, leave."

I look at the arm that caught my fall. I'm lightly scratched up from elbow to shoulder, my skin and the bones underneath throbbing.

"But—"

"Leave." Her eyes are full of tears as she takes in the damaged remains of her hard work. Her tears are going to ruin her perfectly sharp eyeliner. "Please just leave, and I'll talk to you later," she says more evenly now. "I have to go."

I sit up and make sure to angle my arm at her, so she can take in the injury. I give her a moment to feel bad, but she just blinks away tears.

"I hope your dress has sleeves," she chokes out.

Twenty-Two

Clearly, Poppy needs some time to cool off. We've had our fair share of arguments in the past—whose turn it was to drive us to school, who was *really* at fault for Poppy's terrible bangs: me and the scissors, or Poppy and the YouTube tutorial she found—but they never lasted long, and I expect this one to blow over by tonight at the latest; I mean, she said she would talk to me later, so it can't be that bad. Though our arguments have never included raised voices until today. Is this actually a *fight*?

Because there's nothing good waiting for me at home aside from cooled muffins—and totally *not* because Poppy mentioned my now-disfigured arms need covering—I ride into town for a Hail Mary shopping trip. I had been so concerned about finding a date that I forgot I still have nothing to wear to this party. I want to walk in with a smoking-hot date on my arm and a showstopping number on my body.

After risking life and limb biking on the sides of the roads leading to Thrifty, the secondhand shop in Mechanicsburg, I peruse the section dedicated to formal and semiformal dresses for a bit of serotonin and revenge. It's hell shopping for clothes while being fat, especially at thrift stores and vintage boutiques, and extra especially without one's best friend to hype up even the most mediocre of options. I'll find something darling and perfect, look at the tag, and see that it will fit approximately one percent of the population—a percent that does not include me. The benefit of shopping secondhand, though, is that the clothes are cheaper, the environment wins, and the chances of someone else having the same outfit are slim. I cannot and will not show up at Summer's party with a dress someone else is wearing or, worse, a dress someone else is wearing *better than me*.

Despite being donations-based, Thrifty has started leaning toward vintage and other curated selections. The interior is dimly lit and moody, with various lamps around the space, cute vintage runners, and eccentric art on the walls. Pretty much everything is for sale, even if it's serving a purpose for the business. I don't come here often because Poppy gets overwhelmed by all the chaos.

I manage to pull out several viable dresses in the thirty minutes I spend searching through the fabrics. Long-sleeved dresses, short-sleeved dresses, sheer, velvet, floral, polka dot. I don't discriminate; everything in my size is given an equal opportunity to be The One.

In the dressing room, I find reason after reason to not commit to each dress. The velvet dress has Poppy's voice ringing throughout my head, screaming "Velvet in August?!" The long-sleeved dress will make me sweat. The striped dress is too tight on my stomach. *The sheer sleeves don't hide the scratches on your arms*, Imaginary Poppy reminds me in a slightly annoyed voice.

Defeated, I dump my selections on the return rack and start working out how best to message my apology to Poppy from my computer when I get home: Instagram, TikTok, Signal, Twitter—but a swath of bright red hanging innocently by itself catches my interest. I approach it slowly, afraid it'll disappear if I blink. I pull the hanger free and, before I allow myself to get too attached, check the size.

It's fate.

And when I say it's fate, I mean that, technically, it is merely the size the clothing industry—or at least parts of it—has designated me. Whether it actually fits or not is to be seen, but it *should*.

I rush back into the fitting room and peel my clothes off, letting them brush silently against the dingy floor without a care. The dress is made of two layers: a wispy, floral lace with three-quarter-length sleeves and, below that, a tighter, thin red fabric that fits me like a curvy glove. I am bold. I am comfortable. I am summery and fun. I am a walking daydream for Adler and a nightmare for Summer.

My first instinct after handing over six dollars for this majestic dress is to call Poppy. It's entirely inconvenient and uncomfortable to be fighting with her. My mind isn't used to it, nor does it like it, but my phone is still broken anyway. I flash forward to when I arrive at home, knowing that no one there will be excited for me. I can very much see a future in which Liberty lights this dress on fire if I dare to show it to her. Lily just wouldn't care. And I can't tell Adler because we didn't even discuss what we are, if we are anything, yet. We just made out, admitted to feelings, and agreed to show up to Summer's together. It would be very girlfriend-y behavior to send him pictures of the dress—*shit*, right, my phone.

Okay, one problem at a time. I have to get home and send off an apology to Poppy. Then I have to figure out how to cancel my hairstyling plans with Aunt Madison and her spawn, whose angry texts I still have yet to respond to. I definitely don't want to see her before my grand entrance tonight if I can help it.

But in spite of it all, butterflies twitter around in my stomach. For the first time since she told us to save the date, I'm looking forward to my cousin's party.

It turns out I *can't* help seeing Summer before the party. Mom keeps Lily and me busy all day—only giving me a break to wash and dry my pièce de résistance for the night—before taking us both to Aunt Madison's against our will. I didn't even get a moment to apologize to Poppy, and there's as much chance of Lily letting me borrow her phone to do so as there is me running into a mail carrier pigeon with paper, pen, and knowledge of Poppy's whereabouts.

Mom throws the car into park and gets out before Lily and I even take our seat belts off. We stare at each other, daring the other to make the first move and put this disaster into motion. Finally Lily sighs and releases her belt.

"Let's get this over with."

The car jolts as she slams her door shut. Aunt Madison's house—which is how I refer to this place because it makes me angry to think of it as belonging to Summer—is as ridiculous as it is grand. The craftsman-style home was barely a year old when Summer was born, and yet several areas inside have been remodeled . . . twice. The whitewashed brick exterior complements the black shutters and roof, which is covered in massive solar panels they installed three years ago. It's bougie *and* eco-friendly. So annoying.

I don't want to knock Aunt Madison's skills with a pair of hair scissors, but it's safe to say most of these luxuries are provided by Summer's dad. He might not be around, but he *is* loaded and generous—with his money, if not his time. The sad story of it all is that Summer's parents had this home built in anticipation of her being the first of many children to roam the halls. One affair later, and that was no longer the case.

It's probably for the best, if Summer was any indication of what future children would be like. Learn from your mistakes and all that.

We skip knocking and walk into the foyer that looks like it just had a deep clean courtesy of Money Maids—*We don't get paid unless you're happy with the maid*. I can see my frown in the polished floor. I'm assuming they got paid.

If Aunt Madison had asked my opinion, which she unfortunately did not, I probably wouldn't have taken professional black-and-white portraits of Summer every year and then framed them for this space. Sixteen sets of Summer's eyes watch me as I struggle to kick off my Chucks without fully untying them. I'd be lying if I said I haven't been attempting to quickly break them in now that I know they were a present from Adler.

Aunt Madison calls from deeper in the house, and we filter into the living room, where she and Summer sit on the huge white sectional that I've been terrified of even looking at since Lily stained it a few years ago—I tried my best to clean it but ended up flipping the cushion and getting the hell out of there. I still don't know if the mess has ever been found. As always, my aunt jumps up and wraps me into a hug, pulling Lily in when she tries to slip out of reach.

Over my aunt's shoulder, I watch Summer roll her eyes and then meet mine with a glare. Her sour look goes unnoticed by my mom as she tells my cousin happy birthday. A switch flips, and Summer sends her a dazzling smile back. Aunt Madison frees us and offers my mom a glass of wine, which she declines since she's driving us back home after this.

I refused to bring my dress and makeup here to get ready with Summer as if we're friends. Plus, my entrance with Adler needs to be a whole moment, and that can't happen if Summer has witnessed me going from the sloppy mess I am right now into the fairy princess of revenge I will be later. It's like watching your favorite food being made. You are never supposed to see the process; it cheapens the final result.

"So, who's first?" Aunt Madison motions toward the recently gut-renovated guest room en suite off the living room. Aside from a full-sized shower and soaking tub, the bathroom is decked out with floating shelves lined with curling irons, blow dryers, and products I have never heard of. My hair notoriously does not hold curls for more than thirty minutes, but I trust my aunt and her miniature beauty supply store to work miracles.

"Summer," I suggest. I don't want to give my hair a chance to give up before we even get there.

She narrows her eyes at me. "I have to go last. I need my hair to be fresh for the party."

The party is in two hours. *I* need to be last if I stand any chance of my hair doing anything remotely close to a hairstyle by then. I pivot to Lily.

"Lily?"

"Whatever," Lily says from behind the refrigerator door. She cracks open a Pepsi and heads into the bathroom with Aunt Madison's hand on her back, most likely to deter her from running away. The last time Lily let Aunt Madison near her hair, it ended with an unfortunate shag. The haircut was very cute, don't get me wrong. Lily just hated it. She couldn't let the bangs lie how they needed to and touched them so much that she developed forehead acne from all the oil accumulating there between showers.

My mom sits down on the couch right next to Summer even though there is about half a continent's worth of space elsewhere, leaving me standing there awkwardly. I mentally prepare for battle—though I doubt Summer would say something in front of my mom—and plop down on Mom's free side.

"Are you excited for the party?" she asks. "I hear your dad went all out."

"He always does," Summer replies in a slightly uninterested voice.

I want to choke out, "You can't muster any more enthusiasm for fire jugglers? A seven-tier cake?" The version of me in my head shakes her by the shoulders until a little bit of gratitude manages to fall out of her.

"I'm mostly just excited to see him," she adds. "I finished another course for our trip, and I can't wait to show him some of the stuff I learned."

I feel like they're speaking in a secret language.

"Are you in summer school or something?" I interject.

"No, I'm not in *summer school.*" It's impressive how quickly she can switch from kind to cold.

My mom says, "Summer's going on her dad's annual company camping trip next week. They're roughing it in upstate New York."

Summer breathes out a laugh. "It's closer to glamping than camping, but . . . yeah." She reluctantly turns my way. "I wanted to surprise my dad with some stuff. First aid skills, foraging, starting fires. It's the first time he's taking me, and I don't want to be holding him back. We'll be hiking several miles every day in one of the national parks."

"It would sure suck if you got lost. I hear a ton of people go missing in those parks."

"Lahey," my mom says with a laugh. "Knock it off. It's really cool. You could stand to rough it a bit."

"What?" The thought of exerting myself, getting dirty—or *relieving myself in the woods*? "No."

"Summer can show you the ropes when she gets back!" she says.

That's laughable, but Summer frowns. I wonder if she's thinking about Tommy. He would love to do something like this with her—he's the one who likes this kind of thing—but there's the small matter of her lying to him. They've both been uncharacteristically radio silent on social media, and not knowing their official relationship status is driving me up a wall. The only plus side is that it's probably driving Summer up the wall, too, if they haven't spoken since he told her he needed space. Hopefully he needs so much space he can't bear the thought of being around her tonight.

Lily leaves the bathroom, her hair pulled behind her head.

"You're done already?" I ask, trying to peek around her to see what was done.

"She only wanted a fishtail braid," my aunt says with a shrug, stopping at the doorframe.

"It was the safest option," Lily whispers as she throws herself into the seat next to me. I notice the braid is actually made up of teased and curled hair, a few pale pink flowers entwined inside. Aunt Madison doesn't know the definition of simple, but I love that for her. "Your turn."

My aunt starts rubbing her hands together like she can't wait to get them on me. "What's my girl want done? You name it and I'll make it happen."

"Can't go wrong with some classic beach waves, right?" I tug at my limp straight hair. "Maybe we can curl it tighter so it has time to relax?"

She nods. "Exactly what I was going to say. I'm going to make you look like a goddess. We can even make a flower crown or add some in like what I did with Lily's—"

A shrill ring sounds out from the living room. "Dad's calling!" Summer says, much louder than necessary. Attention? Not on her? Not if she can help it.

"Cool, so answer the phone, then," I mutter, stepping into the bathroom. Lily's easy hairstyle somehow caused quite the mess. Hairspray, gel, and hair ties litter the counter around the sink. A bag sits half-full of fake flowers in a variety of colors. When I look back into the living room, Summer is dramatically pacing to take her phone call in front of the couch.

"Hi, Dad," she says loudly, a bright, genuine smile on her face. "I can't wait to see you tonight!"

Her sweet tone makes me want to cringe. I can't remember the last time I said something so sincere to my parents. Truly a daddy's girl in her final form. Wilson would love it.

"Yeah," she says into the phone, breathless. "And I have a surprise for you— Oh, me? Now?"

Her eyes stay shiny, but her smile starts to fade. "What?"

I realize now that Aunt Madison never started getting things ready for my hair. She stands beside me, staring down at her hands on the counter, her crestfallen face frozen in the mirror.

Summer continues. "Oh. Okay. Sure."

She starts wandering away, avoiding eye contact with anyone. Her voice drops. "Yeah, of course. No, it's fine." After a pause: "Yeah," she says, a little sturdier. "I'll get her." She sniffs once and then comes to the bathroom door, hand held out with her phone. "He wants to talk to you."

Aunt Madison takes it for only a moment and stiffly says "Okay" before handing it back. Somehow, Summer's face drops even more when the screen goes black.

"Did he say he was going to call back?" she asks.

"Uh, yeah," Aunt Madison says, collecting herself. "After your party, I think."

"He said he had a surprise delivered."

"Yes, he said it's out front. Let's go!" The forced pep is painful to hear from my aunt, who usually gives it so willingly.

We slowly and all-too-silently shuffle to the front door. Summer doesn't even seem eager to open it and find out what her extremely rich dad sent her for her birthday.

Aunt Madison pushes open the door with a flourish and cries, "Happy birthday!"

There's nothing there on the door mat.

Summer says, "Oh, wow. That's great. I'll have to text him."

The laugh bubbles up inside me, and I fight to suppress it; I wouldn't want Summer to have the satisfaction of me enjoying her joke, but when I spot what stands beyond the front door, the joke's on me. There *is* a gift. A sleek red sedan with a big cheesy ribbon tied around it is parked in the driveway, putting my mom's twelve-year-old car beside it to shame.

"I really like it," Summer says flatly.

I let my eyes bounce from Summer to her displeased mother to my mom and my sister. Everyone is pretty shocked, but I think for different reasons. He really just bought her a car.

"You can't drive," I say. "You barely have your permit."

Summer turns her blank stare toward me. "My mom's been busy. I've only been able to get road hours when your dad has taken me."

She just . . . gets . . . *everything.* And she takes it all for granted.

A flashy car she can't legally drive. A huge party that costs as much as her huge house. A boyfriend she doesn't even know, not really. It's ungrateful. It's infuriating.

"Lily, will you take my picture in front of it?" Summer asks in a monotone voice, handing her phone off to my sister. Dumbfounded, I follow them both out the door, our moms trailing behind and whispering to each other. "I want to show Tommy."

"Tommy?" I ask, shaking out of my stupor. "So, you're talking to him?"

How does one ask if they successfully derailed someone else's relationship without admitting to doing so? What happened to space, Tommy?

"He's my boyfriend," she says sharply, leaning against the new car, "*still.* So, yeah. Were you expecting to hear something else, Lahey?"

There's no way what I said to Tommy didn't cause at least a tremor, if not a full-on earthquake. Tommy might be somewhat of a simpleton, but I don't think he'd just let her lie to his face.

"Won't he just see the car at your party? He's going, isn't he?" I remind myself that I have a date now. Mission accomplished. Summer and Tommy still being together shouldn't bother me as much as it does, but I think if I have to see them chumming it up tonight, I may explode. *I'm* supposed to win tonight. And if I'm winning, that means Summer needs to be *losing*.

She poses for the camera with such confidence and shoots a smirk my way. "Yeah, but there's no harm in giving him a sneak peek."

She got the car. She got the guy.

She will *not* get the satisfaction of humiliating me tonight.

Twenty-Three

Why am I not enjoying my victory?

Not even getting to have full creative control over Lily's look tonight can bring me joy. We're inside her room, mostly to avoid Liberty's sulking in ours, when I pull the wand out of a new mascara and instruct Lily to apply it lightly while I search my makeup bag for the perfect color lipstick—a pale pink called Ballet—to accentuate her skin tone.

Now that I'm sitting in front of Lily's full-length mirror with the late-evening sun blasting through the window, I'm second-guessing my outfit; I'm hot, and my cheeks are darkening into an unflattering color that clashes with my dress, and what color lipstick do I even wear with this? I'm a red-lip girl through and through, but is that too much with the red dress? Is it tacky? I haven't even thought of shoes yet.

Lily rests her chin in my palm when I hold my hand out. "You let her bother you too much," she says without preamble. I am exhausted by this conversation.

I uncap the lipstick one-handed. "I do not."

"You do, too," she says simply.

I apply a layer on her bottom lip and pull away after a moment, waiting for some elaboration, but it doesn't come. "Okay, in what way?"

She blots her lips together. She wasn't supposed to. "Well, this week, you've been acting like a psycho. Trying to get dates and crashing cars and bailing on Poppy."

"Am I not supposed to defend myself when she attacks me?"

"Is that what you're doing?"

God, little sisters are so annoying. They think they know everything and then when it bites them in the butt, they claim to know nothing.

"No, seriously," she adds. "Is that what you think you're doing? Defending yourself?" She takes the lipstick from me and looks in the mirror over her shoulder. "Because it kind of seems like she hit a nerve, and you're just trying to prove a point."

I don't speak up to tell her that I'm not sure I know the difference. I feel like I can defend myself *by* proving a point. And . . . after this absolute week from hell, it feels a little bit like proving it to myself.

I watch Lily finish her lipstick in the mirror and then lock eyes with my reflection. I have a little sweat pooling in unfortunate places on my face, and my curls are nearly nonexistent already. I look sleep-deprived, probably because Lily is right. Summer has run me ragged all week. I'm tired. I'm tired of competing with her. For once, I want Summer to understand what it feels like in my shoes. She's always had pure, undivided attention from everyone—her mom, her dad, her boyfriend. She's got the nice clothes and the expensive straight teeth. She doesn't have to wonder if someone is talking badly about her because of how she looks. She doesn't have to change herself to make people like her—she doesn't even have to wear makeup to look flawless. She just has it so easy. She has it so easy, and yet she still makes things hard for me when they're already hard because I'm a fat middle child with some kind of romance disease.

The only plus side is that Adler seems to be immune to my particular love disorder.

Adler. I have to buck up and get my act together—if not for my own sake, then for his. This is not meant to be a pity date, so I cannot be pathetic. Every time I feel sour tonight, I will remind myself that I won. I won. I won. I did the very thing she didn't think I could, and I did it *well*.

I close my eyes and collect myself.

"Are you meditating?" Lily asks in a skeptical voice. "Right now?"

"I am preparing for battle."

"Nooo," she groans. "No. You're not. It's just a party. Just let it go. I'm only going to this thing for you, anyway. Don't make me regret it."

I balk. "How is that for me?"

"It's moral support. Do I have to spell out everything for you?"

"That's not—" I bite my lip and search the mess of makeup around us. She *did* let me tell her what to do all day, which she knows I like. "Okay. Thank you."

"Yeah, whatever. You're welcome." She stands and opens her closet. "I owed you for the hives."

"You owe me for the hives until you're driving, at *least*."

I consider all the lipstick options before me and decide I can't betray my classic red lipstick—Ferrari. At this point, with the dress and the lips and my burning cheeks, I figure I should just lean into the all-red look. The next time Liberty takes a bathroom break from her wallowing, I zip into our room to find my red suede ankle strap heels in the back of my closet that I thrifted for homecoming last year and call this monochromatic outfit an intentional, self-aware Moment.

After dismissing my parents and Lily to Summer's party an embarrassing ten minutes earlier than what's socially acceptable, I head over to Adler's. I doubt Liberty would crawl out of her cave to see who's at the door, but I couldn't chance him showing up at the house for me before her and I have made up about the previous thing she's mad at me for.

I pause at his front door, my hand frozen pre-knock. My feelings about everything that's happened this week were so numbing that for a moment, I forgot I was going on a *date* with *Adler Altman*.

My final glance in a mirror was surprisingly uplifting, but maybe that was false confidence caused by a last-minute decision to recurl my hair. Panic and doubt start tangoing in my stomach, and it makes me wonder: Will there be dancing at the party? I can't dance, or at least I don't know if I can because no one has ever asked me, and how embarrassing would it be if Adler wanted to dance and I suck at it?

What if he woke up this morning and now regrets yesterday? I haven't spoken to him—I figured because of my broken phone. But if it hadn't been broken, would he have even reached out?

The door swings open, and I drop my hand.

"Hey," he says, breathless and grinning.

"I didn't knock."

"No, I thought maybe you weren't going to."

I blink. "You were just staring at me through the peephole?"

"Yeah, I've been waiting by the door for about ten minutes." He stuffs his hands into his pockets self-consciously. "Why didn't you knock? Having second thoughts?"

"I was having second thoughts that *you* were having second thoughts."

"No. Not a chance."

"Clearly not." I smirk. "Standing at the door for ten minutes? Really?"

With that, I feel like I'm given the proper permission to accept that this is actually happening, and also to check him out. I've seen Adler in so many different states, but I'm almost seeing him in a whole new light now, and it has nothing to do with my lack of prescription sunglasses. He's just . . . beautiful. And I mean he's beautiful in personality, too, which is such an *ick* thing to say, but so true.

I motion to his outfit; he has a simple white button-up with his sleeves rolled to his elbows tucked into plain black jeans. "It's giving emo revival."

He glances down, his hair tumbling forward from behind his ears. "Should I change?"

"No. Never. Please wear this every day."

"Okay, then." His grin turns me hot—hotter. I'm going to sweat off all my makeup at this rate. "Let's get this party started."

Summer's father has outdone himself, and I don't think he'll even know until he gets his credit card statement.

My highly dreamed-about grand entrance doesn't happen at the top of a huge golden staircase or via English-accented introduction by a man in a black tuxedo, but I try not to let that dampen my mood. I have a killer dress and an even better date, so the fact that Adler and I walk into the booming, dark ballroom at the Hilton surrounded by a bunch of other guests arriving at the same time is perfectly fine. I'm kind of hard to miss in my bright red dress, anyway, but even if I had worn black curtains and slid against the wall, I assumed that Summer would find me. But when her eyes meet mine, I don't get the outsized reaction I imagined, but instead a brief expressionless look. She might as well have been looking right through me.

I don't know why I'm so surprised that she's the worst. It's not like it's new.

"This is . . ." Adler trails off.

"Yeah."

We stand, other guests flooding in around us, taking in the spectacle. Me, a little less than Adler because I keep trying to catch Summer's eye. String lights have been draped from the ceiling to create the appearance of a starry night sky that we don't have the privilege of seeing around here. In one corner, there are performers with fire. In another, a massive buffet of food—and mostly desserts—that I instantly want to beeline to, and thankfully, Adler feels the same.

"Let's grab some food?"

"I love you," I blurt out.

He pauses for only a second and then nods to himself, holding out a hand for me to latch on to.

"I meant—"

He laughs. "Yeah, I know."

We pass by the dance floor in the center of the ballroom that Adler doesn't pay much attention to. Maybe he can't dance, either. Before the buffet is a line of various activities: an entire fake living room set up with a few virtual reality headsets from Vice and Virtual; a small but very literal merry-go-round that everyone is mostly using for photo opportunities; an actual photo booth and backdrop for professional photos, and some huge blow-up games that I recognize from local fairs.

The food choices are immediately overwhelming. Brownies? What about brookies? Cake? Ice cream? Do you like pizza? Spaghetti? *Steak?* I look around to see if anyone is actually sitting down with a fork and knife to saw away at a steak but instead make eye contact with Summer again. She's about twenty feet away now, talking animatedly with whoever makes up her social circle these days, a hand wrapped possessively around the arm of *Tommy*, who looks a bit uncomfortable. She won't look away—and if she wants to play this game, I will. Ever since I started wearing glasses, I have had much wetter eyes. I could do this all night—

"—you want?" A tap on my shoulder. "Lahey. What do you want?"

I whirl around to Adler. "Sorry, what?"

He gestures to the endless options in front of us, tongs in his hand. "What do you want?"

"You pick." I tack a smile onto the end of the statement, and he gets started piling a plate with a bunch of chocolate-based items. I'm feeling a bit nauseous now but don't have the heart to tell him. "They have a waffle station," I add monotonously when my eyes catch sight of it.

"You hate waffles," he says offhandedly, collecting a few M&M'S to put atop the hot fudge he put atop my brookie.

"You've got that right."

I turn back to Summer, but she's disappeared. I guess I should find her and say happy birthday or something, like we didn't just see each other an hour ago. Like I care about saying happy birthday to her—it's not even her birthday anymore, but I just know my mother would get mad at me for ignoring Summer all night, and *besides*, I *have* to point out that Adler is here. It wouldn't hurt to have a reason to kiss, either.

"*Lahey.*" It's clear that Adler has been trying to get my attention for some time again.

I don't stop searching the crowd for Summer. "*Wha-a-a-t?*"

Silence. Well, silence if there could be any in this loud room.

I spin, realizing that I just snapped at him. "I'm so sorry."

He hands me a plate that is nearly identical to his and heads to a table without a word. I follow, balancing my candy mountain, as I figure out how to properly apologize for ignoring him and then getting snippy when he tried to get my attention. Maybe, despite my nausea, I *am* hungry.

With a sigh, he throws himself into a seat next to Lily. She's on her phone and basically oblivious to our presence.

"Hey, Lily," he says, overly excited, as I set my plate down and slowly take the seat next to him. "Great party, huh?"

She misses the sarcasm and just nods a distracted greeting to him. I nudge his leg with my foot and when he raises an eyebrow at his plate, I lean in so he can hear me better.

"I'm sorry. There's a lot happening."

His eyes fall from mine to my lips, then drift back. "I forgive you."

"Thank you." It's too soon to look for Summer again, I *know*, but my eyes strain to stay focused on him. "Thank you for coming."

"Thank you for inviting me, kind of."

I laugh and move in to give him a kiss on the cheek. His blush almost instantly overtakes the red lip mark I leave behind.

"Wait." Lily's eyes bounce between us. "When did this happen?"

I glance at Adler, my mouth half-open in an explanation we haven't prepared yet. "Well . . ."

Adler nods. "It's new."

She stares at us for a second, then drops her head toward her phone. "Makes sense," she says. "Does Liberty know?"

"Not yet . . ."

"Forgive me for the hives and I won't say anything."

My eyes roll to the starry-night ceiling, but I feel some relief that I have more time to figure out what to tell my older sister. "Fine."

Adler laughs at the exchange, taking a massive bite of a fluffy marbled cake. He grabs a chocolate-covered pretzel and holds it out to Lily in between her face and phone. She doesn't pause her texting to open her mouth and lean forward to clamp down on it with her teeth.

I'm digging into my sugar coma on a plate when he slides a hand to my knee. I jerk straight in my seat, a piece of the heart attack brookie flying from my fork and to the ground.

He laughs. "Do you want to play?"

"Excuse me?" I'm already shaking from the skin-to-skin contact hidden beneath the table. I can't imagine—*what* is he asking here?

He blinks and then points over his shoulder, freeing me from the clutches of nervous lust. "The games?"

A hysterical laugh slips through my lips. "Oh. You want to load up on sweets and then go jump around?"

"Okay, maybe this wasn't the best plan." He searches the room. "We could . . . dance?"

My stomach drops. "I don't know."

He takes another forkful of cake and talks through the bite. "Okay, that's fine—"

"I just don't know if I can dance." My face grows the hottest it's ever been. It's one thing to *be* this embarrassing but another thing entirely to have to spell it out to a guy I like. "I've never been asked, so . . ."

His grin makes me so weak that I don't think I can stand,

let alone maneuver in any satisfactory way on the dance floor. "Will you dance with me?"

I can't be weak, though. Over Adler's head, I see Summer heading our way, Tommy in tow. If I had gotten even one bite of food, I'd be tossing it from nerves right now.

I lean into Adler, wrapping my arm through his, and smile like an absolute lunatic at Summer. "Hey! Happy birthday!"

"Why are you using a customer service voice?" Adler asks quietly, his brow furrowing.

"Hi," Summer says less enthusiastically because, well, why would she be happy? "Hey, Lily," she says in a lighter tone. Again, Lily just nods.

"Um, Adler, this is my boyfriend," Summer adds. She gestures between them, and I notice the tension. Would *Tommy* still introduce himself as that? "Tommy, this is Adler." The guys exchange an agonized but friendly hello. Summer rushes to add, "He's Liberty's best friend. Where is Liberty?"

"He's my date, and he likes me, a lot. For real," I clarify loudly. "And Liberty isn't here. Lucky her," I add under my breath just for Adler. He grimaces.

"It's a really cool party," Adler says with a smile.

"Thanks. My dad came up with a lot of it."

"And where is he?" I ask, feigning looking around. "I want to tell him he did a great job."

Summer's somewhat smitten expression falls from her face.

"*Lahey*," Lily chides.

"Oh, that's right. Sorry. He didn't come."

Summer's eyes narrow. "It's a good thing my boyfriend did, huh?"

"Totally," I say in an increasingly louder voice. "Tommy, it's super nice of you to look past what Summer did and show up—"

"*Lahey.*" Adler this time. "How about those games, huh?"

I'm not too invested in my war of words with Summer to not notice he's no longer offering a dance. But I *am* too invested in the war of words to end it so soon.

"Yeah," I say, nodding vigorously. "Games. Great idea. You in, Summer?"

Adler's hand entwines with mine. "I think she has to make the rounds to say hi to everyone."

"No, I'd love to take a break from greeting *all. these. peo-ple.*" She cocks her head to the side and squishes up her face in a smile. "It was so sweet of everyone to come just for me. Remind me, how many people came to your party, Lahey?"

"I didn't have a party—I know my mom would have made me invite *you* if I did."

Lily lets her head fall to the table with a thud and stays there, seemingly giving up on us. The mention of my party for two—just Poppy and me—makes me ache to see my best friend. She would be fighting alongside me right now, unlike Adler, and she's so close I could literally (walk to a different part of this hotel and) touch her.

Summer grits her teeth but forces herself to relax when Tommy puts his hands on her shoulders. "What game did you want to play? I'm sure I can beat you at all of them," she says.

I stand up, pulling Adler with me. "Is there a game where I can pull you by your extensions until they rip out?"

"Okay, okay." Adler steps between us. "Let's not—"

"That one." Summer points to a game where two girls

currently stand on small platforms while trying to whack each other with giant Q-tips.

A chance to smack Summer upside the head? "Yes."

We ditch the guys and Lily and head to the game. In another life, we might have been doing this exact thing, but without the intent to kill. One of the girls gets pushed off her platform, her dress swishing around her thighs when she lands, and the other throws her hands up in victory while a small group of friends cheer her on and console the fallen. Some guys with heart eyes for Summer let us jump them in line—she's the birthday girl, after all—and we slip out of our shoes.

As we don the goofy helmets that clash with our outfits, I watch our parents, the boys, and Lily cluster around the edge of the game. Our parents are naively excited, but Tommy and Adler wear the same apprehensive expression. Lily pulls her phone out and the flash turns on. Recording us.

A nervous wave rushes over my insides as we wobble to the platforms in the center of the little arena, big swabs in hand. There are a lot of people watching, and if I *don't* win, I really can't come back from this. My heartbeat drowns out the music and talking until a prerecorded countdown starts at three. When it gets to one, I brace myself on the platform. I'm bigger and top-heavier than Summer, so it should be easy for her to knock me down. But while she may have better balance and a higher chance of winning, I have something better: a lot of pent-up frustration.

I start whaling on her, one end of the weapon knocking into her knee first and then into her shoulder. I had to take my glasses off to wear the helmet, but I manage to see her swinging her Q-tip wildly and without much thought, eyes practically shut. She hits me on the boob first, but it's not enough to unsteady me. As she rears back to charge up, I don't bother to swing. I just fully stab her in the gut with it. She stumbles backward and off her platform, and the crowd around us breaks into smiles and chatter that I can't understand. I feel the energy, though; it's a live wire powering me.

Summer rolls over, fixes her strappy pink dress, then takes her helmet off. The man in charge of the game tells her it's a liability, but she just points her weapon at him and says, "Keep talking like that and you'll need the helmet."

She jumps back up for round two. The countdown has barely reached one when she tries to hit me off guard. I meet her weapon outstretched in front of me, and we fight for dominance. She manages to whack my swab hard enough that I have to choose to lose grip or fall off. I let go, but because I'm weaponless now, she's considered the winner that round.

This last one determines the *champion*.

The number ticks to one.

I use all my power when I smack her wrist.

She drops her weapon, and technically, I've won just like that. These huge stupid swabs are unwieldy and heavy, but Summer still didn't compensate and *hold on tighter*. Probably because she just *assumed* like always, that she would get what she wants. I want to roll my eyes, but instead, I pull the stabbing move again. I believe in not fixing things that aren't broken. Summer, having been hunched over to grab her weapon, accidentally gets slammed in the face.

She goes flying from the impact, her face painted with a gruesome cringe.

My first instinct is to apologize, because I didn't mean to hit her like that. But my second instinct is to laugh, and that's what I do—I hope Lily is still recording. At some point between me delivering the killing blow and being bowed over with laughter, someone stopped the music. Tommy and Aunt Madison clumsily jump the edge of the arena to check on Summer, who has remained surprisingly quiet.

"Lahey, what the hell?"

I lock eyes with Adler, whose stunned expression will probably haunt me forever.

"What?"

He just shakes his head before walking into the crowd, where I quickly lose him.

"Wait!" I toss the weapon aside and rip my helmet off.

"Lahey," Aunt Madison says with a slight laugh. She's on her knees next to Summer, who's dramatically lying there as if I winded her. "Was that totally necessary?"

"It's my birthday," Summer croaks out. She looks fine, maybe a little whiplashed. Her cheek is red, but, of course, she wears it unfairly wonderfully.

"Your birthday was Sunday," I say. "And I didn't make you take off your helmet, tough guy. It was an accident."

Tommy helps Summer sit up, a hand rubbing her back. "Are you okay?"

Yeah, great. That's just what I need. For Summer and

Tommy to be brought closer together because of something I did. I slide out of the blow-up arena and grab my shoes. I fight through the crowd of partygoers, who look less than ecstatic for me, the *winner.*

"Adler!" I catch up to his retreating back, grabbing him by the shoulder. "Wait."

"No, I'd like to be alone right now."

"What, why? I *won*! It feels—"

"How does it feel?" he asks, whirling around. His frown is so loud.

"What's your problem?"

"Are you kidding me?" He gestures back to the scene Summer is still making. "You just beat the shit out of her."

"That's extremely dramatic. It's a game—"

"And before that, you two were in some catty, pointless fight. I thought the whole thing for tonight was just having a date, but it's clearly about more than that."

"*Obviously* it's about more than that." I huff, putting my hands on my hips. "I thought you understood."

"What I understand is that I'll never have your full attention when you're always trying to prove yourself to other people."

"I am *not*—"

"Lahey, you've basically ignored me since we got here. You were downright *rude* to me when I was nice enough to—"

"No. Don't. Don't do that. You said it wasn't a pity date," I say, my voice shaking. It might be from anger, or something else. "You promised it wasn't," I add a little quieter.

He wipes a hand down his face. "I just need to take a walk."

"I think you're turning this into something it's not."

"I don't like this." He gestures helplessly to . . . me. All of me.

The last of my confidence drains away. There isn't a win in the world that could make me feel better right now. "What?"

"I mean, I don't like *you* like this—I just. It's not coming out right. I'm frustrated." He rubs his hands together. "What I'm trying to say is that I don't like that you're happy when other people are sad. You're the girl who used to help people just to be nice, and now . . ."

I don't know what to say. I can't find anything to say in a short enough time to stop him. He walks out of the ballroom and quite possibly out of my life. Because if he doesn't like me like this, like *myself*, then he just won't like me ever.

Out of all the rejections and failures I've experienced in this hectic week, this one hurts the worst.

Twenty-Four

I thought I had experienced heartbreak before. When Holden Michaels held the door open for me one day at school and I interpreted that as him having feelings even though he was a senior and I was a sophomore, and we had basically never spoken. He started dating a cheerleader who wears black lipstick like a week later. When, even though I'm not attracted to girls, I thought Cara Tomlin was going to ask me out to homecoming because she had recently shown an interest in me, just to find out she was trying to get closer to Poppy. But none of that compares to how I feel knowing Adler Altman thought he had feelings for me and I proved him wrong. I took him for granted. I will never have that chance again. He thought I was better than I really am, and now he knows the truth.

I can't beg him to see me for something I'm clearly not, and even if I thought I could, I wouldn't. I've known him long enough to respect the boundaries he's put up. He doesn't like me. I have to—I just have to accept that.

But I can't accept that *here*. It's not exactly the most ideal place for a complete emotional breakdown, and I will find approximately zero sympathetic ears. My parents are probably so embarrassed, and Lily annoyed, and Summer . . . she's Summer; I wouldn't want to talk to her anyway. Poppy's basically down the hall, but even if I was brazen enough to interrupt her working the fundraiser, I haven't had a moment to give her a genuine apology yet.

I seclude myself to a corner of shame and watch as Tommy coddles Summer the whole way to the other side of the room; most of the spectators follow, fawning over her. This is my present to Summer: the attention she always wants. Aunt Madison lingers by the game, talking to the man working it and probably promising him that there won't be any repercussions for Summer's and my spat with an unspoken agreement that he'll be tipped generously. I wait until she breaks away and then rush toward her. My parents have already made it crystal clear that I won't be taking their cars anywhere for a while and I've spent more this week on my emergency credit card than my biweekly allowance will cover.

"Aunt Madison, I'm sorry. I got carried away."

She pulls me into her side tightly, which gives me a forced view of her cleavage. I look up at her face and make sure my expression is primed for pitying.

"I need to get out of here. I'm so embarrassed, and my date left me."

Rubbing one hand down my arm, she says, "No, it's okay. Stay."

"No, really. I need to go. Can I borrow your car?"

She pauses for a second, thinking it over, and then squeezes me one final time. "Of course." She—*Jesus, of course she does*—she pulls keys from inside her bodice. They're warm when she pins them in my hand. "Please drive carefully. I'll pick it up after the party."

"Thank you so much. I'm sorry. Thank you." I'm pulling away with each word, every breath a little easier the closer I get to freedom behind the wheel.

"It's parked on the third level."

I barely acknowledge her as I bolt for the door, my heart pounding. If I can just get home, I can collect myself and regroup. I weave through the hotel, following the signs directing me to the connected entrance of the Walnut Street Garage, and pound down the stairs to the third level with little regard for the safety of my ankles. I had haphazardly strapped my feet back into my shoes but didn't do it tightly enough; my heels keep sliding around, threatening to tip me over at any moment and abandon me with a sprained ankle.

I start slamming on the lock button of the key fob as soon as I leave the stairwell, but it turns out to not be an issue to find the car at all; the bright red Toyota sits innocently a few feet away from me and the horn startles me with its loudness.

Summer's car.

It would infuriate her to know I'm driving her brand-new car, yes, but I can't even enjoy it. All I can think is that this car reminds me that Adler was working on a Toyota just yesterday. It feels like a million years ago that he sort of decided to take me on a disastrous but ultimately fateful triple date. Everything this week was leading to Adler. And I was too distracted by trying to one-up Summer to pay attention to the easiest and best way to one-up Summer: be truly happy with Adler.

I don't remember that Liberty is home tonight, moping, until I open the front door. Maybe a better person would have remembered her older sister's misery at some point between escaping the hotel and walking into the living room to find her buried in the comforts of the couch, but I was a bit distracted.

Liberty pauses whatever sad movie she's watching to glare at me. I deserve it. "What are you doing home already?"

Seeing how pathetic she is just reminds me how pathetic I am, and I can't help myself—I'm an empath. I start crying.

"I'm sorry, Berty." I fling myself onto the couch next to her and bury my face into the balled-up blanket in her lap. Only a second of me crying passes before her hand is brushing back my hair.

"What happened? Are you okay?" She maneuvers over me to pull a tissue free from the box on the coffee table. "Was it Summer?"

"No." I wipe my eyes. "It was me. I'm just—I'm terrible."

I hear her roll her eyes by the tone of her voice. "Dramatic, yes, but nowhere near terrible."

"I really am, though." I throw the used tissue onto the floor, where a pile has already been discarded by Liberty. I don't know how much I should share with her. Is telling her about my misery worth making her friendship with Adler weird, especially when what we had was short-lived and it's over now? "I had a great date for tonight, but then I ruined things by letting Summer get to me and then I kind of assaulted her."

"Lahey . . ." Her brows scrunch together as she looks down at me. "Okay, that's—"

"Terrible! Why am I like this?" I feel too bad already to actually think of an answer to that question. I wouldn't like what it made me see about myself. I know this for a fact.

She sighs. "What do you mean by assaulted?"

I throw my hands into the air. "I hit her with a giant Q-tip! She's fine, but she might have a black eye tomorrow." Her frown is the only indication she heard my explanation. "Which is kind of her fault because she took her helmet off."

"Okay."

"And honestly, I could probably live with that, but the whole time leading up to it, I was basically ignoring my date and so, rightfully, he's not pleased with me or my actions."

"Well," she starts timidly, "he doesn't know you and Summer. I think it might be hard to understand your dynamic—"

"No. No, he does. He understands, and he hates me for it. He hates me, Poppy hates me, *you* hate me. And it all comes back to Summer. It's Summer's fault, really."

"You know that's not true."

Her fingers get tangled in my hair when I yank myself into a sitting position. "Do you hate me?"

"Of course not." She offers me a half-empty bowl of popcorn and M&M'S.

I risk getting a kernel stuck in my teeth for the momentary

serotonin of placing a piece into my mouth and letting the butter soak onto my tongue.

"I just feel like . . ." I think of Poppy's devastated face when her centerpieces crashed to the ground, Lily being grounded because she went through with my suggestion to trick our parents, Liberty having to stay home with her and missing her last day with Sophia. I think of Adler's look of pure disappointment in me earlier. He's right; I used to make people happy, but now . . . "I let everyone down this week, and for nothing. I've got nothing to show for it now."

She bites her lip, thinking through her next words. "I'm sorry for blaming you about Sophia."

"No, I was totally wrong to get you stuck here with Lily all day, and then your *car*—"

"The car is one hundred percent your fault, but not my relationship. That's between me and Sophia, and it was easy to put it all on you instead of on me or her. I'm sorry."

"I'm sorry about your car." I grab her hand and squeeze. "And about your relationship."

"We talked on the phone, but I don't know. Things are weird. We're leaving them really weird."

"I'm sorry," I whisper again.

"It's okay. You didn't let me down."

"Poppy and Adler, though."

"What happened with Poppy and Adler?"

It takes me a moment to realize I said his name instead of "my date."

"I, um, I didn't help Poppy with her centerpieces, and then

I accidentally broke them." I tap Liberty's phone on the coffee table to check the time. The dinner portion of the fundraiser starts in twenty-eight minutes. "I didn't even try to help her after. She told me to go and it was easier to go, so I did. I was too focused on this stupid war with Summer."

"And Adler?" There's hesitation in her question that I don't know how to interpret.

"He was my date tonight." I nod, making it true. "And now we're nothing because he saw firsthand what an awful, selfish idiot I am. I don't think we're even friends anymore."

We're not even *enemies*. Things between us are really bad if I'm romanticizing the tension between us at the beginning of the summer. That was nothing compared to what I'm in for now. A full ice-out.

"Oh." She pulls me into a hug that I'm unsure how to reciprocate because she's doing it through the blanket, and I can't move my arms toward her. "If I had known . . ."

"If you had known, what?" I ask into her shoulder.

"That he was your date."

"What would you have done? Talked him out of it?"

"No." She pulls away. "He was so offended after you tried to match him up with Brighton, so I asked him what his problem was and he told me it was because he liked you. It wasn't my place to say anything at the time. But if I had known he was going with you, I would have told you. Then maybe you wouldn't have—I don't know . . ."

I'm a phenomenal dumbass. I don't know how many times I need to have it spelled out for me tonight before it sinks in by osmosis for Liberty. "No, I *did* know. I knew he liked me, and I still treated him like arm candy."

She blows a gust of air up to her bangs. "*Lahey.*"

"I said I'm terrible."

"I don't really know how to help with that." She sinks back into the couch. "You were all over the place this week; isn't there a version of you in there that can fix these problems?"

She's right. There is another Lahey deep down. The one who doesn't focus on destroying other people's happiness, but on building them up. The me who Poppy expects and loves. The me who Liberty and Lily not only tolerate, but enjoy. The me who Adler likes. The me who *I* like.

"I'm fully prepared to help things with Sophia for you, but I have to fix my own life first." I plant a kiss on the top of her head and sprint to the bay window at the front of our living room. Adler's car isn't in its usual spot, and I'm still phone-less.

"Can you do me a favor and text Adler to find out where he is? Please?" I bound up the stairs, two at a time, and fling myself into our bedroom. So begins my apology tour.

Twenty-Five

I make sure not to change until after my stop at the fundraiser. I've already caused enough damage to Poppy, and the outfit I have planned for Summer and Adler is not exactly appropriate in all scenarios.

With about five minutes to spare until the dinner begins, I rush into the lobby of the Hilton for the second time tonight, but this time sweaty and with several dead plants on a luggage cart behind me. It's the best I can do on short notice.

"Which way to the fundraiser?" I ask the alarmed desk receptionist. His eyes couldn't get wider if they were pulled by people on opposite sides of the planet.

"It's an invitation-only event—"

"I'm with the caterers."

He examines the plant cemetery I brought from Lily's room. "It's in Ballroom B3."

I push my glasses up my nose and examine the closest hotel map.

"It's up one level," he rushes to say. The way his eyes shift from me to the people milling about makes it pretty clear he's trying to get me and my calamity out of here as soon as possible.

I'm happy to oblige. I bolt toward the elevator with my cart squealing, one of the wheels stuck in place and making it harder to steer. A leaf shakes free from one of the fallen Catthews with every bump I hit, but speed is more important than keeping them intact.

Ballroom B3 extends into B4 and even B5. I push my cart to the single opened door and take it in—this event really is a huge deal. Inside, Hilton employees are at the mercy of the fundraiser coordinator and, on a less threatening level, Poppy's parents. At a table across the room, Poppy struggles to make a damaged centerpiece look presentable in comparison to the intact ones. I'm well-versed in reading Poppy's expressions, and I nearly break down into tears seeing how upset she is. Her face matches the shattered work that I ruined.

"Poppy!" I call out, striding into the room like I have a reason to be there. Nearly everyone looks over, but I don't let it deter me. I'm on a mission.

I drag the luggage cart as she rushes over, panic in her eyes when she sees the mess I'm bringing her.

"What are you doing here? What is this?"

There's so much I want to say, tell her, and do, but there's only so much I can manage at once, or in such limited time. I start with the most obvious of apologies:

"I'm sorry for being so shitty this week. I was self-centered and selfish and flaky. I treated you and everyone else around me like minor roles in the movie of my life, and I've faced the facts:

I am no main character. I'm the crusty villain. I broke your centerpieces that you *had to make alone* and I'm so sorry. This was your chance to show your parents that your art belongs in the restaurant and I'll make sure they know it was m—"

"The dead plants, though?" She raises an eyebrow free of jewelry. To see her without it is like someone seeing me without glasses. Unnatural. She needs it.

"It was all I could think of. To go with your theme. We can pretend global warming killed these plants instead of Lily." I glance around the room. Everyone has moved on to continuing their duties, but I spot the tables lacking proper centerpieces quickly. They stick out, in a bad way.

"I don't know if it will help, but . . ." I'm realizing now that this may not make up for being a bad friend this week. It may not even be a good idea or make *sense*—

She pulls me to her chest so quickly that it knocks the wind out of me. "Thank you. I can maybe make this work."

When she releases me, I pull her in again. "I'm sorry I wasn't myself."

I'm the flashiest—and lowest paid (read: free)—server at the event tonight. I look more like someone who should be attending the fundraiser than someone catering it, but I couldn't just help Poppy get dead plants onto the tables and then abandon her. Especially because a text from Liberty with Adler's whereabouts has yet to light up the old iPhone I found in Lily's room and I'm not exactly vibrating with excitement to get back to Summer's party.

So far, I've served three tables chopped salads and refilled seven water glasses. More importantly, I've heard at least nine people commenting on the centerpieces and how they directly relate to Juanita González's green priorities. Each time I hear a hushed praise of the dried leaves and smashed wine bottles—"It must be a statement about recycling"—I rush over to Poppy and relay the comment word for word.

Mrs. Nguyen comes bursting through the server door I was peeking out of, her eyes alight. "The dressing is a hit."

Poppy moves between us with a serving vase of the dressing. "No kidding. This is the third one for table six. I think some of them think it's soup."

"That's not the only thing that's a hit," I chime in before Poppy can leave. She rolls her eyes, a playful smile on her lips, and then nudges the door open with her shoulder. "Poppy's centerpieces are the talk of the ballroom."

"I've heard that, too!" her mom responds excitedly. She turns to address her daughter, but she's disappeared. "That girl."

"She's nervous." I grab another water pitcher to take out. Her mom frowns. "She's scared of what you and Mr. Nguyen think about her art. She didn't want to ruin this night for the restaurant."

"She could never." She clasps her hands together. "We are so proud of her, always. She's so smart and talented."

From a view on tiptoes, she peeks through the small window in the door and watches Poppy. "She doubts herself, but I never do."

She takes the pitcher from me and rushes it out. I lean against the wall and take a break. My feet are killing me by this point, but I won't dare complain. When Poppy pushes through the door with a cart half-full of plates, I join her to the kitchen.

"You don't have to stay," she says with a furrowed brow. "I know you hate Summer, but don't you want to show off your dress?"

I grip the laced top layer in my fist. "Trust me, it's been seen enough. And I don't plan on wearing it to Summer's party. Not again, at least."

She leaves the cart for the dishwasher and tells a Feather coworker she needs to use the restroom. After dragging me into it, she sits me down on the ridiculous bathroom couch and says, "Explain."

We've been so busy since I arrived that I haven't had a chance to catch her up on my day, let alone my entire week. I hadn't wanted to trauma dump it on her when she had just forgiven me for being all about me previously, but since she's asking, I start way back at the point when I left her yesterday and tell her about the car accident, the triple date, and the fight with Liberty that led to alone time with Adler. She squeals and gasps at all the appropriate times, her hand clenched around my wrist like I may run away before I get to the end of the story—and with how embarrassing it is, that seems like a nice option.

"And after I saw you this morning?"

"I went dress shopping." I gesture to the masterpiece adorning my body. "Then I ruined things with Adler and gave Summer a shiner."

Her jaw drops. "A metaphorical one?"

A knock on the door scares both of us into screaming.

"Sorry" comes the muffled voice of Poppy's coworker. "Are you almost done in there, Poppy?"

"No, I have horrible, explosive diarrhea, and it might be contagious because Lahey has it, too. You better not send anyone in here."

I roll my eyes at her bringing *me* into her awful excuse to get out of work.

"Oooookay." We wait until his footsteps fall away to continue our conversation.

"I have about one minute with that flimsy excuse," she says. "My dad has a cure-all he keeps trying to patent that involves putting rhubarb in several orifices."

"Well, I spent all night staring at Summer and waiting for her to ruin the good thing I had going, but by doing that, *I* ruined the good thing I had going on. We ended up on one of those massive blow-up games where you try to knock the other off the platform, and I knocked her into a different universe, I think. I definitely embarrassed her, and maybe hurt her."

She motions for me to continue. "Sounds about right. Hurry up. Think of the rhubarb."

"And . . . then Adler was mad and disappointed, and he left me, so I took Summer's car—*ugh*, she got a brand-new car from her dad—"

She blinks. "You beat her up and stole her car?"

"When you put it that way, it sounds really bad!"

"It *is* really bad. Tell me you didn't actually steal it."

"Of course not. I got the keys from her mom. Summer wasn't even excited when she got the car—she can't drive it yet." I think back to the moment and remember her absolute deflation. *Oh, shit.* It wasn't lack of excitement or gratitude. It was disappointment, exactly like what I saw on Adler's face.

"But I think she would rather have her dad than the car."

Poppy stands and heads to the sink to wash her hands. "You know, if your parents got you a car, they wouldn't let Summer drive it around without asking."

I clasp my hands together in my lap. "Duh."

She locks eyes with me through the mirror. "Meaning your aunt treats you better than her daughter."

"That is *not*—" I cut myself off and start mentally swiping through the photo album of my life. I notice a *lot* of love from Aunt Madison. A lot of attention and compliments. We both love clothes, we love makeup—I guess I've always felt like her favorite of my sisters, but I never considered that I was her favorite, period. "Oh my god. No. I can't even feel good about that."

Poppy dries her hands, solemn. "I would definitely be jealous if I had only one parent around, and they were more focused on somebody else's kid."

"Well, I thought I was done having a good cry earlier, but you're making me reconsider."

All this time, I thought I was competing with Summer. I thought we were on somewhat equal footing, because I wasn't entirely sure what we were fighting for. The truth of the matter is that I had already won the game before it started. I didn't even do anything particularly special. And, to add fuel to the fire, tonight, I showed up with a great dress and an even better date, and then I physically harmed her, charmed her mother into letting me take her car, and did all of it without an apology, or even a birthday gift.

"I'm the worst," I whisper. Poppy sighs, leaning against the counter. "Liberty tried to convince me that I'm not, but I am."

"No more pity party," she says. "I have to get back to work, so what's the plan? What are you going to do?"

"I'm going to change into my pajamas, take off my makeup, and go humble myself."

She freezes, her eyebrows rising slowly.

"No, I will not record it for you," I say.

She scoffs. "Fine, but I'm texting Lily to."

"She'll definitely do that for you."

She heads for the bathroom door. "Can I ask why you're deglamming yourself, though?"

"It's my white flag, to show her I come in peace. And after Summer, I'm tracking down Adler. It's just something he said, about how he likes when I'm just . . . myself. Not trying so hard and not putting on a bunch of masks to please other people. Yadda yadda, he's right."

"His perfection gives me the ick." She fake gags.

"And hey, if he doesn't forgive me, then at least I'm ready for bed. Tomorrow can't be as bad as today, right?"

Twenty-Six

The first part of an apology to Adler is an apology to Summer. A genuine and long overdue one.

I know that math may not add up for some people, but unfortunately, it does for me and this situation—I even double-checked it, since I'm not good at math. I think he'll appreciate that I want to have a mature, and probably very stubborn, conversation with her before I bother even acknowledging how much I messed up with him.

My cousin is not without her own flaws and faults. She has taken part in this little war as equally as I have, but the problem is that I blatantly looked the other way when the reason she was attacking me was right there. Honestly, looking back, it took more effort to ignore her mother's preference for me than it would have to see it.

When I enter her party this time, I do so completely underdressed, alone, and with a huge bag of ice in my hand. I mostly go unnoticed, sticking to the shadows while I try to track down my cousin, but Aunt Madison spots me instantly, a glass of something nearly spilling when she pivots my way.

"Oh, Lahey, baby." She sets the glass down on the nearest table. "What happened? Are you okay? Why are you dressed like that?"

She wraps me into a hug that I can't return. Not this time. I'm on a mission, and Aunt Madison is part of the group of superspies intent on sabotaging it.

"Where's Summer? I got her some ice."

"Oh, that's so sweet."

Not really. It's the absolute least I could do, besides running away, like I did earlier.

She points to the photo area where Summer is draped with friends in front of the camera. Tommy and *Adler* sit at a table behind the camera, talking. My heart seizes at the sight of him. Before I left Poppy, I checked my stolen phone and realized that I wasn't connected to the hotel Wi-Fi, so any chance of Liberty alerting me of his whereabouts was completely destroyed until I got home again.

But, no. He's here. He's still here. Maybe he didn't leave me; I left him.

Without a word, I hand Aunt Madison the car keys and head to Summer, determined to not let anything deter or distract me—even Adler. I'll eventually have to talk to my aunt about how she's part of the reason Summer and I clash, but I first need to make sure Summer is okay. I wait patiently by the camera, avoiding Adler's eyes. I feel them dance along my back, no doubt taking in my disheveled appearance and questioning why he ever had feelings for me.

Another flash and then Summer's eyes adjust, spotting me in an instant. "That's a bold outfit. Does your date like it?"

I pull at my worn pajama shirt and then let it drop, heat pooling in my stomach. "Uh, I hope he does, but I haven't asked yet. I wanted to talk to you."

"Well, I don't want to talk to you," she says with a bite.

"Summer. Please."

Something dims in her expression. It's like when one of the light bulbs in a fixture goes out, but there's another one still holding on strong. She's just a little less right now.

But there's hope in that one light.

She turns to her friends with a big, wide smile. "I'll be back in a few minutes."

"What is it?" Summer steps out of the photo area and crosses her arms like she doesn't have the time or patience for this, but also *desperately* wants it. I know her facial cues as well as Poppy's; I just haven't been looking at them hard enough to see the hurt I helped etch there. The bend in her brows, the wobble of her bottom lip, how she keeps her face tilted away for an easier escape route if this doesn't go her way.

"I'm sorry." I offer the bag of ice.

"I bet you are." She raises an eyebrow at my plaid sleep shorts. "There are a lot of social media accounts here tonight. Hashtag Sweet Summer."

"I'm not sorry for my outfit." It takes a lot of effort not to roll my eyes. "I'm sorry that I hurt you tonight, and that I hurt you all these years. I—I didn't realize."

Her lips part, but nothing comes out. She glances to the door and then back to me. Silently agreeing, we leave the ballroom.

It's quieter out here by half, and there are fewer eyes on our conversation and my terrible outfit.

"Go on," she says.

I exhale through my nose, one short burst. "Okay . . . I . . . I don't want to be your enemy."

"You're not."

"Okay—"

"I don't even think about you."

I snort now, shifting the ice bag into my other hand. It's melting. "I know that's not true, okay? Just—look, stop." I drop the ice bag, wipe my hands on my shorts, and reach out to uncross her arms, keeping ahold of her wrists. "Let's just address things honestly. Do you *like* being miserable?"

She gives her attention to everything in the yellow-tinted hallway except me. "I'm not miserable."

"Around me you are." I think of her laughing with her friends and how open her face was. The smiles she can so easily gift anyone who isn't me. She resents me. She hates me. "I really thought that I was doing something tonight. I thought I could make you regret embarrassing me."

"Seems like you're the embarrassed one now."

"I'm not even that embarrassed. I'm mostly sad." I know she needs something to hold on to, so I don't let go even though sweat builds up between our skin. "You're sad, too."

"What, you just suddenly know everything, Lahey?"

"Not suddenly. I, maybe, knew for a while. About . . . your mom. I mean, I know you guys aren't really close."

"And you just made it worse," she says, breaking away. "You

knew that I was—you knew how I felt. About it."

"You didn't exactly speak up and make it known. You could have told me it bothered you how your mom treated me— treated *you* around me."

"How is that my responsibility, though?" She balls her hands into fists. "Why couldn't . . ."

"Say it. Tell me how you actually feel."

Tears build in her eyes and she tries to blink them away. "How am I supposed to tell the only parent who shows up for me that they make me feel bad? I want her to *like* me."

"She does like you."

"Not as much as she likes you." She wipes her eyes, mascara smudging across her cheeks. "You shove it in my face, and you've never cared that it hurt me, so why should I care when I get the chance to hurt you back?"

"Because why would you want to make someone feel as shitty as you feel?"

"Like *you* did to *Adler*?"

I stare a hole in the carpet. "Yeah, well, why do you think we're having this lovely conversation right now instead of *before* I messed everything up? This whole day has been one mistake after another."

She lets loose a sigh that deflates her. "Just talking about the problem doesn't solve it, though."

"I think it could if we were talking to the right person."

"A therapist?"

I blink. "I was thinking *your mom*, but—"

"No. It's fine."

"It's clearly not."

Noise from the party creates a soundtrack to our lack of conversation. Someone near the door causes a group of people to roar; it sounds like a laugh track on a TV show.

"I think it's already going to be better if you and I agree to stop fighting each other," she says quietly, shifting her weight from one foot to the other. She's joined me in ruining the carpet.

"I think we have to get to the root of the problem, though. I don't want you to resent me more."

She rolls her eyes but says nothing. In this moment, she reminds me so much of the little six-year-old who fell off her bike and scraped her knees in my driveway. The one I tried to make feel better by falling down myself. She was so mad at me after that. Ten years later and I can finally process why. My mom cleaned up and comforted Summer. Aunt Madison did the same to me and bought me a new set of colored pencils. She told me I was brave and kind for what I did. She barely acknowledged Summer except to say that she was okay and she'd get better one day—maybe she'd even be as good as me.

"I'll talk to her with you if you want, or for you."

She sniffs deeply and wipes her eyes. She didn't quite have a black eye from me until now. "Not tonight."

"Okay. It's your birthday present, so you make the call."

She laughs and it spreads warmth to the very tips of my fingers. "That better be a joke."

"I planned on my presence being the present. We don't all have a million dollars, Summer."

She socks me on the arm. "If we're clearing the air and

getting to the *root* of the problem, we should probably acknowledge your rotten attitude toward my dad and his money."

"*Your* money."

"Okay, I can't help that, just like you can't help that my mom likes you better."

"Well, you don't have to flaunt it."

"It's all I have to flaunt."

"That is not true." I take a deep breath. "Because I'm so unused to complimenting you, this might hurt either or both of us, but I'm prepared to face the consequences." I say the next part quickly. "You're funny, beautiful, and super nice to people, and you're generous, and—I am bitterly jealous, but I will try not to be."

She nods, stifling a smile.

"But could you *try* to be less effortlessly pretty—"

"Okay, shut up. That's a little much. It's reading sarcastic."

"Fine. Whenever you're ready to talk with your mom, I'm there—just try not to hate me in the meantime."

"I make no promises."

"I make none not to call you out on it, then."

She narrows her eyes. "I can accept that."

"Now, do I need to fix what I broke with Tommy? Those who can't, teach, right?" I reach into my bag for my mini makeup bag, searching for wipes to clean up Summer's face. If she goes in looking like we brawled again, it won't help my case with Adler or my parents.

She deflates loudly, putting her hands on her hips. "I don't actually think that."

"It's okay. After this week, I really think you were right."

Her eyes widen and a mixture of a scoff and a laugh slides between her lips. "That's a joke, right? Adler is so in love with you. He's been trying to find you since you left. And, earlier this week, at your house. I felt like I walked into a *Euphoria* scene I can't watch with my mom."

"It was *not* like that," I say with a laugh. I appreciate her trying to hype me up, though.

She lets me fix her eye makeup before heading back to the party slowly. Admittedly, I'm taking my time because once we get far enough inside, I have to face not only the public, but Tommy, who I used, and Adler, who I abused. It's not very enticing. Plus, I'm scared this truce bubble between Summer and me will burst.

"I'm just saying," Summer says. "It's like you have invisible little strings connecting you. He moves, you move. I'm not even sure you've noticed."

I hadn't, but hearing it from someone who has nothing to lose by telling me the truth makes me feel a little surer of myself.

During our awkward walk across the room, in which we receive a lot of stares and even one camera flash, Summer fidgets with a few rings on her fingers. She tells me about the new brand of shampoo and conditioner Tommy's been using because it's environmentally friendly, that he's trying to build his own bookshelf, and he's recently bought a record player—clearly trying to fill me in on the latest Tommy facts for our matchmaking needs.

"I hate to admit this," I say with a cringe, "but I've been wrong."

She halts, Tommy a few feet out of reach. His curious eyes glance over us and then quickly away, giving us privacy.

"Meaning?"

"I'm great at getting people together, but I've only done it once without lying, and that relationship is currently in major turmoil."

She blinks. "I don't understand."

"You have to do this yourself. You have to *be* yourself. It's the one thing this week has taught me." Her eyes widen. "More lying isn't going to make up for the lying we did before."

Her hand snaps out to grasp mine tightly. "No. I can't do this. I can't—"

"You can. In the grand scheme of things, I barely did anything to get you two together. Your actual chemistry is what has kept you going and, most importantly, he's *here* tonight. He was already taking space from you and had every excuse not to be here, but he is."

She picks at the strap of her dress before thinking better of it and clasps her hands in front of her. "He's too good for me."

"Well, in my nonexpert opinion, you two are pretty perfect for each other." I pull her over to Tommy before she can resist. "Tommy, this is my cousin Summer. I think you know her."

"Uh . . . I'm not sure if I do," he says softly. "Do I?"

I nudge Summer in the ribs, which wipes the scared look off her face quickly.

"Of course you do." She folds both her hands over his and holds them against her chest. "You know me better than anyone."

"I'm sorry that I matchfaked Summer with you," I cut in. "It was dishonest, but it did come from an honest place. She really liked you and still does, and the only reason I tried to blow up your relationship was because of the bomb about to go off in ours. I'm sorry I put you through all of this, but I hope you can forgive Summer."

His jaw clenches as he looks at her. "I just feel like I can't know what's real about you anymore, or trust that you won't lie—you can't be honest with me."

"Well, she's the most honest person I know," I cut in again. "She tells it like it is, she tells you how she feels, and she has good intentions." I glance at her and then back to him. "Well, maybe not always with me, but we're working through that."

Summer takes a step closer to Tommy and releases a shaky breath. "Now that we've gotten to know each other, I *do* like the things you like. I love that we go hiking and I don't die from exhaustion anymore—it makes me feel so strong and confident, and it's brought me closer with my dad. I used to think reality television was all trash until you and I started watching *The Challenge*. I've just—I don't know. I like myself better when I'm with you. I've changed so much since then; doesn't that count for anything?"

In my opinion, it does. But all that matters right now is Tommy's opinion.

He puts his hands in his pockets and nods. "Okay."

"Okay?" She brightens instantly.

"Yeah, okay. I believe you." He sighs in relief, his shoulders rising. "Anything else you need to admit?"

"Having my cousin set us up was the best thing to happen

to me," she rushes to say, "but I'm sorry that our relationship started off how it did."

He wraps his arms around her shoulders and pulls her into his chest. They are the perfect heights for one another, his chin able to rest on her head. I pull my phone out and snap a picture of them with the twinkle lights blurry behind them. I use the hashtag Summer sarcastically spat at me earlier and close out of Instagram before I can get distracted by any unflattering pictures of me beating up the birthday girl that may have been posted.

Summer, still glued to Tommy, reaches out to stop me from going anywhere. She tips her head up, looking over my shoulder, and says, "Put your newfound skills to use."

Behind me, Adler shuffles awkwardly, his hands in his pockets.

"Can we talk?" I ask him, heart racing. He nods, letting me grab his hand to steer us out of the room. He stays silent the entire way, even when I pull him out of the lobby to the small courtyard area in the front of the hotel.

My legs won't stop shaking with nerves, so I direct us to a bench sitting innocently between a few trees strung romantically with white lights. His gaze meets mine and even though the sun is setting over this chaotic day, there's still hope that it will end better than it's been.

"Um . . ." I struggle to have one single thought that isn't *run!*

"I'm sorry."

"Thank you." He keeps a wary eye on me as I try to put together my next words. It's hard when he's near enough to touch but so very far away.

"I think Summer and I are okay now, or we will be. There was a lot brewing under the surface that neither of us really wanted to talk about."

"Good." He nods. "Great."

"Adler . . ." I stand from the bench and smooth out my shirt, then my shorts. I'm *this* close to regretting my outfit change. "I'm sorry that I treated you like I did. I'm sorry that I wasn't your favorite Lahey."

He gestures to my outfit. "This is for me?"

"Yes. Only you." While extremely cute, in retrospect the all-red outfit was a clear cry for attention and help, and was mostly for Summer's detriment and not even my own benefit. I wasn't dressed for myself, or even Adler.

I spy a small smile threatening to break his grim expression, and I push on.

"I want to introduce you to someone I think you'll like."

"Are you kidding me?" He stands, legitimate anger in his voice, but I place both hands on his shoulders and push him back down.

"No, I'm not matchmaking you with someone—well, maybe myself."

He raises an eyebrow.

"Hi," I say, holding out a hand for him to shake. He does not. "I'm Lahey Johnson. We met at LongHorn Steakhouse. You were my waiter for about five minutes and I was on a date with some guy who was completely wrong for me. In fact, despite being on a date with me, he ended up with another girl."

The corners of his mouth lift.

"That guy had seemed like such a gentleman at first, though."
I sigh, dropping my hand. "The kind of guy who might rescue
a disaster of a girl who got herself into a mess at an ice-skating
rink with a guy whose only personality trait she liked was his
passion for the things he loves."

I sit on the bench again. His eyes track my movements.

"Oh, *hey*," I say. "You work at the cat café, right?"

He smiles fully now. "Yeah, that's me. And you, you're the
girl my coworker can't stop talking about."

"Huh. I remember him, vaguely. I liked that he saved animals." I fake a jaw-drop. "Kind of like *you* saving me from
myself during a horrendous and ill-prepared triple date."

We're grinning so goofily at each other now.

"Is this working?" I ask. "Should I continue?"

"Obviously," he answers.

I turn on the bench so I can't see him anymore and then spin
back quickly. "Oh, there you are! I've been looking for you all
week."

He brushes some hair out of my eyes. My messy bun is lop-
sided and sagging, but I have a feeling I have never looked cuter
to him.

"I just didn't realize it," I continue. "I was trying to find
you in every single guy I saw. I tried to make myself into what
they needed, instead of thinking about what I needed. I needed
you."

"I was there," he says softly. "I'm here."

"You're just—" Tears start to fill my eyes, and I blink them
away, grateful I scrubbed my makeup off already. I sniffle.

"There is no one like you, Adler."

He leans in. "There is no one like my favorite Lahey. She cares about people and has high expectations and will always be honest with me. She tolerates my jokes and blushes at all the right moments."

My eyes dart to his lips, a breath slipping out between mine that is shakier than I'd like to admit. "I'm sorry."

"I forgive you." His nose brushes against mine. The tickle sends a shiver down my spine. "And I do love this outfit, you know."

"I hoped you would."

His hand cradles my head, fingers slipping teasingly between strands of my hair. Our lips connect with an imaginary spark that burns out any lingering shiver from his first touch. He breaks away, eyes still closed, to say, "I did really love that red dress, though."

"Maybe I'll put it back on when we get home." I stand as he's leaning in again. "But now I'm carless, so you have to drive."

"Home? We're not staying?"

I walk backward toward the sidewalk, holding out my hand. He reluctantly follows. "My apology tour has one more pit stop, to try to fix things with Liberty and Sophia."

"Or maybe we stay out of other people's business," he says. "Besides, it wasn't your fault."

"It wasn't *not* my fault. I have to use my powers for good."

Hands connected, we enter the parking garage and walk up four levels to his car. Naturally, I can't stop spitballing extravagant and ridiculous grand gestures for Liberty to show Sophia how she feels. Adler tolerates every silly idea with a smile, but when we get into his car and I plug in his phone so we can listen to every song on Spotify called "Sophia," he cuts me off. Liberty doesn't have a great singing voice anyway.

He disconnects his phone, and the sound system defaults to a CD—an actual physical copy of music that he spent money on—and some type of melancholy piano riff blasts from the speakers.

I pull a face. "Did I say I was sorry? Because I'm sorry. If I had known you'd listen to such tragic music in my absence, I really wouldn't have—"

"Shut up," he says with a grin. He turns the music down just a smidge.

"What is this?"

"Something Corporate."

"What does *that* mean?"

"It's the band's name. They're not really together anymore."

"Of course they aren't; they're awful."

We stop at a red light, the only car around at the four-way stop, and he leans over to me. His hand finds that special place on the back of my head, where his thumb tickles my earlobe and the rest of his fingers stretch out to scratch a metaphorical lusty itch.

"The song's called 'She Paints Me Blue' and it reminds me of you."

"I'll try not to be offended." We're so close that our noses nearly brush when I speak. I'm hypnotized by the way his mouth moves and *agonized* that it's not on mine yet.

"Safety first," I say, reaching between us for the gearshift. I thrust the car momentarily into park and take advantage of the freedom. When we break away again, mouths numb and eyelids heavy, the light has cycled through green and back to red again.

A week ago, I had never gone on a date, nor had I kissed anyone.

Less than a week ago, I was sure I would be alone forever, destined to always be the person planning love instead of falling in it.

A lot can change in a week, though, and who knows what's next? Certainly not me, and I don't even think I'd want to. After all, tomorrow is the start of a brand-new week.

ADLER ALTMAN, 18, through the eyes of Lahey Johnson, who has seen the light

How I know him: my wonderful sister brought him into my life and I owe her (on top of owing her for the car and the breakup)

He likes: learning new things, helping people, eating food like a garbage disposal, cats rool and dogs drool, wearing the same pair of jeans all week, pretending there are bugs crawling up my neck, various family board games and activities, when my glasses are crooked, me

He dislikes: when I am an asshole, mosquitoes

Dating history: I'm more interested in what's in his future

Bio: Adler Altman was born in New Jersey, but we can't hold that against him. During the summer before sixth grade, Adler moved to Pennsylvania, where he found his best friend. Time passed and he formed an extremely great relationship with his best friend's younger sister. Unbeknownst to her, because she does have issues with seeing things (though not typically when they are right in front of her), Adler very much liked her. One week, she desperately needed a date to show her how to be herself and be loved for it. Adler was up for the challenge.

Acknowledgments

Over the years, I've been lucky enough that my list of people to thank for helping me and tolerating me has grown to a ridiculous length. I can't say thank you to everyone for fear of missing someone extremely important. You know who you are, really.

To my editor, Elizabeth Lynch, for being timely, thoughtful, and the best.

To the HarperTeen team: Mikayla Lawrence, Jessica White, Melissa Cicchitelli, Audrey Diestelkamp, and Aubrey Churchward.

To Jessie Gang and Sarah Long, for putting a beautiful fat girl on the cover.

To my agent, Bridget Smith, for being my articulate mouthpiece whenever the situation arises.

To Sonia Hartl, Rachel Lynn Solomon, Carlyn Greenwald, Annette Christie, Andrea Contos, Auriane Desombre, Marisa Kanter, Jennifer Dugan, and Susan Lee, whose words and friendships inspire me.

To my partner, Dylan, for being everything I want wrapped up all in one person.

And lastly, to *What's Your Number?*, the 2011 rom-com starring America's sweethearts Anna Faris and Chris Evans. I will not be explaining further.